Unconventional

ISABEL LOVE

Jennifer,

Don't let anyone define your happiness!

Bella Love
XOXO

July 2017 Edition
Published in the United States of America
ISBN-13: 978-1548286644
ISBN-10: 1548286648

Cover: Najla Qamber Designs, *www.najlaqamberdesigns.com*
Image: Deposit Photos
Editing: Editing by C. Marie, *www.facebook.com/EditingByCMarie*
Proofreading: Bex Kettner at editing.ninja
Formatting: Jersey Girl and Co, *www.jerseygirlandco.com*

Beta Readers: Christy Baldwin, Melissa Buyikian, Felicia Eddy, Saffron Kent, Serena McDonald, Pavlina Michou, Jackie Pinhorn, Desirae Shie, SM West

Dedication

To my readers!!! That's YOU! Thank you so much for taking a chance on a new author. I never thought I'd write a book, so when I get a message from someone telling me they liked my story, it makes me SO freaking happy. Thank you for reading, thank you for leaving a review, thank you for reaching out to me. I hope you like Charlie and Quinn's story!!!

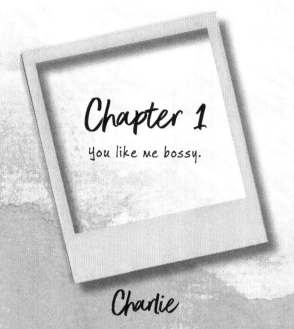

Chapter 1

you like me bossy.

Charlie

The music is loud, the drinks are strong, and the women are beautiful at Club Bailar. I signal the bartender for another round and pass the shots to my best friends, Max and Logan.

"Congrats on your new account!" Max shouts. Picture This, the graphic design firm I work for, just landed a new client—one that specifically requested my photography services and came with a generous bonus. It's one of the best firms in Columbus, Ohio, and I'm pumped that the gears are finally shifting into place. We clink glasses then drink, and the tequila burns its way down my throat. Warmth spreads from my stomach to the rest of my body, adding to my already high spirits.

"Thanks! This is going to be awesome. Maybe I can finally afford to buy a Porsche like Monica's old one now that I'll have some more cash coming in." The thought of Max's girlfriend's old car *still* gives me a boner.

"If you want it, I have a feeling you'll find a way to make it happen," Max says, his bright blue eyes sparkling with pride. Max, Logan, and I have been friends since grade school, and it feels good to have their support.

"How are things with you and Monica?" I ask him. Max and Monica met at this very club, and were surprised to learn soon afterward that Max was a new nurse in the emergency room where Monica works as a physician. Working together definitely made it tricky to have a relationship, but now they are going strong and disgustingly happy.

Max's smile can't be suppressed. "She's amazing. I think I'm going to ask her this weekend." Holy fuck, he's going to propose? I shudder at the thought of getting married. I've been in exactly one serious relationship, when I was too naïve to know better. At 16, I was head over heels in love, planning my future with my high school sweetheart, but it didn't work out the way I'd hoped. Don't get me wrong, the high of being in love was amazing, but the low of having the love of my life rip my heart out was brutal. I won't give another woman the chance to hurt me like that again. I'm single and I plan to stay that way.

"I think you're crazy for wanting only one woman, but I'm so happy you're happy," I tell him.

"What's up with you and Quinn?" Logan asks me, brown eyes dancing with curiosity. I'm surprised they've waited this long to ask me that question.

Quinn Fitzpatrick—or as I like to call her, Red. I look over at the dance floor and find her dancing near Monica and Tate, Logan's girlfriend. All three women are beautiful. Monica's long dark hair falls down her back, her hips moving to the music in a perfect rhythm. Tate is short and petite, with blonde hair in a pixie cut. She reminds me of Tinker Bell, flitting from one foot to the other, dancing with spastic energy and smiling like a goon the whole time. Monica and Tate are attractive, no doubt, but Quinn steals the show. She has wild red hair (hence my nickname for her), creamy pale skin, freckles that make me want to trace patterns on her skin for hours, and luscious lips that look gorgeous wrapped around my cock. Her whiskey brown eyes twinkle with mischief as she shakes her hips to the music. Nearly all of the men on the dance floor are staring at the trio, and one brave soul approaches Quinn. She looks up at him, a slow smile spreading across her face as he whispers in her ear. *Fuck, that smile.* She doesn't even know how sexy it is.

When we first met, Max forbade me from hooking up with his girlfriend's best friend, but making her off limits only made me want to have her—and that was before I saw her. Once I saw her, my cock and I had no intention of staying away. Then she started talking about dick piercings and it was a done deal. I happen to have my dick pierced and she played with it all night that night, and has several times since. That woman enjoys sex almost as much as I do, which is saying something.

"We have fun sometimes, but we aren't together. She's awesome in bed and fun to hang out with, but you know me, I don't want a relationship." I shrug, not wanting to make a thing out of this with Logan and Max.

"So you don't care if she goes home with that guy tonight?" Logan asks, nodding in her direction.

I stare at Quinn as the guy starts to dance with her. She's facing me and I see her lean her head back and laugh at something he says. She must feel us staring at her because she looks our way. When she catches me watching, her smile widens and she winks.

I smirk at Logan. "She can go home with whoever she wants. Doesn't mean she won't be wishing it was me." I must admit, on a few occasions, I've thought about Quinn while having sex with someone else.

Logan and Max laugh and shake their heads.

We do another celebratory shot and I am feeling nice and buzzed. Max can't take his eyes off of Monica tonight and I can tell he's itching to go dance with her.

Sure enough, he turns to us and says, "I'm going to go dance. You guys coming?"

"Nah. You put us to shame, Mr. Salsa King." He took Monica to a salsa dance lesson when they first started dating. They liked it so much, they go regularly now, and I never miss an opportunity to give him shit for it.

"Okay, you guys hold up the bar." He gives us a wave and weaves in between the bodies to get to Monica. He wraps his arms around her and I almost get a toothache at how sweet they look together. I turn to Logan, a sarcastic remark about how pussy-whipped Max is on the tip of my tongue, but find Logan staring intently at Tate.

Jesus Christ. I still can't get used to being the only single guy in our trio. I never thought both of my best friends would be settled down with women at 26.

I lean my elbows back on the bar as I scan the crowd. Clubs are such a great place to people watch. They are also a great place to find a woman willing to celebrate with me, and there's no shortage of hot chicks here tonight. *What am I in the mood for?* I think to myself. Blonde, brunette, redhead, thin, curvy, tall, short—I like every shape and size. In the middle of a group of laughing ladies, I spot a tall blonde with a very nice rack looking right at me. She checks me out from head to toe and I do the same to her.

Very nice. Her tits are pouring out of her pathetic excuse for a tank top, leaving little to the imagination. I know just what I want to do with those tits, and my cock likes the idea a lot. She arches her back, giving me a better view of her ample cleavage, as if the lack of clothing didn't display them well enough for me and everyone else in this club. I meet her eyes, give her a smile so wide my dimples pop, and wink. According to Quinn, I have a "panty-dropping" smile, and I think she's right. Little Miss Look-At-My-Boobs bites her lower lip coyly and smiles back at me, then whispers to her friend and starts heading in my direction.

Well that didn't take long.

"You find what you're looking for tonight?" Logan asks when he sees the girl walking our way.

"Maybe," I tell him with a wolfish grin.

"I'm going to go hang with Tate and leave you to it." He drops some money on the bar to cover the tab.

"Why not stick around and watch me in action? You might learn something," I tease.

"You may think it takes skill to get a new girl all the time, but I have held on to the same girl for *years*. That's where the skill is, my friend—longevity and stamina." He slaps me on my back with a chuckle and heads to the dance floor. *Longevity and stamina.* I roll my eyes. I have plenty of stamina. As for longevity…let's just say I prefer variety.

As I watch Logan's retreating form, I see Quinn. She's still dancing with the same guy and just as my gaze lands on them, he sweeps his finger down her cheek, holds her head in his hands, and kisses her. Her eyes flutter shut in surprise, but I see her sink into the kiss. Her hands clutch at his hair, and they turn their faces to get a better angle. *Damn.* I remember Quinn's kisses, her mouth and tongue warm and wet. *Fucking hell.* She looks so damn sexy, and I'm still staring at her when her eyes open mid-kiss. Surprised to find me watching, her eyes widen a bit. I expect her to close them again, but she doesn't, holding my gaze as she continues to kiss this other man. I watch, transfixed, as her lids become heavy with desire. Kisses turn into licks, then she bites his lower lip and pulls it back a bit, as if to show me. I remember what else she liked to bite.

Sweet baby Jesus. I can't stop watching the little show she's giving me.

"Hi there." A voice breaks into my concentration and I force my eyes away from Quinn to see the tall blonde smiling at me. The thin fabric of her white top leaves absolutely nothing to the imagination.

"Hi sweetheart." I turn to face her, trying my hardest to keep looking

4

into her eyes. "What brings you out tonight?"

She giggles and her tits bounce, drawing my gaze to follow their movement.

Fucking hell. Between Quinn and this girl, my cock is about to explode.

"Spring break just started," she informs me.

Ah, I thought she looked rather young. "Spring break? That's the most amazing time of your college career. How old are you?"

"21," she replies.

Perfect. I look down at her hard nipples and lick my lips. "I like your… shirt."

"Thank you." She smiles and shifts her body weight to one leg, fidgeting the way college girls do. I wonder if she can suck on her own nipples. *Fuck,* that would be hot. I make it my goal to get her to try.

"Can I get you a drink? I'm celebrating tonight, too."

"Absolutely. What are you celebrating?" She touches my forearm and inches closer.

"I had a great day at work," I say, eyeing her lips. They're thin, not like Quinn's full, delectable mouth. The fleeting thought makes me wonder what Quinn is up to. I turn to look at the spot I last saw her dancing and find her watching me. The guy is behind her now, hands on her waist, trying to get as close to her as possible. She's leaning back on his chest but her eyes are hot on me. She nods to my companion and grabs her own boobs, as if to say, *Wow, those are some boobs.* I raise my eyebrows and smirk at her. She points to the girl and mimics grabbing someone's tits in the air, as if challenging me to try to cop a feel.

Challenge accepted.

I nod with a wink and turn back to my new friend. She's twirling a strand of her long blonde hair and staring at the way my bicep strains against my sleeve. Good to know my time at the gym has more than just health benefits.

"What would you like to drink?" I ask her.

"Something sweet," she requests with a smile.

I try to think of a sweet drink, and the only words that come to mind have to do with tits. "Hmmm, what about a Slippery Nipple?"

She giggles again, and I blatantly watch her boobs bounce. I inch closer and she smiles, confessing, "I've never had one."

Visions of making her nipples slippery with my cum clog my thoughts. "Well, we should fix that right away." I turn to signal for the bartender's attention and order two. Once the shots are poured, I hand her one and hold mine up for a toast. "To celebrations and slippery nipples!"

She clinks her shot glass against mine and we tilt our heads back. It's way too sweet for me, but I love the way this girl is licking her lips in appreciation.

"So? What's the verdict?" I place my shot glass down and stand directly in front of her. So far she's getting zero points for conversation. I either need to make my move or take a pass. "How was it?"

"Mmmm, delicious."

"What's your name, sweetheart?"

"Crystal."

I smile at her and lean forward to talk directly into her ear. "Well Crystal, I'd like to celebrate with you tonight by getting my hands, mouth, and cock all over *your* nipples. Do you want to get out of here with me?" She shivers as I run my fingers down her upper arms and steps forward to press her chest against my chest. *Yesss.*

"Yes, I'd love to go home with you." My lust dims a bit at the thought of taking her to my house; history has proven that one-night stands are difficult to get rid of after sex. I prefer to go to their place or get a hotel room.

"Sorry, but my house is getting painted. Can we go to your place?" It's a total lie, but it's my go-to excuse when I'm trying to avoid bringing women home.

"Oh, I live with my parents." *Fuck.*

"Well that's a bummer. What should we do?" I trace the skimpy strap of her top and follow the neckline with my finger. Her nipples point up at me and I would only need to move the fabric over one measly inch to see them.

She arches into my touch and I almost can't take it anymore. My dick is a steel rod in my pants at this point.

"Do you want to find a bathroom?" she suggests helpfully.

Let it be known, a guy can *never* suggest using a seedy bathroom to get down and dirty with a girl, but if she doesn't mind, who am I to complain?

I smile at her and clasp her hand. "Come with me." I lead her toward the hallway with bathrooms. As we're walking, Quinn catches my eye and gives me a thumbs-up. I nod to her boy toy and wink. Max was all worried about things getting awkward after Quinn and I fucked, but he was worried for no reason. I have had my fair share of clingers, but she is not one of them. I love it that we get along so well we can even cheer the other person on when we're hooking up with someone else. That is not a common trait in women.

Crystal follows me through the crowded club until we turn down the hall where the bathrooms are. We can turn right to get to the bathrooms, but they are crazy crowded, and I don't know how much fun we could have with people constantly coming in and out. I look to the left and see a dark hall.

"Let's see what's down here." I try every doorknob we pass, but they're all locked. Near the end of the hall, I see a slightly recessed area with a waist-high file cabinet. If we stand in here, we will be pretty much out of sight.

Crystal reads my mind and hops up on the cabinet, putting her at just the right height. I step in between her legs and run my nose down her cheek. Her arms settle on my shoulders and she sighs sweetly.

"Did you know you have the most amazing tits I have ever seen?" I tell her truthfully.

"Do you like them?" She arches her chest against mine.

I nod rapidly. "Oh yeah. I want to see them, Crystal. Do you want to show them to me?"

She looks from side to side to make sure we're alone down here then giggles and bites her lip. "I don't normally do this kind of thing in a hallway," she tells me.

This girl has known me for all of 12 minutes. We both know I'm not the first random hookup she's ever had, but I don't want to make her feel bad about this. Women should be able to enjoy random hookups just as much as men. There is no shame in two consenting adults giving and taking pleasure from each other. I just need to make sure she wants to do this with me. "No pressure, sweetheart. If you don't like the idea of doing this right here, right now, I can walk you back to your friends and jack off later to the thoughts of what might have happened in this hallway."

"No, no, I want to be here. I'm just nervous about someone catching us, that's all," she says quickly.

Thank fuck. Although, *I* kind of like the idea of someone catching us.

"I'm standing right here, so I'll shield you from view. Besides, if we hear anything we can just stop." I smile my most convincing smile and lean down to kiss her.

Soft kisses at first. They're…nice.

But I need more.

I deepen the kiss, licking at the seam of her lips. She opens her mouth, giving me access, but this makes it worse, not better. It's the wrong ratio of

7

tongue, lips, and teeth. She's trying to touch my tonsils with her tongue, but her lips are so thin that her teeth dig into my lips and gums. This is not working for me. I back away from her mouth and trail kisses down her neck, onto her collarbone, and finally onto the tops of her breasts. *Much better.*

"I'm going to kiss these perfect nipples."

She nods her agreement and leans back against the wall. I mold my hands to her tits, gently massaging and weighing them in my hands. *Jesus Christ*, they're definitely real, so soft and full. I pull the neckline down so her boobs spill up and out of her top.

"Fuuuck. They're perfect."

She moans as I graze the backs of my fingers over her nipples, feeling the hard nubs that have me hypnotized.

Then I hear a soft noise to my side. When I turn to see if anyone is approaching, I find Quinn, standing in the shadows, staring directly at me.

I'm standing here with my hands on a complete stranger's tits and Quinn is watching me with rapt attention. There is no trace of jealousy in her expression, only desire. I glance at Crystal to see if she has noticed Quinn's presence, but her eyes are still closed. My cock throbs at the thought of Quinn watching me in action.

I meet Quinn's eyes. "You want me to keep going?" I ask her. She stares at my hands touching Crystal's nipples and nods.

Crystal, however, thinks I'm talking to her and says, "Yes, please keep going."

Fuck.

Quinn

Holy shit. I can't believe I'm standing here staring at Charlie's masculine hands as they fondle a set of amazing boobs, but my legs seem to be rooted to the floor.

Not 10 minutes ago, I was on the dance floor feeling pretty sure I was about to get lucky with a delicious man, but his friend had some emergency and he had to take off. Monica and Max left a few minutes ago, as did Logan and Tate. I had assumed Charlie and the girl with the giant boobs left when I saw them walking through the club. When my hookup for the night bailed, I decided to go to the bathroom and call it a night.

As I came down the hall to go to the bathroom, a sound coming from the opposite direction caught my attention and I paused to look down the dark hallway. It sounded kind of like a gasp, but I couldn't tell if it was a gasp of pleasure or fear. The lack of lighting made it difficult to see, so I crept down the hall as quietly as I could, the protective side of me wanting to make sure there wasn't someone being taken advantage of. When I heard it again, it was *definitely* a pleasure-filled moan. I froze, ready to turn back around as the girl seemed to be enjoying whatever was happening.

Then I heard the unmistakable voice of Charlie Nelson. Realizing *Charlie* was down the hall getting it on with some random girl did not make me want to leave like a normal person.

No.

My inner pervert wants to stay and watch. See, I've had Charlie's hands on me and I know how talented those hands are. He oozes sex appeal without even trying. With unruly blond hair, mischievous ocean blue eyes, golden skin, and a smile that could melt the panties off a nun, it's hard to resist his pull. The fact that he is honest to a fault, totally unfiltered, and completely up front about what he wants makes him quite charming. He is the perfect choice for no-strings-attached sex.

As my eyes adjust to the dim light, I can see Charlie's face. His cheeks are flushed with arousal and his eyes burn into mine. The girl is leaning back, arching her breasts into his touch with her eyes closed, and I must give props where props are due. Miss Double D has an amazing rack—full, soft boobs with pretty, upturned nipples. Charlie plucks at said nipples, pinching them slightly then lifting each one up toward his mouth.

My own nipples tingle beneath my clothes, and I'm tempted to reach under my shirt and play with them as Charlie starts to lick and suck the stiff peaks in front of him. He leaves them wet, shiny with his saliva, and alternates back and forth between them. Miss Double D whimpers when he bites one and pulls, and her thighs start to rub together. She must be so wet after Charlie's ministrations—I know I am. My body is so turned on, I'm not sure I can wait until I get home to masturbate. My lady bits are all awake and wanting attention.

Charlie grunts in appreciation and turns to look at me. "I bet you're soaking wet for me, aren't you?"

I nod frantically, and part of me wants him to turn his attention on me, but the other part wants to see what he does next. How far will he take it in the hallway of a club? Will she suck his cock? Will he fuck her?

The girl, once again, thinks he's talking to her and responds with, "God, yes."

She isn't much of a talker, but Charlie more than makes up for it.

"You know what would turn me on so much?" he asks her.

I'm afraid she's going to open her eyes, but she doesn't. "Hmm?"

"I want to see you lick your nipples. Have you ever done that before?" He lifts her breasts up, and I can see that it's likely possible. I can't do that, but it's not for lack of trying.

She shakes her head. "No, I've never tried."

"Can you try for me? I'd really like to see it," he tells her in a husky voice as he lifts one breast closer to her face.

She hesitates then leans her head down to see how close she can get. I hug the wall as best I can to stay out of sight but angle my body so I can continue to watch. She stares up at Charlie and tentatively sticks out her tongue to see if she can reach it, then she swipes it across her stiff peak experimentally.

"Fuuuuck," he groans, leaning in to lick it right after her. "Do it again."

They alternate licks until their tongues touch over her nipple, and I'm about to combust.

I'm not a lesbian—my attraction for men has been clearly established.

I've never wanted to kiss a woman, never thought I'd want to lick a girl's nipple, but *fuck*—I can't deny how aroused I am watching this scene unfold.

"I'm going to make you come so hard," he promises her.

Oh my God.

Do I want to watch this?

Yes, I do.

She's wearing a short skirt, so he has easy access. When she nods in agreement, he helps her adjust so she's sitting on the edge of the cabinet, legs spread wide, back leaning on the wall behind her.

"I need you to keep licking those pretty tits for me, okay? You look so hot doing that." She nods and continues, moaning softly as Charlie's hands slide up her thighs. His position makes it difficult for me to see what he's doing, but I can tell when he finally makes contact as they both groan.

Fuck. My own clit is throbbing.

I watch his back muscles shift as he moves his arms. I imagine one hand is holding her underwear to the side and the other hand is busy stroking her. When wet sounds reach my ears, I know I'm right.

Miss Double D moans and stops licking her nipples, only to pinch and pull at them instead. Her head falls back, pleasure softening her expression.

"That's it. I want to feel this tight pussy come around my fingers."

I watch her face and see the moment her orgasm hits. Her face scrunches up, almost in pain, then her mouth falls open and she gasps. She clutches on to Charlie's arms and shakes as he draws out her orgasm.

Charlie looks over his shoulder at me, his fingers still buried inside her, and groans. "Fucking hell, that was hot."

I'm on fire, sweat's trickling down my back, and I ache with the need to come. He must need to come, too.

"Mmmm," she agrees.

All of my senses are so wrapped up in what's happening in front of me, I fail to notice the sound of footsteps behind me until they're right next to me.

"What's going on down here?" a security guard asks.

I step in front of Charlie to give them a moment to put her shirt back on properly and face the tall, suspicious man. "Oh, nothing. I was just looking for my brother," I say louder than necessary. I turn to face Charlie. "Hey, there you are! I just wanted to let you know I'm taking off."

Miss Double D's tits are covered by the flimsiest excuse for a top I've ever seen, her cheeks are pink, and Charlie's erection is making a tent in his pants, but at least all essential parts are covered.

"Don't go," Charlie says to me, stepping away from the girl. "Let me take you home."

The security guard looks between the three of us with narrowed eyes. "You guys can't be down here. Please move along."

"No problem," I tell him and start walking toward the exit.

"Quinn, hang on a second!" Charlie shouts after me. My heart is beating erratically in my chest.

"Who was that?" I hear Miss Double D ask him.

Footsteps follow me and I hear Charlie tell her, "Sorry sweetheart, I have to get going. Thank you for everything."

"Hey wait!" she calls after him. "I didn't get your name!"

Leave it to Charlie to hook up with someone without even telling her his name.

"See you around," he says, dismissing her with a wave as he catches up with me. "Where are you going so fast?" He wraps his arm around my waist and pulls me into his side.

"What are you doing? Why aren't you back there with Miss Double D?" I ask him. He barks out a laugh at my name for her.

"They might have been triple D—did you see those tits?" He groans and looks to the ceiling with a tortured smile.

I did see those tits.

I saw him touch them. And lick them.

And I saw *her* lick them.

And I watched him make her come.

Holy fuck. I'm such a voyeur. It was like witnessing real, live porn, right in front of me.

"Don't you want to take her home and fuck her?" I ask him. Why did he leave her back there?

"What about you? Where is your boy toy for the night?" He smirks at me and pulls me to a stop near the restrooms.

"He had to go." I shrug. "I was just stopping at the bathroom on my way out when I…" I trail off.

"When you decided to watch me in action," he finishes for me.

I laugh. That pretty much sums it up.

"I'm glad you did, it was hot as fuck. Come home with me tonight."

I stop and turn to look at him. His ocean blue eyes are full of lust, desire, and naughty intentions. God, what those eyes do to me.

When I don't answer right away, he flashes me his panty-dropping grin, showing me his dimples and teeth, like a hungry wolf. "Come on, Red," he pleads, using his nickname for me. "My cock is as hard as a rock right now and I know you got all hot and bothered back there watching us. Let's go give each other some orgasms."

I stare into this handsome face and give in to what he wants because I want it just as much.

"Okay, let's."

"I'm going to go to the bathroom real quick. Meet me right here in five minutes." He leans down into my ear and says, "Do *not* get yourself off in the bathroom. I know you're about two seconds away from coming, but that orgasm is mine."

"You're so bossy," I complain. How did he know I was going to try to get some relief in the bathroom?

"You like me bossy."

I do.

Chapter 2

That's some party trick.

Charlie

I'm so worked up right now, I almost can't see straight. I had fully intended to fuck Miss Double D, as Quinn so aptly named her, but once the security guard interrupted us and Quinn bolted, having sex with Crystal lost its appeal. All I could think about was Quinn's gaze on me, watching me touch another woman, watching me make her come. She liked watching. I could tell how turned on she was by the way her chest was rising and falling so rapidly with every breath, the way she couldn't tear her eyes away from me, the sheen of sweat on her upper lip and neck.

My cock throbs in my pants just thinking about it.

Quinn insists on driving as I had a few shots tonight and we decide to go to her place because it's closer. Quinn lives in a condo that's quite nice, actually. Once we're in her car, I adjust my dick so my pants aren't strangling it.

"Congratulations on your new account, hotshot. I don't know if I told you earlier," she says.

"Thank you. You told me earlier, but you can tell me again. I like it when you

praise me."

"I'm not sure there's any room in this car, what with the size of your—"

"Cock?" I interject.

"I was going to say *ego.*"

"My cock is pretty big, too, you have to admit." I look over at her, flashing a naughty grin.

"I do like your cock, you know that. Are you fishing for compliments?"

I chuckle. I love that she admits to liking my cock. Most women shy away from dirty talk, but not Quinn. She's just as blunt as I am and isn't afraid to use words like cock or cunt.

"Isn't there any way you can go any faster? I'm dying over here." I'm two seconds away from pulling my dick out and jacking off while she drives.

"Calm your tits. We're almost there." She rolls her eyes but does push down on the gas pedal a bit harder.

"Speaking of tits, you liked watching me fondle Miss Double D, didn't you?"

"That was one impressive rack," she admits.

"Have you ever…been with a woman?" The way she was watching us made me think she'd like to join in. I could see Quinn experimenting with other women.

"No, I like dick, if you haven't noticed." She smiles and glances over at me. "But I can appreciate that boobs are sexy."

"What about the way she was able to lick her own nipples, wasn't that hot?" I almost came in my pants when I saw that she could do it. That's going in the spank bank, for sure.

"That's some party trick."

"Would you lick your own nipples if you could?" I ask her. Quinn's boobs are amazing, large and perky, though not quite as big as Crystal's.

"Hell yeah I would. That's like asking if you would suck your own dick if you could. Don't even tell me you've never tried to; I won't believe you."

I chuckle. "When I was 14, I tried as hard as I could, but I'm not that flexible."

"There's a sight I would have liked to see." She laughs.

"It wasn't even remotely sexy. I lived in fear that someone would walk in on me and catch an eyeful of me in different contorted positions." I laugh at the memory. "It would seem as though you are a closet voyeur. How did I not know this about you until tonight?"

She chews on her bottom lip. "I didn't know it myself. I mean, I like watching porn, but I've never come across an opportunity to watch re-al-life action."

I file that information away for later and almost weep with relief when we pull into her driveway. We turn to look at each other once the car is parked in her garage, and her eyes roam over my face, stopping on my lips. She leans forward, about to kiss me.

"Is there anything you need to do before I fuck you?" Once I start, I won't be able to stop until I'm balls deep inside of her.

"No."

I promptly get out of the car and walk around the front to open her door. As soon as she's standing, I'm on her, pulling her face toward mine and taking her mouth in a hot, wet kiss. Her lips are perfect, plump, and soft, and this kiss has the perfect ratio of lips, teeth, and tongue. Her tongue dances with mine and she's as ravenous as I am, licking and nip-ping at me. Her hands are busy too, untucking my shirt and reaching for my belt buckle. *Fuck.* I love that she's desperate for my dick, but I reach down and bat her hands away. We need to take this inside. I reach down to palm her ass and pick her up. Her legs wrap around my waist as I carry her to the door, stopping by the security alarm so she can disarm it.

Once the door is open, I stride inside and sit on the couch with Quinn straddling me. She grinds against my erection as I pull her shirt up and off. She reaches for my shirt next, and I reach over my head to tug it off. She sits back on my lap and stares down at my torso, lust and appreciation shining in her eyes. I also take a moment to appreciate my view of her. She wears a red, silky bra, but it seems like some of the material is missing because only the bottom half of her boobs are covered. The top half is ex-posed and I can see the pink skin of her areolas just hinting at where her nipples are. I trail my fingers across the edge of the bra, dragging the ma-terial down a bit to reveal the rest of her nipples. They're tight little nubs and I pinch them, hard. She gasps and arches her back, bringing her chest closer to my face.

"I really like this bra, Red. It seems like you chose the color just for me."

"I chose it for *me*. I like the way it makes me feel," she corrects me, her voice low and throaty.

"How does it make you feel?"

"Sexy."

"You don't need a bra for that. You're sexy all on your own. Stand up, take your pants off. I want to see the rest of you."

She stands and starts to unbutton her pants. "If I'm getting naked, then so are you. Come on, let me see that gorgeous cock of yours."

I comply with her request, grabbing a condom out of my wallet before stripping off my jeans, underwear, socks, and shoes. Quinn makes quick work of her pants and heels then goes to take off her panties but I stop her.

"Wait, *I* want to take those off." I sit back down on the couch and pull her to stand in front of me. The underwear is also silky red, and I love the contrast against her pale skin. Quinn is curvy, her hips flaring out from her waist. I smooth my hands down them before reaching back to squeeze her ass. It bounces when I let go and I can't wait to see it bounce on my cock.

"How wet did you get watching me earlier?" I know she was aroused, but I don't know how much.

"Soaking wet," she tells me.

"I want to see." I reach for the fabric that covers her pussy and run my fingers back and forth, testing the fabric for wetness. Sure enough, it's soaked. "Fuck, Red. I need to taste you."

"So taste me."

I slide her panties down her legs and help her step out of them. I lean forward and nuzzle my nose right in between her legs, inhaling her musky scent, then lick her slit, grabbing her ass and pulling her forward, closer to my mouth. She holds on to my shoulders to steady herself as my tongue laps at her cunt, but I can't quite get the right angle while she's standing up.

I stand, and she whimpers. "Why did you stop?"

I look around her living room and see the ottoman in front of the couch is plush and a decent size. "Lie back on this, I need to bury my face in your pussy."

She shivers at my words and reclines on the ottoman, legs spread wide and leaning up on her elbows so she can watch me. Her red hair is wild, her face is flushed, and her tits are heaving out of her bra as she pants in anticipation.

I kneel in front of her and hold her gaze as I lick her slowly, from opening to clit.

"Fuck, that feels good. Don't stop."

My licks are slow and steady, working her up, but not giving her enough friction to come. She keeps her gaze on me and I watch as she becomes more and more desperate.

"Charlie."

"Hmm?" I ask, like I have all the time in the world.

Quinn likes to be bossy too, and I like to make her beg. She hates begging, which makes me like it even more. She tips her hips up, chasing my tongue, but I move it to lick her folds instead.

"Charlie!" she complains.

"Did I ever tell you how much I love eating your pussy?" I ask her conversationally in between licks. I could eat her out for hours. Her red curls are neatly trimmed, framing her clit and pussy lips. I spread her wide open with my fingers and lick into her opening, pushing my tongue as deep as I can get it, then licking the walls as I come out. Her taste is addictive. Not all women taste the same—some are bitter, some more musky, some sour. Quinn's pussy tastes divine, the right combination of musky, salty, and sweet. I lap up her juices, avoiding her clit, trying to drive her crazy enough to beg me.

"Fuck! Charlie, I need you. Is that what you want to hear?"

Bingo. "What do you need? More of my tongue?" I focus on her clit and she moans loudly.

She doesn't answer me, so I back away.

"Charlie! Please, I need you to fuck me, okay? Please fuck me." She glares at me, pissed that she gave in and begged me, but so turned on.

I chuckle and reach for the condom. "My pleasure. Why didn't you just say so?"

Quinn

My body is so desperate to come but his tongue wasn't enough; I need his cock, and that fucking bastard always likes to make me beg.

He rolls the condom on and tugs on his gorgeous cock a couple of times before lining himself up with my pussy. He pulls me forward slightly, making my ass hang just a bit off the edge of the ottoman, and rubs the head of his dick up and down my folds, coating himself with my wetness. I feel his piercing, a stark contrast to the way a cock feels. The metal of the piercing is unforgiving while his penis is hard but soft at the same time. The combination makes my eyes roll back into my head and my clit throbs as I wait for him to push into me. He doesn't though, not right away. He picks up my legs and drapes them up over his shoulders.

"Charlie!" I bark. "Now. Fuck me *now*."

At my tortured command, he slams into me. I'm so wet, he gains entry easily, but his girth stretches me open, making me gasp at the sudden feeling of fullness.

"Fuck. This is going to be fast."

Thank God.

He leans forward, seeking purchase on the edges of the ottoman to hold on. I grab on to his forearms and he starts to thrust into me.

"Yessss." I love his unrelenting rhythm. His cock is big, and I feel the piercing inside, creating more friction with each movement in and out of me. It reaches all the right places and I'm on the verge of coming.

"I need you to come, Red. Are you close?"

"God, yes."

He leans down and latches on to one nipple, pulling it and biting it. Then he tends to the other nipple, and the extra stimulation pushes me over the edge. Pleasure steals my breath and my vision.

"Fuck!" I shout, wrapping my legs around his waist so I can keep him inside me. My pussy clamps around his dick while I come and he chuckles sexily.

"I love feeling you milk my cock. Was that good?"

"Mmmmm," I tell him, too far gone for words right now.

He kisses me and stays still as I come down from my orgasm. Then he starts moving again and I realize his cock is still rock hard. "You didn't come yet?"

"Not yet. Can you flip over? I need to see your ass."

"I'm not sure I can move," I groan. My body is always a bit paralyzed after an orgasm.

"I've got you." He pulls out of me, helps me sit up, then I turn and face plant into the ottoman. He positions me so I'm kneeling on the carpet, folded over the ottoman for support, ass sticking out at him. He palms my ass and slaps one cheek, the unexpected sting causing me to gasp.

"Don't fall asleep on me."

"Well then, give me something to stay awake for," I retort.

He spreads my ass cheeks apart, so wide I'm completely exposed to his view. I can't see what he's doing, but it seems like he's just looking at me.

"You see something you like?" I ask him, unnerved at his silence and stillness.

"I wish I could take a picture of you right now, all pliant and satisfied, your pussy wet and pink from my cock fucking you," he replies, his voice so husky. "I'd title it *Satisfaction*."

"I bet you have a collection of naughty pictures, don't you?" He is a photographer, after all.

He slides his cock up and down my crack, teasing me. Then he squeezes my ass cheeks together, sandwiching his dick in between them, and pumps up and down. The condom catches on my skin, not slick enough to glide smoothly, so he spits. The sound is so crass, and I feel the *plop* as his saliva lands on my skin, but when he starts moving again, the extra spit allows him to slide easily. *Fuck*, his cock is so big. It makes me squirm every time it passes over my asshole, and that piercing—it's so unyielding.

"You'd think I'd have naughty pictures, but I don't. I'm not much for remembering past hookups, but fuck, I want to keep this image for my viewing pleasure."

"Maybe I'll send you a picture sometime." I've never taken nude photos before, too afraid they would end up online somewhere, but the thought of Charlie jerking off to images of me gets me hot.

"I'd like that." He pulls back, his cockhead trailing down my crack to rub my clit. My nerve endings are still so sensitive from my orgasm that his touch is almost too much.

"Fuck, Charlie," I hiss, squirming away from his attention.

Surprisingly, he heeds my complaint and finally slides into me. It's a slow slide, inch by inch, until his pelvis is flush with my ass, then he stills. Pleasure zings through me at the way he stretches me and my recently sated body wakes up, hungry for more. I need friction, but he isn't moving. I huff in frustration.

"I want you to bounce that luscious ass on my cock," he says in explanation.

That I can do. I lift my upper body off the ottoman and brace myself. Holding on to the sides, I rock forward until I feel he's almost completely out then I back up quickly, loving the way he fills me up.

His hands cradle my hips and pull me back to meet him. "That's it, Red. God, your ass is fantastic."

Nothing is sexier than the sounds this man makes during sex. The deep rumbles, the muttered curses, the bossy commands, even the lewd remarks about my body are all so damn hot.

Charlie Nelson is one sexy beast.

Soon enough, he takes control and reaches around to rub my clit. He can read my body so well, and his fingers plucking my clit while he fucks me triggers an orgasm so intense, I practically pass out. I scream my release and try to grab hold of something to keep me tethered to Earth. He pitches forward on one final thrust and shouts hoarsely along with me. His arms come around me, stilling my flailing movements and holding me close as his dick pulses inside me.

"Fucking hell, that was amazing." He pants into my neck.

"Mmmm," I agree.

"You paralyzed?" He knows this about me—orgasms always steal my coordination and leave me in a heap of spasms and heavy limbs.

"Mmmmhmm."

"Stay here, I'll take care of you." Those words sound so foreign coming out of Charlie's mouth. I know he means he'll take care of my body. Not of *me*. I don't want anyone to take care of me.

I just want orgasms.

And Charlie is good at giving me orgasms.

I'll never depend on any man to take care of me ever again.

Charlie returns moments later with a warm cloth and wipes between my legs gently. Then he lifts me easily into his arms and carries me to my bed.

"Is it okay if I crash here? I can be out of your hair first thing in the morning," he promises.

I usually hate having men stay the night. If it were anyone else, I'd make them leave immediately. In fact, if it were anyone else, I wouldn't have brought them to my house at all, but Charlie is in this strange category. He isn't some random hookup; he's someone I see all the time in my circle of friends. I guess he's my friend with an amazing cock who I like to have sex with on occasion, so I trust him more than a random stranger.

That's the only reason I tug him down into bed with me, snuggle into his side, and promptly fall asleep with the warmth of his arm wrapped around my waist.

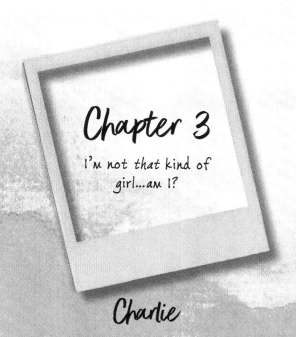

Chapter 3

I'm not that kind of girl...am I?

Charlie

Image 12 is a yes. I move it to the folder titled keep and advance to the next one. Image 13 is too blurry, so I promptly delete it. I'm sitting in my office, reviewing the proofs from my most recent photo shoot when my cell rings and my mom's face flashes across on the phone. Hoping she's calling to congratulate me on my new account, I swipe across the phone to answer the call.

"Hey Mom, did you get my message?" I left my parents a voicemail about my new account last week, but I never heard back from either one of them.

"What message?" she asks.

"I got a new account at work," I remind her, smiling.

"Hmm, what does that mean? I don't understand, is that like getting a new client?" My mom is a lawyer, and so is my dad...as well as my older brother, and my younger sister.

I am the only one in the family that didn't get the lawyer gene, and I'm my parents' biggest disappointment because of it.

They hate that I didn't follow in their footsteps. It would have been forgivable if I didn't go into criminal law like them, but choosing to go into an artistic field like photography? I might as well have committed murder.

"It means I'm getting more work in my firm, expanding my portfolio, and making myself a more valuable asset to the company," I explain.

"That's nice dear," she says, distracted and unimpressed, "Did you get my message?" My smile fades. Her message was about coming to a family dinner next Sunday at the country club they belong to. I hate going to those things. It's all about appearances and making everyone else believe your life is better than theirs, and I hate that shit. Not only was I born without the lawyer gene, I was born without the fake gene, too. I say what I think. When I'm asked a question, I give an honest answer. I don't see why everyone has to pretend to be something they're not. People might balk at my bluntness, but more often than not, they appreciate my directness.

"Yeah, I got your message. I'll be there." I sigh, bracing myself for her warnings.

"Charles, this is going to be a big night for your sister. You need to make an effort to act accordingly," she says meaningfully. Here we go. What she means is, *Come, but don't act like yourself.*

"Mom, if you don't want me there, then don't invite me. I'm not going to pretend to be something I'm not in front of your stuck-up friends who you actually hate."

"You can goof off when you're with your friends. Would it kill you to tone it down a notch when we're in polite company? I know Tabitha is looking forward to seeing you."

That's how she gets me—I have a soft spot for my baby sister. "No worries, Mom. I'll be there, and I'll try not to embarrass you."

"Please bring an appropriate date this time," she adds.

"I'm not bringing a date. I'll be there by myself." Last time a plus one was required, I brought my flavor of the week. Suffice it to say, she did not meet my mother's standards. Also, it gives the wrong impression when you introduce a hookup to your family. She thought it meant she was important to me, and despite my blunt honesty about simply needing a date for a family function, she started looking at me with hearts in her eyes.

I don't do hearts.

"You must bring someone—I've already put the reservation in and marked you down with a plus one," she insists.

"Well, can't you call them and tell them to subtract my plus one? I don't have anyone to bring."

"If we change our headcount then we can't sit at the center table, and I want to sit at the center table," she whines.

The center table. I hate this shit. God forbid I'm the reason we can't sit at the table that affords everyone else the best view of the Nelsons.

I grit my teeth. "Fine, Mom. I'll be there with a plus one." Maybe I'll bring Max with me.

"Thank you, dear. Five o'clock sharp, don't be late."

"See you then."

I hang up and sigh. It's such a chore to deal with my family lately. When we were kids, my brother, Domenic, and my sister, Tabitha, and I were close. Dom and I used to wrestle around and joke all the time, and we totally ganged up on any guys that approached Tabby—she hated every second of it. Then they went to law school and I didn't. I wish I could say we remained close in adulthood, but they're off doing lawyerly things. I miss their camaraderie, and it's probably my fault as I try to avoid family functions as much as possible because of my parents, which means I don't get to see them as much, either. I decide to start a group text with them.

Me: Just got orders from Mom to be at Green Briars Sunday at 5pm.

Dom: You coming?

Tabby: Please say you're coming! I miss you!

Me: I'll be there. She's making me bring a date—how pissed do you think she'll be if I bring Max or Logan?

Dom: Don't tell me you can't find anyone to come with you.

Me: Who are you bringing, D?

Dom: Friend from work.

Tabby: Don't you have a female friend you can bring?

Me: Maybe.

Tabby: I hope your date wears leopard print again. Do you remember Mom's face last time?

Me: Ugh. How could I forget?

Tabby: LOL

Dom: Have a meeting in five, see you Sunday

Me: I'll be the one at the bar.

Tabby: We'll join you. See you then!

Female friend…I don't have many of those. Quinn is the closest thing I have to a female friend, but I'm not sure I can convince her to go to this with me. Maybe I can bribe her with orgasms—surely she'll agree to put up with my family for a couple of hours in exchange for sex.

Quinn

This evening finds me wearing comfortable sweats with my most favorite throw blanket over my lap and a bowl of pistachio ice cream covered with hot fudge in my hand. I take a bite and moan in delight as the combination of sweet and salty melts in my mouth.

"So what's up with you and Charlie?" Monica asks me as she takes a bite of her own ice cream. The question is not a new one.

I give her the same answer I always give her. "Nothing, we just like to fuck. He has an *amazing* cock."

"And you have no romantic notions about him at all?" Her hazel eyes study me as if trying to catch me in a lie. This is her standard follow-up question to my standard answer. We might as well just record the conversation and play it back every so often.

"I don't want a relationship, Monica. You know this. Why is it so hard for you to believe that Charlie and I are just fuck buddies?"

"Well, I guess it's because I don't understand it. You guys have been sleeping together for what, almost seven months now?"

I stop to think back. Has it been that long? "If you're counting from the first night you introduced us, then yes, though we've only had sex a handful of times. It's not like we're exclusive either. I've been with other people and so has he. We just like to have fun," I insist.

"But don't you ever miss being in a relationship?" she asks.

"No, and please don't go there. The only thing I need a man for is sex. Everything else is under control."

"Okay, okay." She holds up her hands in a placating gesture. "I'm sorry. I just worry about you, sweetie. I want you to find your happily ever after."

"Ugh, barf. Reid sabotaged any notion of happily ever after for me."

Reid is my ex-husband, the fucker who promised me forever. He showered me with love and affection, told me it was us against the world, was my number one fan and best friend, made me believe in love.

And then, when I was going through an emotionally tough time, he proceeded to cheat on me with his secretary.

How cliché.

Fucking asshole. I don't want to think about him. He made an ass out of me and taught me a valuable lesson: love is for fools. After I divorced his ass and wallowed in misery for a while, I wised up and decided to use men simply for sex. I've been so much happier ever since. No feelings are involved, only orgasms, a mutual exchange of pleasure (if I'm lucky) and then we both move on. No unmet expectations, no disappointment, no hurt feelings, and no cheating douchebags.

"I just think you're letting him rob you of a chance at something beautiful with someone," she says wistfully.

"I'm glad you have Max, babe, but I'm okay the way I am. I'm 32 years old, I make a living off of my art, and I love my home. I'm happy with my life, honest," I say, trying yet again to convince her. "Tell me about you. How are things with you and Max?"

She blushes—*actually blushes* at the thought of him. "Really good. He says he has a surprise date for us tomorrow."

"Ooooh, maybe he'll take you shopping for sex toys. Have you guys ever played with toys together?" I love watching her squirm. Monica isn't exactly shy, she just hasn't embraced her sexuality as openly as I have.

"No way!" she splutters.

"Maybe he's planning for your first night of anal!" I guess.

"Uhh…" She looks to the side.

"Shut the fuck up! Did he already pop your anal cherry?" I'm impressed—Max is taking good care of my girl.

Her face turns bright red and she bites her lip. That is all the answer I need.

"He so totally did! Was it good? Bad? Tell me all the dirty details!" I press.

She clears her throat and shrugs. "I never thought I'd like that kind of thing, but Max makes everything so good for me."

"So you liked it! I knew you were a closet anal whore!"

"Quinn!" She throws a pillow at me in mock outrage.

"What's the big deal?" I deflect the pillow and save my bowl of ice cream from falling off my lap. "I like anal. If it's done well, it's awesome. It's all about lube and preparation. Toys help, too. If you hold a vibrator against your clit while he's breaching the back door, you barely notice any pain at all," I inform her, matter-of-factly.

"I'll keep that in mind, Miss Sexpert."

"The next step is to put the vibrator in your hooter while Max's dick is in your tooter. That, my friend, feels amazing. Max would love it and so would you. I recommend you surprise him with it next time." I wiggle my eyebrows. "Double penetration for the monogamous."

She laughs at my choice of words and licks her spoon. "Sounds painful."

"You don't know what you're missing unless you try."

"Have you ever?" She raises her eyebrows.

"Used a toy during anal? Yes."

"No, I mean, have you ever had sex with two guys at the same time?"

"Not yet. I've never had the opportunity arise. Have *you*?" I'm 100% sure she hasn't.

"No way, threesomes are a hard limit for me. I'm not that kind of girl." She shakes her head from side to side.

"Listen to you, Miss Hard Limit. Where did you learn that term?"

She rolls her eyes. "I do read you know. I love me some good smut."

"Ooooh, tell me, tell me! What's the kinkiest, filthiest book you've read that you never want anyone to find out you read?" I love reading smut.

"I'm not telling you!"

"I bet I've read it, too. Hey, you want to know what I *just* read that was so good?"

"What?"

"*The Unrequited* by Saffron Kent. It's amazing, you *have* to read it."

"What's it about?"

"Forbidden love. A college student falls in love with her professor— her *married* professor."

Her eyebrows shoot up. "Teacher-student is my favorite."

"It's hot as fuck. She gives him a BJ *under his desk*." A small, secretive smile blossoms on her face at the word desk. "Wait, have you and Max fucked on your desk at work?"

There's that blush again. "I don't know what you're talking about. Oh, look at the time." She checks her wrist that doesn't have a watch on it.

I laugh at her. "Monica! You hussy!"

"Shut up!" She laughs.

We chat about books for a while, then catch up on other less fun topics like work and family.

Once she heads out, I tidy up our mess, wash the ice cream bowls, and wash up for the night. I change into my sleep attire, which consists of a tank top and underwear, and then I slide into bed and burrow into the soft sheets. I reach for my laptop, open my nightstand drawer, and pick out my favorite vibrator.

It's Tumblr time.

As I log in to my account and wait for it to load, my thoughts drift back to that night with Charlie. I remember him watching me when I kissed the sexy guy on the dance floor. He didn't look away when he saw me entwined with someone else, and he didn't look jealous, either. He looked aroused, and he kept watching me. I loved it. Holding his gaze while I was in the arms of someone else…it was intoxicating. I *wanted* him to watch me.

Then later, stumbling on him, seeing him touch that other woman…I should have left right away, but he caught me and his eyes dared me to stay. *Fuck.*

My body warms at the memory. My Tumblr account is my go-to source for porn and I follow a wide variety of pages. I scroll down, skimming over the pictures of male/female couples. Then I see a GIF that catches my eye: a naked woman with a man fucking her from behind. The look on her face is pure pleasure and she stares into the eyes of a second man, seated in the corner of the room. This man is fully dressed, but he has his cock out and is stroking it while he watches the woman get fucked.

I picture myself as the woman, in a room with two men, one fucking me while the other watches. God, why does that turn me on so much? Then I picture Charlie being the man who watches me take another man's cock and my pussy clenches. I imagine him jacking off, watching me come while another man comes inside me. *Whew.*

Time to turn on my vibrator. I run it over my underwear, teasing my clit without giving it too much stimulation. I could come in two seconds, but where's the fun in that? I want to draw it out a bit. Closing my legs around the vibrator, I hold it in place against my panties while I keep scrolling down the website. I want to find a video to watch. I play a little game with myself when I masturbate—I try to see if I can come at the same time the people in the video do. On Tumblr, though, not all videos are created equal. Sometimes it takes a while to find something that strikes my fancy.

A few scrolls later, a video gets my attention. This time, it's a brunette woman watching while a man fucks a busty blonde. *Yes.* I scoot my underwear down and touch the vibrator directly against my wet folds, moving it up and down while I watch. The man is nowhere near as hot as Charlie is, but the blonde kind of resembles Miss Double D. The brunette is sitting back against the headboard while the couple fucking is lying across the bed sideways, right in front of her. She strums her clit as the man thrusts into the blonde over and over again. *Fuck,* I like that. I push the vibrator inside me and pump it in time with the man on the video. He comes all over the girls' tits, and the brunette crawls over to them and licks it off her. My eyes widen as I watch her lick the man's cum off another woman's chest and I can't hold back my orgasm. Pleasure so intense it almost hurts courses through me and I tremble through my release. I turn my vibrator off, the sensation quickly becoming too much for my pulsating clit, and catch my breath.

Fuck, that was hot.

Would I ever want to do that? Watch Charlie fuck someone else?

Lick his cum off of someone else?

Or would I want him to watch *me*? See him stroke his cock while I suck some other man's dick?

My imagination goes wild with the possibilities.

But that's all it is—a fantasy. Just my imagination.

So what if I get off to thoughts of a threesome?

That doesn't mean I want it to happen in real life.

I mean, I'm not *that* kind of girl.

Am I?

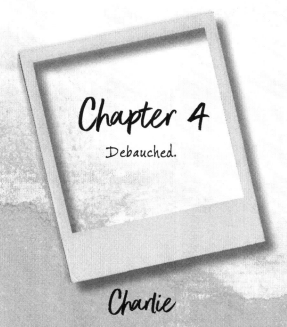

Chapter 4

Debauched.

Charlie

Logan, Max, and I have a long standing date at O'Malley's for happy hour on Fridays, and we all try to make it unless there's a legitimate reason to miss.

"Look what the cat dragged in," Logan comments when I arrive 15 minutes late.

"Yeah, yeah, sorry I'm late. I'll buy the next round." I greet each of them with a hearty hug, giving Max an extra squeeze. "Congratulations, buddy. I can't believe you're getting married!!" I tell him. He beams at me and I can't help but smile back at him as I take a seat and start pouring a beer into the empty cup waiting for me.

"Thanks. It feels a bit too good to be true."

"I always thought Logan and Tate would be the first ones to get married." I look over at Logan. "What gives? You guys have been together for a million years. What are you waiting for?"

Logan throws a peanut at me. "Fuck off, dude. Why aren't you getting married? Oh, that's right, because you can't keep a woman around long enough."

I burst out laughing. "It's not that I can't keep a woman around long enough, it's that I don't *want* to."

"Well there you go," Logan points out. "You have your life choices and I have mine."

Point taken. "Wow, I didn't realize you were on your period," I mutter. Turning my attention back to Max, I ask him, "So when will you guys tie the knot?"

"We haven't planned that far ahead, but I'd marry her tomorrow if she'd let me. Will you guys be my best men?" He looks from me to Logan.

"Both of us?" I ask him, surprised. The three of us have been best friends since grade school, but I always figured he'd ask Logan—he's way better at adulting than I am.

"Of course!"

"You know I'll probably make inappropriate comments in my best man speech, right? Are you sure you don't want to limit my duties to just a regular groomsman? I think I can handle that without fucking it up."

"You're not going to fuck anything up, Charlie. I want you to be my best man, inappropriate comments and all." He smiles at me.

"But you know *my* speech is going to be better, right?" Logan asks him.

"Fuck you, Logan. My speech is going to kick your speech's ass," I say, puffing out my chest in mock seriousness.

Max chuckles. "*Both* of your speeches are going to be awesome."

I narrow my eyes at Logan, who smirks at me with confidence. *It's on.* I need to start working on mine immediately.

"So how's work going?" Max asks Logan.

As he tells us about the latest with his job, my cell vibrates in my pocket. I take it out and see it's a text from Quinn. *Hmmm.* She usually doesn't get in touch with me unless she's feeling frisky. I click on the notification to open the text, curious to see what she said.

Instead of a text, I find that she has sent me a picture. It's of her right shoulder, and her bare skin peeks out from beneath the strands of her wavy red hair. The picture is not explicit—no private parts are exposed—but fuck if it isn't sexy, sensual even. My cock twitches as I zoom in to look at her creamy white skin covered in freckles. I want to touch her hair, sweep it behind her shoulder, trace the path those freckles make with my tongue. My fingers swipe at the keyboard to text her back.

Me: Mmmm, Red. Thank you for this picture.

Red: You're welcome. What are you up to?

Me: Happy hour with the boys.

Red: What are you doing later?

Me: What did you have in mind?

Red: Your cock in my mouth.

Me: That can be arranged.

Red: Come over when you're done.

Me: Sounds good.

Me: Actually, I have a favor to ask of you, too.

Red: A sexual favor? A BJ isn't a good enough favor?

Me: A non-sexual favor.

Red: Hmmm, it'll cost you.

Me: I'm willing to pay you in orgasms.

Red: We'll talk when you get here.

"Seriously, Charlie. Who are you texting over there with that grin on your face? You setting up a play date?" Logan says, drawing my attention back to the conversation.

"Uuuuuhhh, yes. If you want to know the truth, I am."

"Please tell me it isn't with someone like that one chick you dated. Candi? You know, the one with the high-pitched giggle?" Max comments, groaning.

I cringe. That giggle was unfortunate, but she had a thing for anal, which kept my attention for a couple weeks until I couldn't stand listening to her laugh anymore.

"No. I admit Candi wasn't one of my best decisions, but we both had fun while it lasted," I tell them. I don't mention Quinn's name because then they will think there is more going on with us than there really is.

"I can't wait until the day you fall for someone." Max grins.

"You're going to be waiting a long time, then," I tell Max. Been there, done that, and I have no desire to repeat that fiasco ever again.

"I bet he falls hard," Logan says to Max, like I'm not even here.

"He won't even know what hit him," Max agrees, grinning.

"Have you met me? What about my track record for the past 10 years says I'm a relationship kind of guy?" I ask.

"I think there's a lid for every pot," Max tells me.

"And sometimes the best things happen when you least expect them," Logan adds helpfully.

"When did you two start working for Hallmark? I need to find some single friends." I shake my head in mock disgust. "I'm going to go to the bathroom to make sure my balls didn't run away from this conversation." I stand. "I suggest you guys find yours." Logan and Max bust up laughing as I make my way to the bathroom.

My cell vibrates in my pocket again and I pull it out, hoping Quinn has sent me another picture.

The universe is smiling at me because that's exactly what it is. Like the first one, it's not explicit. It's a picture of her waist—well, half of it anyway. It starts just under her breast, capturing the curve of her waist and the flare of her hips. No nipple is showing, no pubic hair is exposed, only milky white skin with the sexiest freckles ever. I can tell she's naked and lying in bed, her silky purple sheets contrasting against her fair skin. *Mmmm.* I make a folder in my phone labeled *Red* and save both pictures for easy access later.

Fuck. I check my watch and see that I've only been here 45 minutes. Max and Logan will probably give me grief for arriving late and leaving early, but my cock is eager to get in between Quinn's cherry red lips.

I go to the bathroom then make my way back to the table, an excuse to leave on the tip of my tongue. It dies when Max says, "You're not leaving yet, right?"

"Uh, no, of course not." I sink down into my chair and deflate.

"Are we keeping you from your play date?" Logan smirks at me knowingly.

I scratch my forehead with my middle finger.

"You guys would never believe how much work having a dog is. I feel like we have a newborn for all the attention Sparky requires." Logan says, changing the subject when I don't answer.

One subject leads to another, and I covertly check the time on my phone. 20 minutes have passed, and I *really* want to leave. Just as I begin to make my excuse for real this time, I look over Max's shoulder to find Monica, Tate, and Quinn approaching the table. Half of me wants to bitch that the ladies are crashing happy hour, but the other half is so excited to see Quinn, I want to throw her over my shoulder and go back to her place.

I raise my eyebrow at her questioningly.

"Ladies, how nice of you to join us," I comment, flashing them my most charming grin.

"Sorry we're crashing happy hour," Monica apologizes to me, giving me big puppy dog eyes. I chuckle and give her my usual greeting, picking her up and spinning her around. "No worries, beautiful. Congratulations on your engagement to the male nurse."

"Easy there," Max growls. I love seeing him get so riled up whenever I touch Monica—as if I'd ever be interested in my best friend's girl.

"Relax, you lovesick fool," I tell Max, setting Monica down and holding up my hands. Then it's Tate's turn. She's been with Logan far longer than Monica has been with Max, so Logan doesn't even blink at my over-zealous greeting. Finally, I step in front of Quinn. Her eyes are lined in purple and her lips are painted cherry red. It might look stupid on some other woman, but it just makes Quinn look exotic.

"Red," I say in greeting, a smile spreading slowly across my face at the thought of getting her alone later.

"Just so you know, this wasn't my idea," she whispers in my ear as I give her the same greeting.

"Whose idea was it?" I ask, setting her down. The only empty seat happens to be next to me, and I press my leg against hers as we sit.

"I thought we should celebrate Max and Monica's engagement," Tate pipes up, "so we stopped by to pick Quinn up."

"Well, what are you drinking? Let me get us some spirits." I collect drink orders from everyone and Quinn volunteers to help me get the drinks from the bar.

On our way there, I grab her hand and duck down the back hall, pressing her up against the wall with my body.

"I was just about to make excuses to leave and come over," I tell her.

"Eager to see me, are you?" She smiles up at me.

"Definitely. Thank you for the pictures." I stare down at her lips, so sexy painted in red lipstick. I don't kiss her, though, as that would definitely transfer to my lips. For some fucked up reason, I want to see it smeared all over my dick.

She laughs. "It's not like I sent you anything exciting."

"I beg to differ." I take her hand and bring it down to my erection. "I *really* liked them."

She squeezes my cock and blows out a breath. "How long do you think we have to stay?"

"Let's go have a drink and get out of here."

"Agreed."

Quinn

Charlie and I bring back a pitcher of margaritas and one of beer and begin pouring. I know Monica loves margaritas, and the bartender even gave us salt-rimmed glasses, my favorite. I pour margaritas for the ladies and Charlie pours beer for the guys. Then we raise our glasses and give a hearty, "To Max and Monica!"

I clink glasses with everyone, smiling despite myself. I'm not the biggest fan of marriage, but Monica looks so damn happy. I notice she puts her drink down without taking a sip. *Huh, that's weird.* Then Max pulls her into his lap to kiss her soundly and her drink is forgotten.

"So when are you thinking about having the wedding?" Tate asks the happy couple.

"I'm not sure yet," Monica tells her, looking over at Max.

"Well, let me know so I have enough time to plan my awesome speech," Charlie says, narrowing his eyes at Logan.

"You should just start planning now since you'll need all the time you can get," Logan retorts.

I sense a bit of friendly competition between Logan and Charlie. I can't even imagine what Charlie would say in a best man speech, and the thought makes me chuckle.

"Hey, can I be in charge of planning the bachelor party?" Charlie asks Monica.

Monica stares at Charlie and blinks. "As long as you promise me it won't be another episode of *The Hangover*."

"You know, I don't think—" Max starts to shake his head at Charlie.

"Fuck that, Max. You're *having* a bachelor party," Charlie interrupts.

"No worries, because *I'll* plan your bachelorette party," I tell Monica as I sip my drink. This is right up my alley.

Charlie smirks at me, and I raise my drink to signal for him to take a sip as well. My body is revved up and I want to get out of here. His smirk turns into a knowing grin and he tilts his head back to gulp down his beer. I watch the way his lips mold to the glass and his Adam's apple bobs as he swallows. God, that Adam's apple—why is it *so* sexy?

The next 30 minutes of conversation are the slowest of my life, especially because Charlie starts touching me. I know I should discourage this public display, as this is fodder for our friends—especially Monica, who gives me a look like she thinks we make a cute couple—but I don't care what they think. I'm desperate for his touch and if that makes them think we're more than just fuck buddies, so be it.

Finally, after we've discussed the pros and cons of separate versus joint bachelor and bachelorette parties (Monica and Max vote for a joint party, Charlie and I insist they be separate), Charlie tugs me to a standing position and announces that we're leaving. *Thank God*. My underwear is soaked, the fabric sticking to my skin, and I can't stop thinking about sucking his cock.

We decide to go to his place this time, as it's closer to O'Malley's. On the way out, Charlie orders a car to pick us up since we've both been drinking, and the second we step outside, his big body cages me against the exterior brick wall of the club.

"I thought we'd never get out of there," he says breathlessly against my ear, licking my neck.

I sigh and angle my head up, giving him better access. He licks up to my mouth and kisses me, our bodies pressed together so tight. He's hard, and his erection presses into my belly. It's like a magnet, and I can't resist reaching down to cup him through his pants.

"Fuck, Red, you can't do that out here. You trying to get us arrested?" he teases, biting my lower lip and sucking it into his mouth. He tastes like the beer he was drinking but his mouth is still delicious. He pins me against the wall with his pelvis and I feel the scratch of the brick against my back. Somehow, it makes me burn hotter for him.

Minutes pass while we make out on the street like teenagers. Finally, a car pulls up to the sidewalk and beeps. Charlie looks over his shoulder and recognizes the make and model from the service he ordered. "Come on, let's take this to my place."

The driver looks at us warily as we slide into the backseat. "No sex in my car," he warns us.

Charlie chuckles and raises his hands in the air. "No worries, we can wait 10 minutes," he reassures the driver. No matter how horny we are, the rank smell of body odor and stale sweat kills our libido pretty quickly. I cover my nose and make a face at Charlie. He flares his nostrils in disgust, making a gagging face, and we chuckle while we endure the short drive to his place.

I was amazed to learn that Charlie has his own house—for some reason I pictured him living in an apartment. When he brought me here for the first time, I expected a frat house vibe, maybe even a keg in his kitchen, but surprisingly, Charlie has furnished his house to feel like a home. The decor is decidedly masculine, but the furniture is contemporary and comfortable and the walls are decorated with what I assume is his photography.

Charlie unlocks the front door, letting me pass in front of him. Once he locks it, he turns to me, a wicked sexy grin on his face.

"How many times have you masturbated thinking about that night?" Charlie asks, his voice a husky rasp in my ear.

"So many times," I admit.

"God, me too." His eyes glow with arousal and he stares at me like he wants to eat me up. "Kneel down, Red. I want your mouth on my cock. You can decorate it with that lipstick of yours, make it into a work of art."

I don't balk at his command only because I want him in my mouth just as bad as he does. I lower myself to the floor and kneel in front of him, reaching for the buckle on his pants. My mouth practically salivates as I carefully unzip and lower his pants and boxers. He's already hard, his erection catching on the fabric then springing up to salute me once free from the confines of his clothes.

Charlie Nelson is well endowed. I want a picture of his magnificent penis for my masturbation material. I've searched Tumblr high and low for a dick as pretty as his, but I can't find a good match. He's thick and long, his pubic hair dark blond and sparse at the base. The skin is golden and soft, stretched taut around his hard shaft. It's a smooth cock, too, no angry bulbous veins protruding, and I'm always drawn to the pierced head. He has an apadravya, a barbell that runs vertically through the head of his penis. One ball sits on the underside, right where the head meets the shaft, and the other ball is on the top, right in between the shaft and the tip. So, no matter what position we're in, there are two points of extra stimulation.

Charlie's voice interrupts my reverie. "While I love the way you're staring at my cock right now, I'd love it even more if you touched it—preferably with your lips or tongue."

I look up into his face and see him watching me, muscles corded with tension, hands balled into fists at his sides. He towers over me like a Greek god. Some might think the man is in the position of power in this situation, but he isn't. I have all the power right now, and I want to drive him crazy.

"I think I like the idea of your cock being my canvas," I tell him, gripping the base of him. I lean in close and rest it on my face, loving the heat and weight of it on my cheek. He grunts at the contact, swiveling his hips to get more friction. Meeting his gaze, I position his penis just so, and land a purposeful kiss at the base, stamping my red lipstick on him. His eyes flare and he smiles, his dimple popping out on one side. Then I drag my lips up the side of the shaft, pulling the red color in a smeared line. I'm sure it's smeared all over my mouth, too, but I don't care. I place another kiss around the barbell on the top of his head, stamping my lipstick around his piercing. My tongue sneaks out to touch the piercing as I do this, unable to resist pushing on it in the process.

A hasty, "*Fuck*," is my reward, and the sound goes straight to my clit.

I sit back and admire my handiwork. The sight of his penis with red lips at the tip and the base with lipstick smeared down the side should look ridiculous, but it doesn't. We both groan in appreciation and I need more.

Before my tongue touches his tip, he reaches down and angles my chin up, inspecting the mess my lipstick made on my face, I'm guessing. "This is a good look on you, Red. If I could take a picture, I'd title it *Debauched*."

The thought of him taking my picture shoots a tingle through me. I actually liked sending him those pictures earlier, though I purposefully left out my face. Do I trust him enough to take a picture of my face?

"Do you want to take pictures?" I ask him.

"Fuck yes, can I?"

"Only if you promise not to get my full face, keep them to yourself, and password protect them on your phone."

"Done." He reaches down into his pants pocket and finds his cell. The screen lights up as he unlocks it then he holds it above me, positioning it to get a shot.

"One more thing." I hold my hand up to cover my face. He lowers the phone and looks at me expectantly. "I need a picture of your dick."

He smirks, surprised by my request. "I'll send you all of them."

I put my hand down and lean my face up at him. He focuses intently on the screen, tapping to change a few settings. His eyes gleam, as if he likes what he sees, and it makes me so hot. The sound of the shutter going off makes it real—I've officially lost my mind—but I don't care. I reach forward and pull his cock close to my lips.

"Don't forget to get this," I remind him. His cock jumps in my hand, his excitement impossible to ignore. I tongue the bottom ball of his piercing and lick all around it, loving the texture of the cool metal on my tongue and also loving the feel of his skin so warm in contrast. I trace the line up from his piercing to tongue the slit of his opening. I wiggle my tongue around it, licking off the pre-cum that gathers there.

The shutter continues to go off and the sound only ramps up my arousal. I feel so brazen, so naughty, getting my picture taken like this.

"I want a picture with your lips stretched wide around my dick." He grunts and bucks his hips, seeking entrance into my mouth. I smile at his bossiness, but do as he says. His girth does stretch my mouth and I definitely can't take all of him. I wrap my hand around the base and take in as much of him as I can then stop to look up at him with my mouth so full. His eyes glitter as he stares into the screen, now snapping pictures every few seconds.

I swallow around the head of his cock and he curses, closing his eyes as the sensation draws his focus away from the camera. This is what I love to see—Charlie out of control.

I get to work, bobbing slowly on his cock, tugging on his shaft with my hand then sneaking my other hand beneath his balls to play with the skin there. He's so sensitive and I feel his cock pulse in my mouth when I sneak my finger closer to his asshole.

A lot of guys love ass play, though I've never gone very far in that department with Charlie. His reaction now makes me want to see how much he'll let me do. I turn my focus to his balls, licking all around to get them nice and wet. Then I nuzzle under them, licking the skin between his balls and his ass as far as I can reach with my tongue.

"Fuck, that feels good," he praises as he widens his stance.

I can reach farther and don't hesitate to bite the crease of skin where his ass meets his leg then I lick away the sting with my tongue and tease all around his hole. Before I return to his cock, I coat my finger in saliva. Then I reverse my path, licking around his balls and up his shaft, opening my mouth as wide as I can around his cock. He groans, closing his eyes and leaning back against the door.

As I work the tip of his cock with my mouth and the base with my hand, I sneak the wet finger in between his ass cheeks, finding the puckered skin. It clenches tight at the attention and he grunts, eyes flying open to look down at me. I keep my finger still, just resting on his asshole.

"Red?" he questions. I don't answer him with words, but I hold his gaze as I continue to stroke his shaft. My saliva has dripped down his cock so my hand slides easily up and down, matching the movements of my mouth.

He relaxes as I blow him, and he slowly starts to thrust into my mouth, his dick hitting the back of my throat. I try to relax my throat as best as I can, but he's so big, my gag reflex threatens to surface. I swallow, hoping to keep it under control. He must feel the movement of my throat swallowing against him because he curses.

"Your mouth is so perfect," he tells me. "I want to come down your throat."

I moan around his cock in agreement. I want him to come down my throat, too.

He picks up the pace, fucking my mouth. The cell phone slips from his fingers and he reaches down, holding my face in his hands, watching his dick slide in and out of my mouth. The constant poke of his dick to the back of my throat makes me tear up.

He's close; I can tell by the way his cock swells in my mouth and his balls draw up. My finger is forgotten by him, but not by me. I push forward slowly, breaching his hole just to the first knuckle. His eyes widen in surprise and the added sensation pushes him over the edge. He shouts as his orgasm hits and his cock jerks, semen flooding into my mouth. I swallow as fast as I can, but I'm not fast enough. Some of his cum leaks out of my mouth, leaving a warm trail down my chin and neck. His muscles clench around my finger as his dick pulses and I lick his cock like a lollipop, cleaning him off as he comes down from his orgasm.

"Sweet baby Jesus, Red, that almost killed me," he wheezes, pulling out of my mouth. He tilts my chin up to look at my face, and I'm sure I look like a hot mess—my mascara smeared by my tears, lipstick smudged all over my face, and semen dripping down my chin. He makes note of all this, eyes trailing up and down my face. Then he bends over to pick up the fallen cell phone. Holding my face with one hand, he snaps a shot of me. "Now *this*, this is the one I will call *Debauched*."

Then he does something I never expected him to do: he kneels in front of me and *licks* my face clean. He licks his cum off my neck and chin, licks my tears off my cheeks. Then he licks into my mouth and kisses me like he can't get enough of me.

If I wasn't turned on before, I'm approaching combustible levels of arousal now.

"Hey, Red?"

"Yes, Charlie?"

"I want you to ride my face."

So I do.

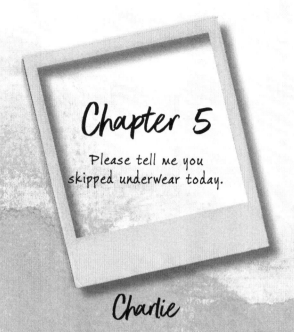

Chapter 5

Please tell me you skipped underwear today.

Charlie

Quinn lies across my body, drowsy and spent after I made her come twice with my tongue and then again with my dick.

"You alive, Red?" I ask her, tracing patterns on her back and shoulders, connecting the dots her freckles make on her skin.

"Mmmm," is the only response she can muster.

I chuckle, enjoying her like this, pliable and relaxed. Her skin is so soft under my fingertips and I don't want to stop touching her.

"You need anything before we go to sleep?" I ask her.

"I can leave if you give me a minute," she mumbles, eyes still closed.

"Don't be ridiculous. Just stay," I insist, kiss-ing her shoulder. If it were any other woman, I'd be collecting her clothes and getting a car to come pick her up. Scratch that, if it were any other woman, I wouldn't have brought her to my house to begin with, but it's Quinn. She's practically asleep already and besides, I still need to ask her if she'll go with me to my family dinner on Sunday.

I quickly brush my teeth and wash my face, make sure the house is locked up, then slide back into bed next to Quinn. Still in the same position, she's now asleep, breathing slow and even. I plug in my cell and open up my gallery to look at the pictures I took of her tonight. It starts with the last picture.

It's my favorite.

Her face is a mess. Eye makeup ruined, a red blur around her lips from her smeared lipstick, a clear wet trail from the corner of her mouth down her chin and neck. She's truly *debauched*.

Fuck. My cock stirs looking at her like this. She asked me not to take any pictures of her face, but my brain wasn't working well as I had just come in her mouth. I'll never show anyone this picture—that's not my style—but I can't delete it.

I scroll through the rest, stopping on one with her lips stretched around my cock. I zoom in, noticing how wet my dick is with her saliva, how perfect her lips look on my shaft. The next one is her tonguing my piercing.

Fuuuck.

I swipe to the next one, finding an image of her holding my cock in her hands, lipstick decorating it.

These pictures capture how unbelievably sexy Quinn is.

As promised, I select each one, put them in the folder with the other pictures she sent me earlier, and mark the folder as private, locking it with my fingerprint. Then I put my phone on the nightstand and try to fall asleep…only I can't get comfortable, tossing and turning. I even punch my pillow a couple of times but it doesn't help.

All of my movement causes Quinn to stir and she rolls over, draping herself across my chest, burrowing her face into my neck. Her bare tits mold into me, her hair more soft than ticklish on my skin. I turn, pulling her into me with my arm around her back and my leg between hers. Finally comfortable, I fall asleep.

Consciousness filters through me in stages. First, I notice the light shining in through my bedroom window. Then I feel the silky skin underneath my fingers, the warmth radiating from soft curves tucked up against my chest. Finally, I realize my cock is wedged in between two butt cheeks. The power of deductive reasoning helps me figure out I'm in bed with a woman. This is not common.

Cracking my eyes open just a bit, I see red hair and a smattering of freckles all over her pale creamy skin. *Mmmm.* I think back and remember my night with Quinn.

My cock likes these memories a lot. I thrust my hips experimentally, testing to see if Quinn will push back into my touch, but she lets out a small snore and rolls over, throwing her leg over my hip. She looks so young in her slumber, no mischievous grin, no sassy mouth, no smart comeback hurled in my direction. In sleep, her expression is peaceful and relaxed.

Though I'd like to wake Quinn up with my mouth between her legs, I don't want to disturb her. My bladder and stomach both complain at once, one too full and the other too empty. So, I get up, do my thing in the bathroom, and then get started on breakfast. Maybe pancakes and bacon will help my case when I ask her to be my date tomorrow.

I'm flipping the last pancake and turning off the pan of sizzling bacon when she appears in the kitchen, wearing one of my white t-shirts. It's so big on her that one shoulder peeks out of the neck. Her hair is disheveled and her face is scrubbed free from makeup, but she still looks delicious.

"Morning," I greet cheerfully, plating her breakfast.

"What's all this? I never knew you gave the royal treatment to your hookups in the morning."

"I don't have hookups over if I can help it, but I was hungry and thought you might be too. Besides, you're not just a hookup, you're my friend. Now, would you like two slices of bacon or three?"

"How about four?" She quirks an eyebrow.

"Greedy little thing, aren't you?" I tease, putting four slices on her plate.

She steals one off the plate before I can set it down on the table, moaning loudly when she takes a bite. "Wow, I'm impressed you know how to cook."

"It comes in handy when I'm hungry. Getting takeout for every meal wreaks havoc on my stomach." I dig into my own plate and decide there's no time like the present to bring up my request. "I have a favor to ask you."

"Aha! *That's* why you're feeding me," she exclaims.

"Maybe…but seriously, my family has this dinner at Green Briars tomorrow to celebrate my sister's new job, and my mother has insisted I bring a date, lest I screw up the headcount and ruin the seating arrangement. I thought about asking Max, but my mom might have a conniption." I risk a glance at Quinn's face to see her reaction. She's staring at me warily.

I raise my hands up, placating. "I'm not trying to make this into anything, Red, I swear. A girlfriend is the last thing I want, and I know you aren't looking for anything serious either. Meeting my family does not mean I want more with you, I'm just in need of a date and other girls tend to get clingy when I ask them. I figured I wouldn't have that problem with you."

"Phew, you scared me there for a second." She grabs her chest.

"My parents are stuck-up lawyers, but my brother and sister are pretty cool. It would be two, three hours of your life, tops. Then I'll pay you back any way you want, preferably in orgasms." I look down at her chest to where her nipples are saluting me under my shirt.

"Hmmm." She fingers her lip then takes another bite of bacon. "Maybe you're onto something. My parents have this tendency to invite my ex to family get-togethers. I hate seeing him there, and it makes it worse if I'm alone. If I go with you to this thing, will you come with me to one of mine?"

"Done." I smile at her.

"Okay hotshot, give me the lowdown. Where are we going? Who will I meet? How should I dress? What's our story?"

We make a plan over breakfast and I find that the thought of going to this dinner has become a little less painful knowing Quinn will be there, too.

Quinn

Charlie said to dress conservatively, so I scan my closet to see if I even own anything conservative. It's not that I dress provocatively, but my clothes tend to be…unique and artistic. I end up choosing a black silk top paired with a mint green pencil skirt and finish the ensemble with black ankle boots. I keep my makeup simple and wrangle my unruly hair into the only up-do I know how to style. Looking myself over in the full-length mirror, I think I could totally pass for conservative.

My doorbell rings at four PM on the dot, and Charlie whistles appreciatively when I open the door.

"Sweet baby Jesus, Red, you look edible. Please tell me you skipped underwear today." He has yet to make eye contact with all of the ogling.

"How did you know?" Any kind of underwear, even thongs, only manage to create lines under this skirt.

"Wishful thinking." He chuckles, finally meeting my eyes. I appreciate the heat I see in his gaze, but it makes me worry I've missed the conservative mark.

I clear my throat. "Am I dressed okay?" I ask. I'm mentally scanning the contents of my wardrobe again, but I don't think I have anything better than this to wear today.

"You look perfect." He winks. "Ready to go?"

"Yes, just let me get my purse." As we walk to his car, I appreciate the back view of Charlie. He, too, looks edible, but in a polished way I've never seen him dress before. Charcoal grey slacks with a matching suit jacket and a white dress shirt make it look like we might be going to a wedding, but his tie is electric blue with a little design on it that I can't quite make out.

The way he opens my car door and closes it after I sit makes this feel like a date, and strangely enough, that thought makes my palms sweat. I have let this man do all manner of naughty things to my body—not to mention the things I've done to his—but a simple opening of the door makes me queasy. *This isn't a date. It's only a favor.*

"Don't look so scared. Our first stop will be the bar for some fortification. We'll stay a couple hours, then I'll give you orgasms as payment," he promises, and it makes me relax. Despite the dapper clothes and gentlemanly manners, he's still the same old Charlie.

"Sounds good."

The drive isn't long and before I'm ready, we stop in front of an ornate building. Valet takes the car and Charlie takes my hand as we walk inside. "Remember, you're my date. We're supposed to hold hands and act all coupley."

"Is coupley a word?" I ask him.

"Probably not." He shrugs with a smile, wrapping his arm around my shoulder.

After the employee manning the door checks Charlie's name off of a list, we enter the dining room. This place is fancy. He warned me that everyone in his family is a lawyer and we're dining at an actual country club, so I had clues that his family is wealthy, but I'm still taken aback by just how posh this place is.

"Holy fuck. Where are we, the royal palace?" I mutter to him as we enter the dining room.

"Hardly. I know it's fancy, but it's just stuff."

Just stuff. Right. He must have grown up surrounded by nice things to have become accustomed to luxury like this.

Charlie leads me to the bar, as promised, and quirks an eyebrow at me. "What's your pleasure?"

"A shot of tequila, please, and a rum and coke," I tell the bartender.

The bartender looks to Charlie. "Make that two shots of tequila and a seven and seven."

He leans one elbow on the bar and faces me, hooking his arm around my waist to pull me into his space. He smells so good, a heady combination of woods and spice.

"Take a breath, you look uncharacteristically scared right now. Want to sneak into the bathroom for a quickie?"

I snort. "Maybe later."

"That's what I like to hear." His eyes twinkle with mischief and we both take in our surroundings for a minute. "You know what I hate most about this place?" he asks me.

"What's that?"

"It's full of fake people. Everyone is putting on a show for everyone else. I can't stand it here." He gestures to a man down the bar. "Take that guy, for instance. I know he's gay, but he's here with a fake fiancée because his family wants to keep him in the closet."

"Seems like it isn't a very good cover if you know about it."

"Exactly."

"But aren't we doing the same thing? Pretending?" I gesture between us.

"Please." He sighs. "It's not the same at all. We're fuck buddies on a date. This isn't much of a stretch, Red. I can't wait to get under that skirt today, and I'm not lying to anyone about us being engaged. My mom told me I need a date, I asked you, and you came, end of story."

"So you don't want me to be fake? Act conservative, proper, and polite?"

"Fuck no. I want you to be yourself, and I'm going to be myself. They're just going to have to deal with us."

I nod, feeling better about my role here today.

The bartender places our drinks in front of us and we get ready for the shots of tequila.

"Allow me." Charlie takes my hand, licks it, and sprinkles salt on the wet patch of skin, and then his left hand gets the same treatment. Armed with a lemon wedge in one hand and the shot glass in the other, he toasts me. "To surviving this dinner." We clink glasses, lick the salt, down the shot, and bite into the lemons. The alcohol burns its way down my throat and warms my belly, and I reach for the rum and coke to chase the taste out of my mouth. I'm hoping the shot takes the edge off of my nerves.

"Well, look who it is!" exclaims a deep voice behind me. "You weren't lying when you said you'd be at the bar."

I turn and find a man who can only be Charlie's brother. He has Charlie's blond hair, though his is slicked back while Charlie's is unruly, the same blue eyes, though less mischievous, and even the same dimples pull at his cheeks when he smiles. I can tell he's older and more serious than Charlie, but he's still absolutely stunning.

"Dom!" Charlie greets his brother with a hug and takes my hand to introduce me. "This is Quinn Fitzpatrick. Quinn, this is my brother Domenic."

Domenic smiles at me, his blue eyes warm and friendly, and shakes my hand. "Nice to meet you Quinn." He looks back at his brother. "I'm glad you didn't bring Max as your date."

"Yeah, me too. Quinn's much prettier than Max."

"This is Samantha." Domenic steps aside to reveal his date, and Charlie and I shake Samantha's hand. She's a tall brunette with harsh features and a serious demeanor.

"What are you guys drinking?" Charlie asks them.

"You are aware it's only 4:30, right?" Domenic quirks an eyebrow at him.

Charlie blinks. "And?"

Domenic laughs. "Sam, you want anything?" he asks his date.

"No, thank you," she says, eyeing my drink with displeasure.

Whatever. I pick it up and take a big sip. I don't think Serious Sam and I are going to be friends, so I turn to look at the boys instead. *What a view.* Charlie is taller by a couple of inches and Domenic is slimmer, but they both fill out a suit very well.

"I have a feeling Ben is going to propose tonight," Domenic tells Charlie.

Charlie looks shocked. "What? I thought we were celebrating Tabby's job at the firm." That's what he told me on the way over. Tabby recently graduated from law school, passed the bar exam, and was just hired by a prestigious firm.

"I thought so, too, but then Ben showed up at work to talk to Dad, and Mom has been acting extra neurotic."

"When is she not neurotic?" Charlie asks. "Tabby's too young to get married." He looks worried.

"Yeah maybe, but Ben's parents are joining us for dinner, so just brace yourself, okay?" Domenic bumps shoulders with Charlie. "Let's go find the table."

"Okay, we'll be right there."

Domenic and Sam walk into the sea of tables. "Hey, you okay?" I ask Charlie, who has lost his usual spark.

"I just can't believe my baby sister might get married. She's only 23 years old." Seeing Charlie look anxious is just wrong.

"Do you not like her boyfriend?"

"Ben?" He shrugs. "Honestly, I can't imagine anyone being good enough for my baby sister. I just don't want her to give up on her dreams for a guy, you know?" He runs his hand through his hair.

"Well, maybe she won't. Maybe Ben makes her happy." Look at me, defending the idea of marriage—who am I? He doesn't look convinced.

Blowing out a breath, he picks up his drink and takes my hand. "Let's do this."

I pick up my drink as well and we walk over to the table right in the center of the room. Everyone we pass is dressed to the nines and they all peer at us intently, making me feel like I'm on display.

"Do I have something on my face?" I whisper to Charlie.

He gives me a onceover. "No, why?"

"Everyone is staring at us."

"Just part of the experience when you dine at Green Briars," he tells me.

We find that the seats have been assigned, so we set our drinks down at the places labeled *Charles* and *Quinn*. My eyebrows rise at the use of Charlie's full name—it does not suit him at all. Despite being early, we are the last ones to take our seats. As I scan the people at the table, I see an older man who must be Charlie's dad—the genes are strong in this family. Mr. Nelson is quite the silver fox, and when he greets me, I can see what Charlie and Domenic are going to look like in 30 years. The only feature he doesn't share with his sons is a set of dimples.

When I meet Mrs. Nelson, I find the source of their dimples. "Thank you for joining us for dinner, Quinn." The words are kind enough, but I don't see warmth in her blue eyes. Instead, it feels like she's studying me, cataloging all the ways I don't fit in here. *Don't worry lady*, I think, *I'm well aware already.*

"Thank you for having me, Mrs. Nelson, Mr. Nelson." I can't *not* be polite to Charlie's parents.

"Come meet my sister." Charlie steers me away from his parents before they can say anything else. Tabby is tiny compared to her brothers, and dressed in a powder blue shift dress and navy skyscraper heels, she looks elegant and young all at the same time. "Tabby Cat!" Charlie shouts as the girl launches herself into his arms. He spins her around like he usually does with Monica, and she laughs and hugs him right back. The sight makes my heart squeeze.

"I told you to stop calling me that like 10 years ago, Charlie," she complains. Her twinkling eyes and wide smile betray her annoyance with her brother.

"Aw, you know you love it when I call you Tabby Cat." He turns to find my hand and pulls me forward. "This is Quinn. Quinn, this is my sister, Tabby."

She smiles and instead of shaking my hand, she leans in to give me a hug, squeezing me tight. "Nice to meet you, Quinn. This is my boyfriend, Ben," she indicates the man beside her, "and Ben's parents, Mr. and Mrs. Collins."

After the introductions are complete, we take our seats. Luckily, Charlie is next to his sister, and I'm in between Charlie and Domenic. This seating arrangement is definitely giving me ideas about being in a Charlie and Domenic sandwich—*wow*, that would be something, but I have a feeling Domenic is not quite as much fun in bed as Charlie is.

"How are things going at work, Domenic?" Mrs. Nelson asks him. He responds with some lawyer talk that goes straight over my head.

"And what about that high-profile case you took on? Any breakthroughs yet?" Mr. Nelson chimes in. Domenic answers again with the lawyer talk, although he's pretty evasive. My guess is that he isn't supposed to be talking about whatever high-profile case he has.

After they finish interrogating him, they move on to Ben, Tabby's boyfriend. He is—you guessed it—also a lawyer. At least the wait staff has now started serving the food, and I dig into my salad and bread roll, absolutely starving. I must not be using the right fork because Mrs. Nelson frowns at me. *Whatever.* I smile up at her, hoping I don't have lettuce stuck in my teeth.

Once Ben has updated the table about his latest wins in court, the topic changes to Tabby, and I can't help but notice no one has asked Charlie about his job and his latest account. It isn't easy to be a successful photographer, and Charlie is doing so well.

When Tabby is done talking about her new job, I decide I can't take any more lawyer talk. "Did you guys hear about Charlie's new account? They personally requested Charlie to handle all the photography," I say to the table.

Charlie stiffens in his seat, the easy smile slipping into a cautious expression.

"That's great, Charlie!" Tabby flashes him a warm smile.

"Congratulations," Domenic adds.

A disinterested Mr. Nelson asks Mr. Collins about setting up a golf match with some of his clients next month and I look around, surprised no one is going to ask Charlie about his good news.

I peer at Charlie and see his resigned expression. Reaching my hand down to his thigh, I squeeze, letting him know I'm here.

"Tough crowd," I mutter to him.

He nods, looking way too morose.

"Want to sneak to the bathroom for a quickie?" I suggest quietly, hoping to see his smile again.

"What about you, Quinn?" Mrs. Nelson interrupts my whispers. "What is it that you do for a living?"

"I'm an artist," I tell her, and the table goes quiet. It's like I confessed to being a prostitute.

"How interesting," she says, clearly uninterested.

"Quinn is very talented," Charlie defends. "Her work is for sale at Art Redefined, the gallery downtown."

"I'll have to come check out your work some time," Tabby smiles at me. Bless her heart for trying, but Mrs. Nelson is on a mission.

"Do you make a living off of your art?" she asks.

It takes me a beat to grasp that she just said that out loud. "Uh, yes. While I may have started out as a starving artist, after a couple of years I found the right gallery and the right niche for my art. It pays the bills." I smile stiffly.

Charlie goes for my thigh this time, squeezing me to let me know he's here.

"Good for you," Domenic chimes in this time. "I'm impressed that you and Charlie can tap into your creativity on demand. That would snuff my creativity right out, too much pressure."

"It isn't always easy, but I've learned to follow my muse wherever he takes me. I'll sometimes go weeks without any inspiration, but when it hits, I have to drop everything—cancel lunch dates, forget meals, forgo sleep—so I can make up for lost time." That's what Reid had the hardest time dealing with—being ignored when my muse stole all of my attention—but if I don't create, I don't get paid.

"So you work from home?" Mrs. Nelson asks me.

"Yes, I have a studio in my house."

"Must be nice to be able to work from home," Tabby comments.

"It works well for me."

"I need a drink. Quinn, do you want to come with me?" Charlie asks.

He doesn't have to ask me twice, and we head back to the bar for another shot and drink.

"Sorry about the inquisition back there," he apologizes.

"Hey, it's no sweat off my back. I can see why it's so rough being the *only* one in your family who didn't go into law. It's like they don't even know how to talk about anything else."

"Right? All the shoptalk drives me crazy. I can't wait to get out of here."

"So what's on the agenda after this?"

"We can go back to my place, where I'll take my frustrations out on your pretty pussy."

"Check please."

He chuckles.

We take our shots and linger by the bar, neither one of us wanting to go back to the table to finish our dinner. Charlie is standing very close to me, which is how I feel him stiffen. My eyes fly up to his face to see what's wrong, and I notice him looking over my shoulder. I set my drink down, peer behind me, and see a slender brunette approaching us. She's hauntingly beautiful with big, brown doe eyes and glossy chestnut hair on a face that stares at Charlie with guilt and fear.

I look back to Charlie and see him clench his jaw so hard, I'm afraid he may chip a tooth. This is obviously someone he does not want to see.

I wonder who she is.

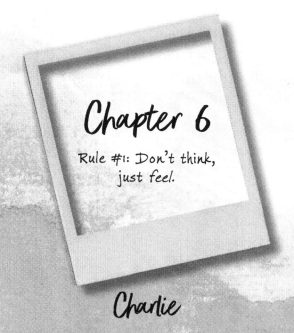

Chapter 6

Rule #1: Don't think, just feel.

Charlie

Fuck, this dinner just keeps getting better. First, there's the awkward conversation with my family—it's like they do it on purpose to make sure I can't contribute to the conversation. Would it kill them to talk about anything other than work? Then, my mom interrogates Quinn, making her feel like a weirdo for being an artist.

And now this—the only woman I've ever loved is walking my way. Anna.

It's been eight years since I last saw her, 10 years since she broke my heart.

I don't want to notice how beautiful she is. I don't want to acknowledge that she's grown up as I have, but she still looks like the same girl I fell in love with. Her big brown eyes scan my face, taking me in. I don't want to remember how I used to get lost in those eyes. I don't want to see the hurt reflected in them as she looks at me. I don't want to notice how pale she is and worry that she isn't taking care of herself. I don't want to feel the pain in my chest as I think about

what she did to me, *to us.*

As she approaches, I can't control my body's reaction. All my muscles stiffen, my jaw clenching painfully. I know Quinn notices my reaction to Anna and she's looking back and forth between us, waiting for me to tell her who is approaching us, but I've lost the ability to talk.

Anna steps right in front of me, her arms wrapped protectively around her waist, as if I'm the one that hurt her. I don't want to notice the birthmark she has on her shoulder, the one she thought was ugly, the one I used to kiss every time I saw it.

"Hi Charlie." Her voice is barely above a whisper.

"Anna." My voice is steel.

She flinches at my animosity. *Tough shit.* I want her to just say what she has to say and leave. Looking at her hurts too much.

"How are you?" she asks quietly, taking in my face, my neck, my body. She sees Quinn then glances at our hands, maybe checking for rings.

"I'm fine." I bite out the words, firing them at her like a weapon. "What do you want?"

She waivers, looking around and noticing the attention we've gathered with this short exchange. She was never one to put on a show, but she soldiers on, turning back to face me.

"It's been a long time, Charlie. I just…I need you to know how sorry I am." She looks right at me, her gaze begging me for forgiveness. Her eyes shine with unshed tears and she bites her upper lip to stop herself from crying. It's the same thing she used to do when she was upset, and I don't want to remember these things about her. 10 years may have passed, but what she did to me will always be unforgivable.

I chuckle and it's a dark, ugly sound. Quinn steps closer to me, putting her hand on my back, trying to comfort me. I take a deep breath in an effort to calm down. "Time doesn't change what you did, Anna."

She flinches again, and a tear drops down her cheek, leaving a wet trail on her pretty face. There was a time in my life when I would have done anything to prevent Anna from crying. I loved her so much, seeing her upset caused me physical pain. Now, though, the sight of her tears does nothing to me. My heart is a piece of stone.

She looks to Quinn and I know I'm being rude by not introducing her, but fuck manners. It's all I can do to stand here, in front of Anna, and not lose my shit.

"I know, Charlie. I wish I could go back in time. I would do so many things differently." She sounds sincere, and maybe she is, but that doesn't change the fact that she lied to me. She took a choice away from me, shattered my heart, and changed my outlook on relationships for the rest of my life.

"Yeah, me too. I wish I never would have fallen for a selfish liar like you." My words are knives and I fling them at her. I can see them land, too, as she gasps with pain and more tears start to fall. She wipes them away quickly, struggling not to fall apart. Footsteps approach and I see a familiar face. It's her older brother's best friend, Weston maybe? I can't remember his name. He stares at Anna, concern etched in his expression.

"Anna, you okay?" he asks her, standing close by her side.

She squares her shoulders and raises her head, gaze still fixed on me. "I'm okay, Wesley."

Wesley (I was close) sees the tears falling and knows it's a lie. He narrows his eyes at me, like I'm the one in the wrong here, because I made her cry.

Anna's desperation for forgiveness is a palpable thing, but I don't have forgiveness in my heart. I'm not sure I ever will where she's concerned.

"Careful with this one," I tell Wesley, wanting to lash out at Anna some more. "She's a liar."

He steps protectively in front of her, fists clenched at his sides. "That's enough," he growls. "I know you two have history and I know it ended badly, but you have no idea what she's gone through since then."

"And you have no idea what the fuck you're talking about. If you did, you wouldn't be looking at me like that," I fire back, my voice rising above the rest of the chatter. The surrounding tables quiet and heads turn in our direction, trying to hear what's going on. I need to get out of here. My collar all of the sudden feels like it's choking me.

Quinn takes my hand and squeezes it. "Hey, I think we need to get back to dinner." That's the exact opposite of what I want to do after a run-in with the most painful part of my past, but I don't resist when she leads me back to the table. I need to get this dinner over with. Then I plan to get drunk. This is why I avoid relationships—the only thing love ever gave me was a broken heart.

"Told you he would propose," Dom elbows me on the way out. It was all I could do to stay at the table until after dinner, when Ben did indeed propose to Tabby. The crowd sucked it up just as eagerly as they did the scene between Anna and me at the bar. The minute I could get away without risking my mom's fury, Quinn and I said our goodbyes, and I was surprised to see Dom and Samantha right behind us.

"You called it. I just hope Tabby is happy," I say.

"Did you see her face? She's glowing," Quinn points out.

"She did look happy," I admit. We turn in our tickets to the valet attendant and wait for them to bring our cars up.

"Hey, you okay?" Dom asks.

Fucking hell. "I'm fine," I grunt, hoping he isn't going to bring up Anna.

He raises his hands in a *don't shoot* manner. "Sorry, I just know how messed up you were after you two broke it off. It had to be hard to see her."

"It was unexpected. I should have figured she might be there, though. Her parents were members at Green Briars when we were younger, too." Back then, Anna and I were so happy that our parents were members of the same country club because sometimes we could sneak off and fuck in the bathrooms.

"It's a shame she never went to medical school like she planned."

There are a lot of things about Anna that I would call a shame; her change in career plans is not one of them.

"Yeah, it's a real pity," I retort wryly.

"Well, at least you followed your dreams." Dom smiles at me, meeting my eyes. "You've wanted to be a photographer since you got your very first camera. I'm proud of you, Charlie."

He's proud of me. Not once in all my life have my parents uttered those words. There's a strange burning sensation in the back of my throat and my eyes feel hot as I nod, unable to speak around the lump in my throat.

I'm saved by the valet, who hands Dom his keys. He hugs me, slapping my shoulder, and we say our goodbyes. Then it's just me and Quinn. She's been quiet this whole time, not asking for any answers. I'm grateful, as I don't want to give them.

"So, you have two options," she tells me.

"Only two?" I try to bring some levity to my voice, but the last couple of hours have me feeling raw. "And what might they be?"

"Option one: I can take you to a bar, get you drunk, and take advantage of you."

"I like the sound of that one, Red. What's option two?"

"You can come back to my place, get drunk, and paint with me."

"Paint with you?" I raise my eyebrows. I am not talented with a paintbrush.

"Painting is fun. Plus, you'll get drunk no matter which option you choose."

"Hmmm. Decisions, decisions." I rub my fingers together, watching her. "Will you still take advantage of me at your house?"

"Definitely."

"I'll take option two please." I surprise myself with my choice, but I need a distraction right now. Being in public around people does not sound very appealing, and the idea of watching Quinn paint has my curiosity piqued.

"Excellent."

———

20 minutes later, Quinn has stripped me down to my underwear so I don't mess up my clothes, poured us each a drink, and led me to her art studio. I've never been in here before and I'm impressed with how tidy it is—I imagined it to be a mess. She has several easels, three of them with pieces in different states of completion. Waist-high carts sit next to each one so she can keep the items she needs for each piece handy, and one wall has a massive shelving system with supplies. There is even a sink and short countertop for cleanup. The room has huge windows, and I can imagine she gets a lot of natural light in here during the day.

We're in here to paint, but my fingers itch to get out my camera and take pictures of everything. Quinn puts a blank canvas on one of the easels, gives me a palette, and pours a healthy heap of different colors on it.

"Are you ready for the rules?" She quirks her eyebrow at me.

"Rules? You should have told me there were rules before. I'm not much for following rules, Red."

"You'll like these, I promise."

"Okay, tell me the rules." I take a healthy swig of my drink before she collects it, puts it on the counter, and hands me a paintbrush.

"Rule number one: don't think, just *feel*."

I sigh. Well that kind of defeats the idea of distraction. I don't want to feel.

"Rule number two: there are no mistakes."

I laugh at this. "I'm pretty sure you're wrong about that one."

"I'm not wrong. Those are the rules of *my* studio," she huffs. I take Quinn in as she sets herself up. She doesn't have a canvas on her easel like I do; instead she has a gigantic pad of paper and a charcoal set on her cart.

She's wearing a paint-splattered t-shirt that falls to mid-thigh and leggings—also paint splattered—in combination with her makeup and fancy hairdo. Anyone else might look ridiculous, but she manages to look carefree and sexy.

"Is there a rule number three?" I ask her.

"Nope, that's it. Okay hotstuff, I need music when I create, so what's your pleasure tonight?"

"Heavy metal." I need something angry.

"Perfect. I have just the thing." She links her phone up to a stereo system I didn't notice before and the sounds of Metallica blare through little speakers placed all over the room. *Wow.*

"Okay, no more talking. Become one with your brush. Dip it in some paint and smear it on the paper. I don't care what it looks like," she orders me.

The heavy beat vibrates in my chest and I stare at the blank canvas in front of me. I'm not much for drawing people or landscapes. I look over to Quinn and see she has turned her easel so she's facing me and I can't see what she's drawing. She's busy, picking up different pieces of charcoal, bobbing her head to the beat. She isn't watching what I'm doing at all. *Don't think.*

I take a deep breath, smear my paintbrush in some red paint, and splatter the wet paint onto the canvas. Red drops land with plopping sounds and it looks like blood. I do it again, and again, and again. Some of the drops begin to drip, and it makes me want to connect them on the bottom of the canvas. I drag the brush through the lower half, and it feels good to see the angry slash my brush makes. I drag it back and forth. Minutes pass and I find myself singing to the music and sweating.

I look back over my shoulder to find Quinn watching me, smiling.

My canvas looks like a murder scene. It screams rage. Horror. Anger.

But surprisingly, I feel better. It's like I ejected all my feelings out of me and they landed on the canvas.

Huh. Maybe there's something to this painting thing. It's quite cathartic.

Now that I'm done with my piece, I can't help but want to see what Quinn has drawn.

Quinn

It's not every day I have a living, breathing muse right in front of me. I started with his eyes; those are always the hardest to draw. I tried to capture the intensity of his gaze as he worked on his piece. He was in pain.

Then I got distracted by his hands, the way they gripped the paintbrush. They're strong masculine hands, hands that know how to pluck and pinch and stroke my body in all the right ways.

Now I'm working on his torso. He has sculpted his body with just the perfect amount of muscle—not too bulky, but not too lean either. I blend the charcoal to try to capture the contour of his muscles when he leans forward to paint.

I love watching him get lost in his piece. He hasn't drawn a picture; rather, he's captured feelings of anger and pain in an abstract way. I'm sure he'll think it's garbage, but it's amazing.

I'm dying to know what happened with him and that girl, Anna. I know better than to ask him, though; he'll tell me if he wants me to know. Just like I don't want to talk about Reid, I can respect if he doesn't want to talk about his past.

He puts his brush down and looks over at me, raising an eyebrow. There's a light sheen of sweat on his body from his efforts.

"Not too shabby, hotshot," I compliment.

He looks a bit embarrassed. "I'm not quite sure what it is, but it did make me feel better. Is art therapeutic for you?"

"Of course, that's why I started painting. It was an escape from real life. Now, I crave it."

"Can I see what you made?" he asks me.

"Come on over." I collect the two previous pieces and lay all three next to each other. Charcoal is so much fun to work with.

Charlie makes his way over to my easel and his eyes widen in surprise.

"I had no idea you drew people so well. This is amazing," he says sincerely.

"You make a good muse." I bump his shoulder.

"Obviously."

We chuckle. "Don't worry, you can have these. I'm not going to sell them or anything."

"What am I going to do with drawings of myself? You can do whatever you want with them, Red. It's your talent."

"Okay. What do you want to do with your piece?" I ask him.

"Burn it?" He laughs. "It's hideous."

"No way. Can I try to sell it at my next showing? I'll give you the money," I offer.

"No one is going to want that thing. I am not an artist," he protests.

"I beg to differ, but if no one wants it then it won't sell, no harm done." I shrug.

"Fine," he concedes, if a bit grumpily.

"I think you forgot about our other mission tonight," I point out. His glass is still half full of the drink I poured him earlier.

"Is this the part where I get to take advantage of you?" He quirks an eyebrow up, smiling at me with his devilish grin.

"I was referring to the getting drunk part, but I won't complain if you want to take advantage of me." I smile coyly back at him.

"Can I fuck you here, in this room?" he asks me, his gaze traveling down my form. I'm a total mess. I'm wearing paint-splattered clothes and charcoal must be everywhere. I blend and shade with my fingers, so I always find smudges all over my body after I work with it.

"I'm a mess, Charlie. Let me at least clean up."

"You're perfect." His eyes blaze with hunger and my protest dies a sudden death at the way he's looking at me. He takes my charcoal-smeared fingers and places them on his sweaty chest. "Besides, don't you remember how much I like being your canvas?"

I think back to his cock smeared with my red lipstick all over it. *Fuck, that was hot.* "Speaking of which, I never got those pictures," I complain.

"I'll send them to you right now," he offers.

I slide my hands down his chest and abs, diving right into his underwear. His cock is not yet fully erect, but it's getting there, and I give it a tentative squeeze.

"Send them to me later."

He grunts as I stroke his dick. "I need your pussy, Red," he whispers into my ear, palming my ass.

"My pussy just so happens to be available."

He picks me up abruptly and walks us over to the counter. He sets me down, crouches in front of me, and leans his face into my crotch. My hands go to his head, fingers running through his hair as he rests there for a second, nuzzling the apex of my thighs. I can't get a good read on what he's feeling right now. Painting seemed to help clear his head, but he still isn't quite back to normal after his run-in this afternoon.

He reaches for the waist of my pants and looks up. He stares at me so intensely it makes my pulse kick up. Slowly, he takes my clothes off, holding my gaze with every movement he makes. I feel like I'm caught in a trap.

Once I'm completely naked, he lifts me and sets me on the counter. The surface is cold, but it feels good on my overheated skin. Music still pours out of the speakers, heavy and angry. He touches me, fingers tracing my lips, then my chin, down my neck, leaving goose bumps in their wake. He watches his fingers move, making patterns on my skin, and I realize he's tracing my freckles.

"Spread your legs," he orders. I'm so glad for him to be bossing me around like his usual self that I forget to be annoyed. I comply, leaning back on the counter and spreading my legs open. My cunt is soaking wet; I'm sure he can see it glistening.

Instead of stepping between my legs like I want him to, he backs up, looking at the supplies I have stocked on my shelves next to us. He looks side to side, scanning each shelf, then sees a new package of paintbrushes. He quirks an eyebrow up at me and goes to retrieve it.

"Mind if I open this?" he asks.

"You planning on using a paintbrush?" I ask him, confused.

"Yes," he says, without further explanation.

"Okay," I say, curious as to what he's going to do next. My nipples have hardened to tight little nubs and my clit is a live wire, begging for relief. As he opens up the package and takes out a brush, I shift, closing my legs to rub my thighs together.

"Keep them open," he corrects in a deep, authoritative tone. *Fuck, that's hot.*

"I need you to touch me," I complain, spreading my legs as open as I can comfortably have them on this counter.

He ignores this and rinses one of the brushes in the sink then dries it with a towel, trying to squeeze all the water out of the bristles. Taking the newly cleaned paintbrush in hand, he goes to collect a stool and sets it in front of me. He sits and his head ends up right in between my legs. *Yes.* I want his mouth on me, his fingers, anything at this point.

"Close your eyes," he instructs.

"What are you—" I begin to ask.

"Red," he interrupts. "I'm going to get a condom. Just lean back, close your eyes, and relax. I'm going to make you feel good," he promises.

I nod and do as he says. His footsteps pad to the door and through it, leaving me in silence for a couple minutes. I try to just empty my mind. I feel the way my lungs expand with each breath, the excited thrum of my pulse, the hard wall behind my head, the cool surface of the counter under my hands and legs. The smell of paint lingers in the air, but instead of being unpleasant, it's familiar. I relax into the moment and try to imagine what Charlie is doing right now. Is he back yet? What's taking so long?

The song changes and "Closer" by Nine Inch Nails comes on. *Fuck*, what a good song. The insistent beat of the music fills the room, seemingly louder than the last song, and it makes me feel electric. My skin tingles, waiting for something, *anything*.

Then I feel something cold and soft and wet on the inside of my thigh, right next to my knee. *Must be the paintbrush*, I realize. It feels…good, not what I expected. He drags it up my leg, the damp bristles causing goose bumps. *Higher*, I think, *touch my pussy*. But when he reaches the crease where my thigh meets my sex, he skips over and drags the brush down the other thigh. *Bastard*.

"Charlie," I whine.

"Shhh." The brush travels lazily along my other leg and back up again, over my hip this time, circling my navel, then up toward my nipple. *Yes*. I welcome the attention to my nipples, loving the feel of the soft, wet bristles on the sensitive skin. I lean into this touch, needing more.

The lyrics start and they ratchet up my arousal. This is the absolute sexiest song to fuck to. I need him. My *clit* needs him. I spread my legs farther apart, tilting my hips up as if to show him my pussy.

"Please," I whisper.

"Trying to show me something? I see it, Red. Your pussy is soaked for me."

I shiver at his words, his voice smooth velvet. My focus is on the one point of contact he has—that paintbrush. It swirls around both nipples, going back and forth, and then finally it travels toward my pelvis. *Keep going*.

It brushes over my pubic hair then travels down the crease of my right thigh and up the crease of my left thigh, just missing all the parts that are screaming for attention. He is torturing me, and my thighs start to tremble with need. I move my hips to chase the paintbrush, but he chuckles and moves it out of reach. My eyes are still closed, so I can't see him, but I feel his breath on my thigh, just inches away from where I want him to bury his tongue—or his cock.

Fuck, I'd even take the paintbrush right now.

I'm desperate.

He's apparently a mind reader because the next thing I feel is a swipe of the paintbrush up the center of my pussy. He circles my opening, collecting my arousal, and then sweeps it up and over my clit, painting my pussy with my desire. Up and down, around my clit, then up and down again.

"Oh, God," I cry. I rock my hips, seeking out more friction. My entire pussy is slick, but the paintbrush is too soft. I won't be able to come like this. I need more.

I think Charlie finally needs more, too, because I hear the paintbrush clatter on the countertop, then the rustle of the condom wrapper. He steps in between my legs, gripping my hips to pull me closer to the edge of the counter, and our skin collides. His skin is hot, his touch strong. His mouth meets mine in a sloppy kiss as he thrusts inside. I'm so wet he slides all the way in.

"Fuck," he curses. "This is going to be fast, Red. Hold on."

I wrap my arms and legs around him as he cradles my head in one hand and takes hold of my waist in the other. Then he fucks me.

It's fast.

It's hard.

It's animalistic.

It's fucking amazing.

His sweat drips onto my skin as he pounds into me and I clutch at his back, holding on tight. The backdrop of the music feeds our frenzy. We're eating at each other's mouths, grunting, pleading, moaning, cursing. Before I know it I'm there, right on the edge of orgasm. I buck up, trying to chase my pleasure, but it remains just out of my reach. With an agonized groan, Charlie's movements begin to get uncoordinated and he leans down to bite my shoulder. The unexpected burst of pain does it, and I teeter over the precipice of pleasure, shattering in his arms. His orgasm hits right after mine and he clutches me to him, slowly pumping his cock in and out, milking the high.

That was intense.

We hold each other, panting as our senses return.

"Welcome to the Jungle" by Guns and Roses starts and the intense, animalistic, I-want-to-devour-you mood is broken. Charlie chuckles. I love hearing that light sound.

"Feel better?" I ask him.

"Definitely."

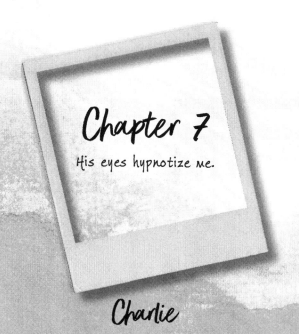

Chapter 7

His eyes hypnotize me.

Charlie

Anna has the most delicious mouth. I kiss her, licking her lips, sucking the top one in my mouth, then the bottom one. I sweep my tongue inside, seeking out her tongue to play with mine. I can't get enough of her.

A noise startles me and I pause, listening for the sound. "Did you hear that?" I ask Anna.

She laughs, her brown eyes twinkling at me. "Hear what?"

"It sounds like a baby crying." I focus on the faint noise, but just as soon as I hear it, it goes away.

"No, silly. Why would you hear a baby crying? There's no baby here."

I nod, knowing she's right, of course. After waiting a beat longer and hearing nothing, I relax and capture her lips once more.

"Mmm, I love your lips, sweets," I murmur.

"I love you, Charlie, so much," she tells me, sighing sweetly.

Then I hear it again, louder this time. It's a baby crying for sure. I freeze and pull back. "You have to hear that."

She looks up at me, confused. "I don't hear anything."

"I have to go find it." This baby is upset, wailing. I don't know anything about babies, but I know something must be wrong. I get up and leave Anna in her bed to search for the source of that horrible cry.

I exit her bedroom and go down the hall, pausing near each door to see if the cry gets louder or quieter, but it seems to be getting farther away. I open every door anyway, just to check. My heart is hammering in my chest, anxiety spiking over what could be wrong. I have to get to that baby.

The closer I get to Anna's room, the louder it gets.

Huh, that's weird. I started in Anna's room, so I know there's no baby in there.

But I step closer, and sure enough, the sound is louder.

Wails turn into screams and I feel full-on panic. I have to find this baby.

I open the door to Anna's room and find a crib has been placed in the corner. A little baby is lying in it, arms and legs flailing wildly, screaming to get someone's attention.

"Hey, shhhh, it's okay little baby, I'm here now." I talk to the infant as I approach it, hoping if it hears the sound of my voice it'll know that help is on the way. I lean over the crib, peering down to see the smallest baby I've ever seen. He's wrapped in a blue blanket, so I'm assuming it's a boy. Red faced and sweaty, he continues to kick and squirm, helpless to do anything but lie there and cry.

I've never held a baby before, but how hard could it be? I reach into the crib to pick him up, but as I reach over the railing, the bed drops, putting the baby just out of my reach. I stretch my arms farther, but still, I can't reach him.

What is going on?

I jostle the crib rail, unsure how to lower it. I squeeze every button and try to lift and lower it, but I can't figure it out.

His screams are piercing my brain.

"Anna? Can you help me?"

She appears next to me, clicks a latch, and lowers the crib railing without a problem. She reaches down and scoops up the baby. He quiets instantly and my panic starts to subside. Thank God for Anna, she'll know what to do.

"What do you think is wrong with him?" I ask her. She's facing away from me, so I can't see the baby anymore. She starts to move her arm around, jostling the baby, making him cry again.

"Hey, what are you doing?" I ask her, worried she might hurt the baby. Don't newborn babies need you to support their head?

"Don't worry," she says. "I'll take care of it."

All of a sudden, the cries stop, and the silence that follows is deafening. The panic comes back, clawing at my insides, squeezing my chest—what the fuck just happened? I have to hold that baby. I circle around to the front of Anna and freeze.

"What the fuck?"

"I'm so sorry, Charlie." Anna says, frantic. "I didn't know what else to do."

"No!" I shout. "What did you do?"

"I'm so sorry."

"NO!"

Quinn

A scream yanks me out of sleep and I bolt up to a sitting position, worried there's an intruder. Blinking rapidly, I search the room for a bad guy. It takes a couple seconds to clear the sleep from my brain, but as my vision comes into focus, I can tell no one else is in my bedroom except for me and Charlie.

"No, no, no, no. *WHY*?" Charlie shouts, the words being ripped from him, saturated in agony. His eyes are still closed, but his face contorts in pain. His chest rises and falls rapidly as he shakes his head back and forth.

"Charlie?" I touch his shoulder tentatively. Are you not supposed to wake someone up when they're having a bad dream? I can never remember. He's hot, covered in sweat, and his fingers clutch the sheets, trying to get a hold of something.

"How could you?" he whimpers, sounding utterly broken.

I lean over him and smooth his hair out of his forehead. "Shhh," I whisper. "It's okay, Charlie."

He turns toward me and wraps his arms around my waist, burying his head in my chest. I think he's still asleep as he hasn't opened his eyes yet. I just wrap my arms around him and hold him tight. What on earth is he dreaming about?

"Anna," he moans. It's not a sexual moan; it's a heartbreaking one.

Ah. He's dreaming about the woman from the country club, Anna. Seeing her must have brought back some heck of a memory because this dream has him deep under.

"It's Quinn. I'm here with you, Charlie. It's okay," I murmur in his ear.

"Oh, God," he sobs, his whole body shaking. *Is he crying?*

My heart squeezes painfully at the thought of someone hurting this strong, sexy man in my arms. She must have done quite a number on him, and I hate her for whatever she did.

"Charlie, it's okay. I have you," I say, louder this time, wrapping my whole body around him. I need him to wake up, but I don't know how to snap him out of this dream. I kiss his forehead, rubbing my hands up and down his back and arms.

He rolls us so he's on top of me, but he's still clinging to my body as if he's drowning. I keep petting him, hoping my touch will wake him. I touch his face, startled to find his cheeks are wet. My lungs collapse at the realization that he really is crying. I wipe his tears away, their presence so wrong on the face of this man. Charlie is jokes and innuendo and inappropriate remarks. He isn't a serious or sad kind of guy—he's light and laughter, so full of life, so full of fun.

But right now, in my arms, this six-foot-tall, golden-haired man with ocean blue eyes and irresistible dimples is falling apart. He pants, trying to catch his breath. My eyes burn at the sight, my heart breaking for whatever he went through.

I kiss him again, my lips touching his warm skin wherever I can reach—his forehead, his hair, his temple. I shift, trying to reach more of his face. His breath, hot and humid, hits my skin with every shudder. I cradle him as he cries in his sleep, and I can't stop the tears from overflowing. It's stupid—I don't know what I'm crying for—but Charlie is in pain, and somehow, his pain hurts me, too.

He gasps all of a sudden, jerking awake. Wild frantic eyes look all around and settle on me.

"Quinn?" he croaks, voice thick with emotion.

"I'm here, Charlie," I reassure him.

"What happened?" he asks, looking so vulnerable I could cry all over again.

"You had a bad dream," I tell him gently, continuing to pet and soothe him. He's like a spooked wild animal, and I can't bear the thought of him retreating. I need to make sure he's okay.

He stares at me, his pulse hammering wildly in his neck, his heart pounding so hard I can feel it on my stomach where he's lying on me. He takes a deep breath and settles back down, his head on my chest. We're naked, having gone to sleep shortly after sex last night, and his sweat-slicked skin slides over mine. I run my fingers through his hair and wait to see if he will fall back asleep. We lie in silence, entwined together for a while. It could be five minutes or an hour, but I'm too wound up to fall back to sleep.

"You still awake?" he whispers.

"I am."

"I can't sleep."

"You okay?" I ask.

He sighs. "That dream, it took me back in time. I can't shake it."

"You don't have to tell me about it, but I'm a good listener if you want to get it off your chest," I offer quietly.

He's silent for so long, I assume he doesn't want to talk about it. Then he sighs again and shifts us, pulling me over him so my head is pillowed on his chest this time. "It's about that girl we saw at dinner, Anna," he starts.

I stay quiet, letting him have the time he needs to say what he needs to say.

"She was my high school girlfriend. We dated freshman, sophomore, and most of junior year. We were each other's firsts and we were so in love. We had our whole lives planned out. She wanted to be an obstetrician and we were going to get an apartment while she went to a pre-med college and I went to art school for photography. Then I'd support her while she finished med school and residency. We were going to have four kids and live happily ever after."

Knowing the Charlie I know now, the one who hates relationships and has sex with many different women, I'm surprised to hear about this younger version of himself. How did he go from totally in love to who he is now?

"I was devoted to her. She was my best friend and I would have done anything to make her dreams come true, anything to make her happy." He says the words with such sincerity that my heart hurts.

"What happened?" I have to ask.

"She got sick, told me she had the flu. So, I took care of her, brought her soup, missed assignments from school, the whole nine yards. I did anything I could think of to make her feel more comfortable. Then she had to go to the doctor because she didn't get better, and I offered to take her, but she dodged me, telling me she was fine to go by herself. I didn't think anything of it at the time, other than wishing I could have taken her because I wanted to be there for her, but I was busy with school, too, so I shrugged it off.

"But after her doctor's appointment, she...changed, became withdrawn and sad. She couldn't look me in the eye. I kept asking her what was wrong and she kept saying she was fine, but I knew she wasn't. She stopped running track, stopped wearing makeup, started wearing baggy clothes instead of the pretty, girlie things she used to wear. Up until then we'd had sex all the time. We were 16 years old and inseparable, sneaking away every chance we could to find a place to be together, but then she just…wasn't interested.

"Finally, I confronted her. I was worried sick and threatened to involve her parents if she wouldn't tell me what was going on." His muscles tense and his tone becomes incensed.

My stomach hurts at the thought of what he's going to tell me, and I wrap my arms around his waist for comfort.

"It turns out that when she supposedly had the flu, she wasn't sick at all. She was *pregnant*," he spits.

Oh, Charlie. I squeeze him, distressed by what he had to go through. The words echo in my head and I can't think of anything to say. He used past tense, so I'm assuming she didn't stay pregnant. Did she have a miscarriage? An abortion? Either way, my heart squeezes at the devastation of losing a baby at such a young age. I wait patiently for him to continue.

"I don't even know how it happened. I used a condom every single time. In fact, I've never once had sex without a condom." He laughs and it's a brittle sound. "So, while I was buying her soup and taking care of her, she was pregnant. While I was rubbing her back as she vomited and asking if there was anything I could do for her, she was carrying my baby, and she never once mentioned it. We told each other *everything*—or at least I did—every mundane thought, every hope, every dream, everything. How could she not tell me? I go over it again and again and it makes no sense. We wanted kids, we even picked names out for them, for crying out loud." He's pissed now, his voice getting louder and louder with outrage. I'm outraged on his behalf.

"And when she went to the doctor, it was to have an abortion." He chokes on the last word, swallowing thickly. I feel his chest cave in as he struggles to control his emotions, and my eyes burn with tears for him.

"Now, I believe in the woman's right to choose, but what about the father? What happened to *my* choice? Didn't I deserve to even *know* about it?" He's definitely crying now, his voice guttural and broken. There's no stopping my tears from overflowing at the sound of his anguish. I'm trying to picture Charlie at 16, hearing that his girlfriend aborted their baby without telling him.

"The thing is, I don't know what my choice would have been. Maybe I would have agreed with her. We were way too young to be parents. We had

70

all these goals, and having a baby definitely would have put a kink in them.

"But maybe I wouldn't have cared if the timing was off. There was nothing I wanted more than to have a family with her. I could have gone to school first then stayed home with the baby while she went to school, or I could have changed aspirations, gotten a different job right out of high school. I don't know, we could have figured something out, but she lied to me. She had the abortion without giving me a chance to weigh in on the subject. I didn't even know about it until two months later. Two entire fucking months, she saw me every day and never told me. I *hate* her for what she did."

So do I, I think. Though she was in a difficult position, I can't believe she didn't tell him.

"After that, I started having dreams about babies. I dream that I hear a baby crying, but I can't find him, or I can find the baby, but he's just out of my reach. Or he's about to fall out of an open window, and I can't get there in time to save him, so I have to watch him plummet to his death. If I'm especially lucky, Anna is there and kills the baby. They're all different variations of the same thing: my baby needs me, but I'm too late to save him."

Oh, Charlie. How horrifying. I can't imagine those dreams; my stomach churns just thinking about it.

"I'm so sorry, Charlie." Lifting my head up, I look at his face, so serious and sad in the darkness. He shrugs and looks away, not sure what to say.

I'm not quite sure what to say either, but I want to comfort him. I throw my leg over his waist and straddle him. His hands land on my waist, but his grip is tentative; I'm not sure if he's going to push me off or hold me close. Leaning forward, I kiss his lips gently. He doesn't kiss me back, but he doesn't push me away either. I decide to push my luck.

"I'm so sorry she hurt you," I murmur then kiss his cheek. "I'm so sorry you never had a choice." I kiss his other cheek, and then his forehead. "I'm so sorry for your loss," I tell him. I feel it more than he could imagine. Gingerly wiping his tears away, I kiss his lips again. My kisses aren't sexual; they're sweet, affectionate. I want to take his pain away. He squeezes his eyes shut and breathes heavily, chest rapidly rising and falling.

His fingers tighten on my skin and his muscles tense—his thighs, his abs, up to his chest and arms. He's liked a caged animal, torn between flight and fight. He still hasn't kissed me back but our lips are connected, breathing into each other's mouth.

I place my hand on his chest, right over his heart. "It's not your fault, Charlie. You know that, right? It's not your fault."

Tortured blue orbs meet mine. "Quinn." The use of my actual name as opposed to his nickname for me is a warning.

"You are a good man. I know you are. You need to forgive yourself for something you didn't do."

He shudders. "I don't know how."

"Have you ever told anyone about this?" I ask gently. I suspect he's bottled it all up inside.

He confirms my suspicion with a shake of the head.

"Not even Max or Logan?"

He shakes his head again.

"Maybe you should. Maybe it might help to grieve properly for what you lost. Let your friends lighten the load you carry."

"I don't want anyone to see me like this," he admits, looking at me warily.

"It's okay, Charlie. I won't ever tell a soul," I promise him. "This is your story, but thank you for sharing it with me." I kiss him softly again.

This time, he kisses me back. His strong arms wrap solidly around my upper body, crushing me to him, and he pours his pain into his kiss. I gladly accept, wrapping my arms around him. The kiss is angry and desperate at first, him eating at my mouth and me letting him. He flips us over so he's on top of me, and I cradle him with my body. Minutes pass and he gentles, kissing me languidly with slow licks and deep breaths.

We roll again, our bodies entwined, and I try not to get turned on. I want to keep sex out of this moment of comfort. Nothing about this situation is sexy. My heart is bruised from the story he's told me, and my mind is on the past and the pain of losing a child.

But we're naked.

And kissing.

Our bodies rub together, creating a delicious friction in between my legs.

I ignore it, determined to let him seek comfort from me. *This is not about you*, I remind myself. My nipples harden, screaming for attention. My pussy is so wet, I swear I can smell the faint musk of my arousal in the air. My heart rate escalates, but I keep my kisses slow and gentle.

Another roll puts him on top of me again, and I feel his cock as we move. It's hard and hot, a steel brand on the inside of my thigh. *Oh, fuck.*

Ignore it. This is not about sex. This is about comfort.

My pelvis tilts up without my permission, seeking out his erection, drawn to it like a moth to a flame. He shifts slightly and all of a sudden, it's right in between my legs, his length resting on top of my slippery slit. I wrap my legs around him, holding him in place. His cock throbs, and I can't stop my hips from moving, sliding up ever so slightly, then down. The small amount of friction is bliss.

Charlie groans, a deep, masculine rumble, and his hips start to shift with me, sliding his cock through my wetness. His piercing rubs my clit and my breath catches at the sensation.

"Quinn," he murmurs into my mouth.

"Charlie," I say with a sigh.

The next shift of his hips brings his cock farther back, and the forward thrust causes it to notch right into the entrance of my pussy. He freezes, realizing that any more forward movement will result with him inside of me. He isn't wearing a condom, something he is always so careful about. Now I know why he's so careful, but I'm clean; I get tested routinely and I know he does too, as we share our test results every time. As for birth control, he's safe from pregnancy with me.

"Quinn?" Lust-filled eyes meet mine, searching for my answer.

I hold his gaze and nod my consent.

I haven't had sex without a condom in a very long time, not since I was married, and I forgot how much more you can feel without that thin barrier. Charlie pushes in agonizingly slowly, looking into my eyes the entire time. I watch his face, rapt, as his expression changes from lust to wonder. This is the first time he's ever had sex without a condom, and I realize he's placing an awful lot of trust in me right now. He's trusting me to be clean and to be safe.

It's humbling, his trust.

When he's finally buried inside, he stills, his eyes closing for a brief second of bliss. A beat later, he opens them and watches me as he pumps in and out of me, torturously slowly, dragging his piercing along the sensitive walls of my pussy. His eyes hypnotize me. I'm entranced, unable to look away, and I see every bit of pleasure wash over his face, every bit of emotion.

He doesn't say a word, not one dirty command, not one filthy request. He just stares into my eyes as he feels me from the inside.

My orgasm is a surprise, stealing my breath as blinding pleasure crashes into me. I clench around his erection rhythmically and he grunts at the feel of it, watching me fall apart as if it's the most amazing sight he's ever seen. When I can open my eyes again, I hold his gaze and push on his chest, telling him I want to be on top. He sinks deep, rolling us without separating our bodies.

Then I ride him, continuing his slow, languid pace. The angle hits a new spot deep within me and though I wasn't expecting to come again, a second orgasm is approaching. I ignore it, focusing only on making Charlie feel as good as he just made me feel. Soon, though, the pleasure becomes too much and I lose my coordination. I lean down, laying my chest on top of his, and kiss him, conveying how amazing this is with my lips and tongue. I try to keep moving, but he senses my difficulty, grabs hold of my hips, and takes over, thrusting up into me.

The movements are so slow that I can feel his orgasm approach. His cock swells, his strokes stutter, and he grunts, burying himself as deep as he can while he fills me up with his cum. The pulsations of his cock push me over the edge and I follow him into bliss.

My orgasm paralyzes me and I sink on top of him, resting my head on his skin as we catch our breath. I can feel his heart thump against my chest. Once I feel like I can move again, I attempt to get off of him, but he wraps his arms around me, keeping me draped over his body, so I settle back down.

My eyelids suddenly weigh a thousand pounds. I close them and try to stop myself from yawning, but it's no use. I drift off to sleep, surrounded by Charlie's warm embrace, his cock still inside me. This time it's my past that haunts me when we fall asleep.

Chapter 8

Sweet baby Jesus.

Charlie

My job takes me to New York City for meetings with current and prospective clients. I'm happy to get away, actually. Things with Quinn are getting a bit…intense, and some distance is just what I need to put things into perspective.

I don't want a relationship—absolutely not. The word alone is enough to give me hives.

But…

I can't stop thinking about Quinn, especially that last night with her.

Her sketching me. Fucking her in her studio. Waking up from my nightmare surrounded by her scent. Telling her about Anna and the baby then sinking into her body as I shared my pain with her. I woke up feeling amazing, light and happy. I caught myself whistling on my way home.

Whistling.

I'm getting attached, and that won't do.

So here I am, at the bar in my hotel, nursing a scotch. Dim lights paint everyone in shadows, and slow, sultry music charges the atmosphere with sex—the perfect sce-

nario to find a random hookup. A month ago, I'd already be balls deep in some willing woman.

Now?

I'm scrolling through pictures of Quinn.

Fuck. Me.

I stop resisting and text her.

Me: Hey.

Could I be any lamer? *Shit.* I cringe at the stupid message, wishing I could take it back, but texting does not have an unsend option, so I'm forced to sit here and see whether or not she texts back.

As I wait for Quinn's response like a little puppy waiting for scraps of food under the dinner table, a woman slides onto the barstool next to mine. Her perfume wafts in my direction, tickling my nose with the citrusy scent. I look over, smiling politely as she orders a drink from the bartender. She's probably mid-twenties, and from the looks of it, she's wealthy. Her dark brown hair is glossy and perfectly coifed, makeup flawless, clothes expensive, and sparkling jewelry winks at me from her ears, neck, and wrists.

She catches me taking her in and her eyes flare with interest. She's actually quite gorgeous.

But my dick doesn't respond.

Nothing.

Not one twitch.

"Hey handsome," she croons.

Who the hell says that? "Hi," I respond tersely. My cell phone is a beacon and I can't stop myself from checking to see if Quinn has responded.

Nothing yet.

"Waiting for someone?" she asks, eyeing my phone.

"No." *Yes, but just a text message.*

"I'm Topaz." She sticks out her hand for me to shake, looking at me expectantly.

Oh, I guess this is the part where I tell her my name. "I'm Charlie."

"Mind if I keep you company, Charlie?" She licks her lips, gaze lowered to my mouth. Topaz is definitely down to fuck, or at least she's giving me some signals, and *still* no response in my pants. My cock is soft, maybe even retreating at the thought of fucking this woman.

"Sure." I shrug. What else am I going to do other than sit here like a pathetic fool and wait for Quinn's text? What is she doing tonight anyway? Is she out at a bar on a Monday night hooking up with someone? We never discussed making things exclusive, so she's free to fuck someone else.

Maybe that's what *I* need to do—fuck someone else to get Quinn off my brain.

I pocket my phone, trying to force my attention away from the unanswered text. I turn to give Topaz my full attention and notice that her drink is half empty. "Can I get you another drink?"

She smiles a model-perfect smile. "A cosmo would be great, thank you."

I signal the bartender and order another round for both of us. "So what brings you to New York?"

"Work."

"Me too."

"And what is it that you do?"

"I'm a photographer," I tell her.

"Well, that's interesting. I'm a model."

I knew it. "So you must be sick of photographers, then."

Her eyes travel down my form but my cock remains unaffected by this woman.

"I might like to be photographed by you," she purrs.

Her flirting fails horribly because now all I can think about are the pictures I took of Quinn. I smile stiffly. *Come on, get your head in the game.* "Sorry, I'm off duty tonight."

"Well, that's a bummer." She sidles up to me, placing her hand on my chest. My nose tickles again with the heavy scent of her perfume, and instead of wanting to pull those lush curves into my body, I just want her to stop touching me.

"You okay over there?" Topaz runs her hands up my chest to my neck, and I reach up to grab her wrists, preventing her from touching me anymore.

"Huh? Oh, yeah, just thinking," I mutter.

"Do you have a girlfriend? Wife?"

"No." The denial sounds hollow, but it's the truth—Quinn *isn't* my girlfriend.

Just then, I feel my cell vibrate in my pocket. I don't even try to act cool. I back up, giving myself some space to reach into my pocket and bring the screen to life. My lips curve up when I see Quinn's name.

"Excuse me, this is important," I tell Topaz as I sit at my barstool and open up Quinn's text.

Red: Hey hotstuff, I was just thinking about you.

Me: What were you thinking about?

Red: Well, I was scrolling through Tumblr, getting ready for my self-love session of the night, wishing someone would have sent me those pictures...

Sweet baby Jesus. I don't know which part of that statement to focus on first. My dick stirs to life, quickly hardening in my pants as I imagine Quinn lying in bed, playing with herself as she watches porn.

Me: Let's break that statement down and deal with it one scintillating part at a time, shall we?

Red: Did you just text the word scintillating?

Me: I did. Autocorrect helped me spell it. ;-)

Red: Me too.

Me: I want to talk about your self-love session.

Red: What's to talk about? I like orgasms and you weren't available to give me any, so I'm going to give myself some.

Me: And you have a Tumblr account?

Red: Yeah, don't you? Tumblr is the best.

Me: Yes, what's your account?

Red: You show me yours, I'll show you mine.

Me: Pierced&Horny

Red: Ha! I might already follow you!

Me: What's yours?

Red: I don't know if I want to tell you.

Me: Hey, that's not fair. I showed you mine, now you show me yours.

Red: You may find some surprises on my page.

Now I'm curious. What does she have on there that she doesn't want me to see?

Me: I promise not to judge. I just want to see what turns your crank.

Red: A variety of things.

Me: Red...

Red: Red_Hot&Horny

Me: Ha! We're both horny.

Red: Well, we already knew that.

Me: Give me a minute to look you up.

Without thinking, I open my Tumblr app then look around. I completely forgot about Topaz but find that at some point while I was texting Quinn, she got up and left. It's just as well—I wasn't into her at all. I throw some money on the bar then get up to go to my room.

Alone in the elevator, I open the app and search for *Red_Hot&Horny*. I find it right away and start scrolling through her posts. *Does she post pictures of herself?* I wonder, but I don't see anything that resembles her. The first couple of pictures are pretty standard—a close-up of a man's cock inside a wet pussy, a man with a woman's hair wrapped in his fist, pulling her hair as he fucks her from behind. *Nice.* I tap the heart, liking her post.

I stop scrolling when I see the next one. It's a video, but I spy *three* people. Curiosity burns through me. *Does Quinn like the idea of a threesome?* The elevator dings, notifying me that we're on my floor. I ignore the video for a second so I can step off the elevator and find my room without running into a wall. As soon as I lock the door, I throw myself on the bed and hit play.

A brunette woman sits on a bed with her back against the headboard, her legs splayed wide open. She's strumming her clit while staring intently at the couple fucking right in front of her. The man is really pounding a blonde chick with gigantic tits, almost reminiscent of Miss Double D. The blonde is lying on her back, boobs bouncing with every thrust. Then the man pulls out and comes all over her tits. I'm hypnotized as the brunette crawls toward them and starts licking the cum off the blonde's skin.

My cock is rock hard.

I hit share on the post and text it to Quinn.

Me: Red. This video is very naughty.

Red: Thought you might like that one. Does the blonde remind you of anyone?

Me: Did you find this after that night with Miss Double D?

Red: Yes.

Me: Would you have liked to watch me fuck her?

Red: Is it weird if I say yes?

Me: Is it weird if I like the idea?

Red: Do you?

Me: My dick is so hard right now just thinking about it.

Red: Mmm. Did you see anything else you like on my page?

Me: I'm checking it out now. In the meantime, check these out.

I go to my private gallery and send Quinn the file with the pictures I took of her when she sucked me off. Then I go back to Tumblr and scroll down. The next picture is also of a threesome, but this time, it's two men and one woman. One man is sitting in the corner, fully dressed, but his fly is open and he's stroking his cock. He's a one-man audience, watching a naked woman getting fucked from behind. The woman is staring at him, blissed out in the ecstasy of another man buried balls deep inside her.

I groan and palm my dick, desperate for some friction. In fact, why have I not taken my pants off yet? I unzip and free my cock. It's so hard it stands straight up, pointing to the ceiling. I squeeze the base then stroke up, applying pressure on my piercing, and the sharp tug of the metal makes me hiss. I could come in two seconds, but I don't want to. I ignore my aching erection and share this picture with Quinn, too.

Me: Fuck, Red. You're killing me.

Red: What do you think of that...scenario?

Me: It looks hot as fuck.

Red: You like to watch, too?

Me: I don't know, to be honest, but the thought of me sitting there, watching you get fucked, with your eyes on me...let's just say, my cock likes that scenario a lot.

Red: I think I'd like your eyes on me.

Me: What do you think of the pictures?

Red: They're...filthy. I look like a porn star.

Me: Nah, you're way hotter.

Quinn

I scroll through the pictures Charlie just sent me. There are so many, and I'm the star in all of them—well, me and his magnificent penis. The first couple images show me with red lipstick smeared on my face, kissing and tonguing his cock, which is decorated with my red lipstick.

Fuck, that's so hot.

Then I see a picture with my lips stretched wide around his shaft, his skin wet and shiny with my saliva. Looking at these pictures is hotter than looking at Tumblr, hands down. My clit throbs, reminding me that this was supposed to be a masturbation session, but I'm too focused on looking at these pictures. I need to see all of them before I can think about anything else.

Swiping across my screen to look through the next pictures, I stop when I see the one he called *Debauched*. The title is fitting; I do look completely debauched. This is the only one of my full face, something I had requested him not to take a picture of, but I love the picture so much, I don't care that he took it. There's mascara smudged under my eyes, trails of tears on my face, lips swollen with a blur of red tint remaining from the lipstick that smeared everywhere, and a trail of his cum dripping down my chin and neck.

What I notice most of all are my eyes. They're blazing with need, desire, and pride. I had just made him come so hard and I'd loved every second of it. I had no idea I looked like this. Seeing myself so well used and so needy at the same time...it makes my skin hot.

I minimize the pictures and open my messenger to text Charlie.

Me: You took a picture of my full face.

Charlie: I know. To be fair, you had just sucked my brains out of my cock, so I wasn't thinking clearly, and once I saw it, I couldn't bring myself to delete it. It's my favorite one. If you want me to delete it, I will.

Me: It's...so dirty. I can't stop looking at it.

Charlie: I've jacked off while looking at it too many times to count.

Me: Would it be weird to get myself off...looking at myself?

Charlie: Fucking hell, Red. Do it. Are you touching yourself right now?

Me: Not yet.

Charlie: Because I want to touch my cock. I'll be lonely if you don't join me.

Me: Can't have that.

Charlie: Tell me how wet you are.

I split the screen on my phone so the picture of me debauched so wonderfully by Charlie is on top and the texting app is on the bottom. Then I hold the phone in my right hand and reach down with my left. I can't remember the last time I had phone sex with someone. Wait, is this phone sex? Or sexting? Whatever it is, it makes me feel like a teenager.

I'm naked, having already shed my clothes and retrieved my vibrator for my date with Tumblr. My skin tingles in anticipation, even though it's only my hand gliding down my waist. Charlie knows what I'm doing. *He's doing the same thing.* That thought makes me burn hotter, imagining him stroking himself.

Trailing my fingers along my abdomen, through my curls, and in between my lips, I find myself soaking wet. *Mmmm.* My fingers slip through easily and I gather up some of my wetness to circle around my clit. *Yess.*

Me: I'm soaked.

Charlie: Fuck. I want to see. Send me a picture.

My eyes widen. Do I want to take a picture of myself to show him? My heart rate kicks up. *Yes, I do.* Instead of taking a picture of my pussy, I hold up the fingers that were just sliding through my wetness and snap a shot of them. The flash picks up the shine, showing that my fingers are indeed wet, so I send it to him.

Charlie: If I were there, I'd lick those fingers.

Me: If you were here, I'd want you to lick more than that.

Charlie: Where would you want me to start?

Me: You can start by sending me a picture of how hard you are.

Charlie: You want a dick pic? I just sent you a whole bunch of them. Not enough for you?

Me: None of those were pictures of you RIGHT NOW.

I wait, anticipating his picture. Then a box appears as the picture downloads, and the sight that greets me makes my mouth water. Charlie is lying on a bed, his pants gathered just under his crotch, his dick standing proudly at attention. It's thick and long, with the silver metal of his piercing glinting at me. I don't know what it is about that piercing, but I love playing with it.

Me: Very nice, hotshot. Have I told you lately how pretty your cock is?

Charlie: Pretty? Pfft. He's NOT pretty.

Me: He's very pretty. And that piercing...why am I so obsessed with it?

Charlie: Because it makes you feel so good.

Me: Yes, yes it does.

Charlie: I love it when you beg for my cock.

Me: I don't beg.

Charlie: Ha! I've heard you beg—for my cock, for me to fuck you harder— and I love the sound of it.

While my mind is annoyed by the fact that he does reduce me to begging, my pussy likes it. My clit is pulsing in time with my heartbeat, so aroused by the visual stimulation of the pictures and the texts from Charlie. I strum it gently, just teasing myself, but seeing the picture he sent me of his cock makes my pussy feel empty. I get my vibrator and rub it gently up and down, loving the feel of the cool temperature against my hot flesh. *Mmm.*

Me: If only you could see me now, you might do some begging yourself.

Charlie: What are you doing? Are your fingers busy?

Me: No.

Charlie: ??

Me: It's my vibrator.

Charlie: Fuck me. You're using a vibrator? Is it inside you?

Me: Not yet, just getting it nice and slick.

Charlie: What color is it?

Me: Red.

Charlie: How appropriate. You're right, I want to see it.

Me: Maybe if you say please.

Charlie: You know you want to show it to me. Don't you want me to see you fucking yourself with your red vibrator? You're such a dirty, dirty girl.

Me: Nice try.

Charlie: I bet it would slip right inside without a problem because you're so wet.

I move the vibrator toward my opening and play there a moment, wanting to draw out that first stroke in. The first stroke is always the best, feeling the stretch then the fullness that follows. I inch it in, then back out, giving myself some shallow strokes.

Charlie: You must be busy over there. Is it all the way in yet? Or are you teasing yourself like I tease you?

Me: You are a tease.

Charlie: Is it all the way in? Show me.

Me: Just one inch.

Me: Now two.

Charlie: Fuck, how big is that thing? I need to see it.

Me: If you say please.

Instead of saying please, he sends me another picture, this time of his hand wrapped around his dick, mid-stroke. *Holy fuck.* That's so hot. Why is it so hot when guys touch themselves? Especially Charlie. His hand is so masculine, the dim light in the room glinting off his piercing.

I slide the vibrator deeper, imagining it's him filling me.

Me: That still isn't please.

Charlie: Fine, PLEASE, Red. Show me that dirty pussy full of your fuck toy. I'm DYING. PLEASE.

His words make me burn hotter. I push the vibrator all the way in, sighing at how good it feels to be full. I can't resist pumping it in and out a couple times, needing the friction. Then I sit up, point the phone at my cunt, and awkwardly try to snap a few pictures. The first two suck, not capturing the right angle to show exactly what I'm doing, so I have to spread my legs as far open as I can and tilt my pelvis up. Turning the phone a bit to the side shows exactly what I want him to see—my folds wet with arousal, the red vibrator half in, the exposed "shaft" shiny from being inside me, my pussy stretched around the girth.

Without thinking too hard about it, I share the photo with him.

Charlie: Fuuuuuck. I need you to fuck that pretty pussy. Fuck it fast and hard, because I'm about to come at the sight of you like this.

I do just that, turning the end piece to power it on. My hips buck up at the jolt of sensation and my clit pulses, almost like it's jealous of my pussy. I slide the vibrator out of me and circle my clit with it. Direct contact is too much, but subtle swipes add to the pleasure sweeping over my body.

Did Charlie come yet? Is he fucking his hand? Is he squeezing hard? Is his hand moving so fast it's a blur or does he stroke it slowly?

Me: I want to see you come.

Charlie: Ditto

Me: Video chat?

Charlie: Fuck yes.

I hit the button that has a video camera to turn our exchange into a video call. Then I see it. Charlie's dick is shiny with…lube? Spit? It's slick so his hand glides over the skin easily. He's stroking slowly, squeezing it harder than I would ever feel comfortable squeezing. Then when he reaches the tip, he applies pressure to the piercing, almost tugging it.

"Red," he pants, voice tight with need. "Show me. I need to see it."

I was so preoccupied with getting my first view of him, I forgot to angle my phone the right way. I sit up and try to hold the phone over my crotch, but it's awkward to keep this pose and work the vibrator, too. Instead, I put a pillow in front of me and prop the phone against it, right in front of my pussy, giving him the best view and freeing up both of my hands.

"Fuuuck," he grunts, squeezing the base of his dick. "Put it inside."

"What if I don't want to?" I tease, sliding the vibrator up and down the outside of my sex, circling my clit when I get to the top.

"Is that how you get yourself off? You don't put it inside?"

"No, I do, but I like to tease my clit too," I tell him, breathless. My screen shows a smaller box in the corner with my video, and the combination of seeing Charlie tug on his cock along with me stroking my pussy amps up my arousal. I'm so close.

"Put it inside. I need to see it. Do it slowly."

"You're so bossy for someone who is in a different state."

"You know you want to."

"What's my reward if I do?" I ask him. I do want to put it inside—my pussy's now jealous of my clit, and my nipples are tingling. My boobs are visible on the screen as the phone is angled up a bit, and the tips are firm, erect points.

"I'll probably come all over my hand."

"*That's* my reward?"

He chuckles, the sound deep and wicked. "You love it when I come."

Yes, I do. He knows me so well. I position the vibrator at my entrance, circling the sensitive skin, hesitating before pushing inside.

"Yes, nice and slow," he instructs. His hand is picking up speed, working his cock diligently now.

I go slow, but only because that's what *I* want.

"Fucking hell, that's the hottest thing I've ever seen. Look at you, you dirty girl, fucking yourself so I can watch you."

His hips start bucking up now so he's truly fucking his hand. Then his hand disappears for a second, abandoning his erection, leaving it to sway and twitch on its own. I hear an unexpected sound and realize he's spitting onto his hand, the wet plop of the saliva hitting his skin sounding so crass. His hand comes into view again and he spreads the spit around. It must not be enough though, because the view changes angles, like he's sitting up, and he spits directly onto his dick. The spittle lands messily, a blob of saliva and bubbles right in the center of his shaft.

Why is that so hot? In any other circumstance, I think it's gross when guys spit, but seeing Charlie's erection shiny, watching him spread it all over from tip to base—it makes me push the vibrator in the rest of the way.

"Yesss," he hisses.

My moan escapes without my permission, but I'm so close to coming I don't care. It's not like I need to preserve my dignity at this point. We're having phone sex; getting each other off *is* the point. I push the vibrator in and out, swiping up to circle my clit after every couple of strokes. The tingling of my nipples can't be ignored anymore, so I use my free hand to pinch the right one, then the left.

"Oh, God. Those pretty nipples need attention, don't they? I want to bite them. You'd like that, wouldn't you, Red? The sting of my bite followed by the thrust of my cock."

I nod in agreement, so far gone that words escape me. He's fucking his hand in earnest, now, and the up and down movement of his hips is hypnotic.

"Fuck, I'm going to come," he announces. I stop moving, transfixed as he stops all motion, brings the camera closer to his cock and gives one final stroke. His dick pulses in his hand, a jet of semen erupting from the tip and landing…somewhere. A masculine grunt, deep and erotic, hits me in my clit, reminding me that I stopped moving. His cock is still jerking and spurting, the semen now running onto his hand, adding to the lubrication. He fingers the ball of his piercing at the base of his head and the picture on my screen jumps as his movements get choppy and stuttered.

He sighs blissfully. "Do it. I need you to come now."

My orgasm is unstoppable. One stroke of the vibrator across my clit and back into my pussy takes me over the edge, my gaze still locked on his spent cock, wet with his cum. I moan and buck, trying to keep still so he can see the muscles in my vagina clench around the vibrator. I turn it off quickly but keep it inside, moving it in and out so slowly until I stop pulsing with pleasure.

When I've come back to Earth, seeing my pussy on the screen is a bit awkward. I remove the vibrator, drop it on the bed next to me, and pick up the camera. He does the same, and our faces come into view. We're both flushed and a bit sweaty. My hair is an absolute disaster, the wild curls sticking up everywhere.

I bite my lip and he smiles broadly, dimples flashing at me.

"That. Was. Awesome." He emphasizes each word like a 14-year-old boy who just got his first blow job.

I laugh. "Yes, it was definitely more exciting than what I had planned for tonight."

"Will you give me a sec?" He waves his semen-coated hand around. "I need to take care of this, but don't hang up, okay?"

"Sure. Me too." I lay the phone on my bed, go to the bathroom to wash my hands and put on a robe, then lie back down and pick the phone back up. Charlie's smiling face greets me.

"Hi," he says, as if we just started talking.

"Hi." I chuckle.

"Aww, you covered up the fun parts."

"You had a pretty good view of my fun parts just a moment ago."

His smile turns naughty. "Yes, I did."

"So, how's your trip? You winning the new clients over with those dimples?"

"Today went well…"

I fall asleep with Charlie's deep voice rumbling in my ear as he tells me about his day.

Chapter 9

Humble is boring.

Charlie

Well, Mr. Nelson, this sounds like an amazing plan. When can you start working on our project?" Roger Diamond slaps his hands together with excitement.

My smile is hard to contain, so I don't even try. "Thank you, Mr. Diamond. I'll check my calendar and email you some dates. If memory serves me right, I have some time free next month, but I'll verify and we can pick some dates that work for us both."

"Good man. I look forward to it." Mr. Diamond shakes my hand. "I hate to cut this short, but I need to get going."

"No problem. We'll talk soon," I assure him.

"Sounds good." He smiles broadly and with a final nod, heads out of the restaurant.

I'm three for three—every prospective client I met with on this trip decided to book my services. Pride surges through me and I itch to tell someone about it.

Without thinking too hard, I pick up my cell and text Quinn.

Me: Hey.

Red: Hey yourself. What's up?

Me: Did you know I'm awesome?

Red: And so humble, too.

Me: Humble is boring.

Red: You are anything but boring.

Me: Seriously, though, this trip was a success. I'm three for three.

Red: I expected no less from the awesome Charlie Nelson.

Me: So you do know I'm awesome.

Red: Did you flash them the panty-dropping smile?

Me: I keep telling you, my dimples don't work on men.

Red: How do you know? Did you smile at them, dimples and all?

Me: I guess I did.

Red: See, it works on men and women. No one can resist those dimples.

Me: Now you're doling out the compliments. Keep them coming.

Red: I'm proud of you, Charlie. I knew you would sign them all, though. You're so talented, they'd be stupid not to work with *you*.

Warmth blooms in my belly, and my lips curve up in a small smile. It feels good to know she's proud of me and thinks I'm talented.

Red: What are you going to do to celebrate?

Me: I know what I want to do to celebrate.

Red: ??

Now this is new territory for me. I know we texted about it a bit last night, what with the contents of her Tumblr page, but how do I tell her I want to watch her get down and dirty with someone else?

I open the Tumblr app, scroll through her feed, and find the threesome video with the man watching the woman get fucked by another man. I hit the share button and send it to her.

Subtle, Charlie. Real subtle.

I fidget, staring at the screen as I wait for her response.

Red: You want to watch?

Me: Yes.

Red: Would you want to...participate?

Holy shit. A threesome? Do I want a threesome with Quinn and some other guy? I think about this. A threesome with two girls is a definite yes—two girls kneeling at my feet, taking turns sucking me off, kissing, rubbing their nipples together, one riding my face while the other rides my dick.

Hell.

Yes.

But me, Quinn, and another guy? What if she sucked my cock while she got fucked? I imagine it, how she would jostle as he—whoever *he* is— thrusts into her, her big whiskey brown eyes locked on mine. Or...I could fuck her as she sucked on his cock, and there's always the whole double penetration scene, but that would involve me getting very up close and personal with the guy.

I can *say* those scenes don't turn me on all I want, but my dick doesn't lie, and he's telling me threesomes with Quinn—with either another girl *or* another guy—sound fun.

Me: Possibly, but I want to start with watching you.

A beat goes by with no response and I'm afraid she's not into it. *Shit.* Does she think I'm a total pig for suggesting it? Well, I guess I am a total pig, but still, I hope I didn't offend her. I thought she was into it last night. She has all this stuff on her Tumblr page, after all, so the thought of it must be arousing to her, and she *just asked* if I wanted to participate.

I start typing out a message, trying to backtrack and apologize, but my phone buzzes in my hand before I hit send.

Red: *When?*

I exhale a sigh of relief. I half expected her to start giving me a piece of her mind.

Me: I get back into town Friday.

Red: So, Friday night then?

A laugh bubbles out of me at her response.

Me: Anxious much?

Red: It sounds fun, and you do need a proper celebration for your new accounts.

Me: I couldn't agree more.

Red: Okay, we have two days to work out the details. I need to get back to work.

Me: Work hard so we can play hard later. ;-)

Sweet baby Jesus. My heart is pounding in my chest with excitement. Despite my vast experience with females, I have never done anything like this. I mean, I've watched my fair share of porn, but I've never wanted to watch a woman actually have sex with someone else before.

Then I get stuck on one thought: who are we going to find that would be okay with me watching? Do we need to set it up as an accident, like the way Quinn ended up watching me? What if the guy spots me and gets upset?

We definitely need to work out the details.

Quinn

Studying the finished pieces in my studio, I try to decide which ones I want to bring in to the gallery today. Every month, I go through this process. You'd think I'd want to sell all of my pieces—it is, after all, my source of income—but I pour my soul into my art, and it isn't always easy to part with pieces of my soul.

Charlie's piece is going for sure. I'm so excited to see what Suzanne, my manager at the gallery, thinks of it. Running my hands through my hair, I blow out a breath and just gather up all my finished pieces except for the charcoal drawings I did of Charlie. I can't part with those yet—and I'm not sure if I ever want to.

After loading everything up into my car, I drive to Art Redefined. I've been working with this gallery for a couple of years now, and we seem to be a good fit for each other. I can't make the same style art every time I create, and Suzanne loves that I produce variety. What I make all depends on my mood and frame of mind; plus, I'd get bored to death being stuck in one style.

She squeals at the sight of my full arms. "Ooooh! What do you have for me today?"

"Have a look at these while I get the rest from the car." I carry them into the back room and head back out for my second load. When I get back, I see her staring at Charlie's piece. "What do you think of that one?" I ask her without telling her it isn't mine.

She can't tear her eyes away, awestruck. "This is magnificent, so painful and raw. What happened to you since I saw you last, Quinn?"

I beam at her. "I knew you'd like it. That isn't my work, it's by a friend of mine. He didn't want it and didn't think it was very good, but I love it."

"Where does he usually sell his art?"

"Actually, he's a photographer, not a painter. He works in marketing, but after a particularly rough night, I suggested we paint to relieve some stress, and this is what he came up with."

Her eyebrows rise in surprise. "Can I sell it?"

"Absolutely."

"Can he make more?"

I laugh. "Not sure about that, but I'll work on it."

"You do that. I think this piece will go fast."

Happy with Suzanne's response, I go about unwrapping the other pieces. The bell rings, indicating that a customer has walked in.

"I'm going to go man the front, can you give me your inventory list when you're done here?"

"No problem, meet you out there in a bit." Each piece has to get photographed and added to a list so she knows what's available, and I busy myself with the simple tasks. Every month Suzanne rearranges all of the pieces on display, exchanging old inventory for new, or just rotating the pieces to a different spot to keep the look fresh and new. Once the gallery has been rearranged, there is an open house for members, an insider's first peek at new art. We're encouraged to attend to mingle with buyers, but I've only been a handful of times—too much schmoozing for my taste.

"Hey gorgeous," a deep voice says from behind me. I spin to find a tall man wheeling a cart carrying several canvases and sculptures into the room. He's clad in faded jeans torn at the knees and a paint splattered t-shirt, soft from use and so well worn it's almost see-through. On anyone else, the outfit might make you think he's homeless, but this man is fit and muscular, and the shirt only makes you notice what's underneath—the broad shoulders, firm chest, and flat stomach. My eyes roam up to his face, noticing the dark stubble decorating his square jaw and upper lip. His long black hair is a mess, as usual, but the rumpled look only makes him that much sexier. Tobias notices my roaming eyes and grins at me.

"Hey, I was hoping I'd find you here." I grin back at him. "Want to have lunch with me?"

"Lunch?" One eyebrow quirks up. "Is that what we're calling it these days?"

Right. So, Tobias and I have had sex a few times since my divorce. He's fun, laid back, and so good at oral, it makes my toes curl just remembering. We haven't gotten together in a long while, though, but when Charlie texted me that he wants to watch me with another guy, Tobias came to mind.

I chuckle at his confusion. "No, I actually mean lunch—you know, where we go to a restaurant, sit down, and exchange conversation while we eat food?"

"Is *eat food* code, too?" His eyes roam my body, and I have to stop myself from squirming at his attention. I keep thinking about Charlie watching me suck Tobias's cock—or even better, Charlie feeding me his cock while Tobias eats my pussy.

"Have you ever known me to beat around the bush?" I quirk my eyebrow up at him.

He sighs. "No, you're as direct as they come. You sure I can't convince you to come to my place instead?" His pretty lips pout and he blinks at me with puppy dog eyes.

"Don't worry, I think you're going to like what I want to talk to you about."

"Well, now you're talking." He rubs his hands together with a wicked grin. "I'll be done here in five minutes."

I laugh, looking at his cart so full of pieces. "No you won't, but don't worry, I'll help you when I'm done."

20 minutes later, we're walking down the street to my favorite sandwich shop. We chat about nonsense while we order at the counter and pick out a table, the aroma of fresh bread making my stomach grumble.

"All right already, Quinn. The suspense is killing me. Out with it." He bites into his BLT and stares at me with curiosity.

I swallow the delicious bite of chicken sandwich and contemplate how to begin. Hell, Tobias already knows I'm not subtle, so I just spit it out. "My friend and I are looking for a third, someone to play with me while he watches. Would you like to play with us?" I pretend my heart isn't beating a mile a minute and take another bite of my sandwich, feigning indifference to his response. If I'm being honest, I want Tobias to say yes. I know him, I feel comfortable with him, and I've already had sex with him. I might be secure in my sexuality, but I'm not sure how to go about picking up a stranger to play with me and Charlie.

He doesn't make me wait long for his answer. "Fuck yes. I'm in. Tell me more about your friend."

I put down my sandwich and blow out a breath I hadn't realized I was holding. "Have you ever done anything like this before?"

"I've had a couple of threesomes before. Does your friend want to partake?" He wiggles his eyebrows suggestively.

That's the other thing—Tobias is bisexual. He doesn't let a silly thing like gender get in the way of acting on attraction.

"I don't think so, at least maybe not right off the bat. Charlie is…" I trail off, trying to find the words to describe him. "He's young and fun, sexy and charming. We hook up every now and then, more often as of late. One night at Club Bailar, I happened to stumble upon him with another girl. I meant to turn around and leave, I promise I did, but he caught me standing there watching them and kept going while staring at me. It was the hottest thing."

Tobias's green eyes glitter with delight as I tell him about my accidental foray into voyeurism. "So now he wants to watch you?"

"Yes."

"Are you in love with him?"

My heart stutters in my chest—it's been doing that ever since Charlie shared his painful past with me. I think of his nightmare and after, how he opened up to me and let me see his vulnerability, and my chest squeezes. Then I remember my past with Reid, how he promised to be there for me and when faced with a choice, he didn't choose me. I ignore my stupid heart's reaction to Charlie.

"No, don't be silly. We're just friends—friends who fuck a lot."

He looks dubious. "Are you sure? Because I'm down to fuck, but I don't want to step in the middle of a relationship."

"I promise, you're not stepping in the middle of anything. We just want a fun night full of orgasms and depravity," I reassure him, also trying to reassure myself, too.

An elderly woman at the table next to us splutters. *Shit*, I may have said that too loud in my efforts to be convincing.

"Well, how could I pass up orgasms and depravity? Let's meet up for drinks. If we all get along and want to take it further, we can progress from there."

"Sounds perfect." I smile at him, excitement tickling my belly.

This is going to be fun.

Charlie: You around?

Me: I am. In fact, I think I have a plan.

Charlie: Tell me.

Me: So I have this friend, someone fun and unattached, and he's interested in joining us.

Charlie: Who is he?

Me: His name is Tobias. He's 30, sells his art at the same gallery I do.

Charlie: Have you fucked him before?

Me: Yes. Not for a while now, though. The last time was probably six months ago.

Charlie: And he knows I want to watch? He's cool with it?

Me: Yes. He suggested we get together for drinks first to make sure everyone can play nice and then go from there.

Charlie: You trust him? I mean, is he clean?

Me: He has a condom rule, never goes without, but we can exchange test results if you want.

Charlie: Yes, I want.

Me: No problem.

Charlie: I have to go, but Red?

Me: Yes?

Charlie: I can't wait.

Me: Me either.

I swear I've never been this horny in all my life. Thoughts of meeting up with Charlie and Tobias tomorrow night are never too far from my mind. I went to the spa today to get waxed and buffed and polished, and my nails are painted red, so shiny and sexy. My legs are hairless and soft, my pubes trimmed and tamed, with the hair directly around my delicate bits waxed and bare for extra exposure. It's so smooth and sensitive down there, I can now feel my underwear against my skin. Not going to lie, it feels so good I get turned on just walking.

Charlie sent me a Tumblr video earlier depicting a delicious threesome that had me shoving my hand in my underwear to get some relief instantly. Despite masturbating mere hours ago, I'm still horny. It's like I have this itch that won't go away until it's scratched.

So, even though it's only eight PM and I want to do some work in my studio, I know I won't be able to focus until I masturbate again. Just as I strip off my clothes and settle into bed with my vibrator in hand and finger ready on the Tumblr app, my phone rings in my hand. The picture of my mother is like a cold shower, instantly dousing my libido. I debate ignoring her, but that never works well.

I draw the sheets up to cover my nakedness and throw the vibrator back into the nightstand drawer. Then I take a deep breath and swipe to answer.

"Hello."

"Oh my goodness, you actually answered. I'm shocked." My mother's sarcastic voice is like a needle to my brain. So she's starting with the guilt this time—I guess it's better than leading up to it.

"You say that like I never answer your calls."

"You usually don't."

"That's because you always make me feel guilty, like you are right now."

"Well, if the shoe fits."

Wow, it only took 3.2 seconds for the conversation to go downhill. I sigh and try to find an ounce of patience.

"Let's start over, Mom. How are you?"

"I'm fine, dear. I'm calling to tell you we're having a family dinner on Sunday. Your sister is coming up and it would be nice if you could join us."

Damn. I dread family dinners. My parents take every chance they get to point out that I abandoned my wedding vows—though they fail to acknowledge that Reid *also* abandoned our wedding vows when he cheated on me. Half the time, they actually invite Reid, so I have to see his shitty face and try not to punch him. I think if they could, my parents would just adopt him and boot me out of my family. You'd think they'd be on my side after what I went through, but they hold fast to the claim that wedding vows are forever and divorce is taking the easy way out.

"Did you invite Reid?"

"Your father had lunch with him today, and I imagine he did extend the invitation," she informs me.

Fuck. Every time, it's like a punch to my gut.

"Why do you do this to me, Mom? Reid is my *ex-husband*, the man I found fucking some other woman *in my bed*," I screech.

"Language, Quinn. You don't have to be so crass," she scolds.

"I'm not being crass, I'm stating the facts. You and dad continue to treat him like he's still a part of the family, and he isn't. We're *divorced.* If you want me to come to family dinners, stop inviting him." My blood pressure is escalating by the second, but I can't help it. This drives me *insane.*

"He's our son-in-law." She sniffs. "There's nothing wrong with us hoping you two might get back together, and you can't get back together if you never see each other."

I open my mouth to correct her—he was their son-in-law. *Was* being the operative word.

But then an idea comes to mind.

"If I come to dinner, can I bring a friend?"

"Of course."

"Okay, see you Sunday."

I'm going to see if Charlie will return the favor and come with me—that should put a smile on my parents' and Reid's faces. I snicker at the thought of sticking it to Reid.

Getting out of bed, I throw on some painting clothes then lose myself in my work.

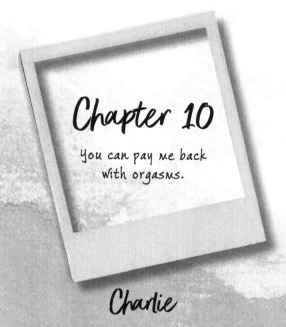

Chapter 10

You can pay me back with orgasms.

Charlie

I wake up on Friday with a spring in my step. Usually when I'm out of town for work, I'm depressed to go home, especially when I visit New York City, but not this time. I scan the hotel room. My bag is packed and waiting by the door. No chargers left in the plugs. No toiletries in the bathroom. My cell beeps with an incoming text to tell me my ride to the airport is waiting downstairs, and I'm 30 minutes early.

I never run early.

Also, not sure I'm proud to admit this, but I've never come to New York and not found a willing woman to keep me company during my stay.

Guess there's a first time for everything.

Waiting on my phone is a queue of videos to be sent to Quinn. I had my own Tumblr session last night—for research purposes, of course—and man, did I find some great ideas. I scroll through the list and hit share on the first one, careful to type Quinn's name in the *to* field. This is not something I want to accidentally send to my mom or sister.

I hope she's still in bed when she gets

this. I imagine her naked and tangled up in her sheets, getting so horny from watching the porn I just sent her that she has to rub one out before she gets out of bed. My pants get tight at the thought. The video shows a woman positioned on all fours sideways on a bed with one man behind her, getting ready to fuck her, and one man at the foot of the bed, watching. She stares at the observer as he unzips his pants and pulls out his erection. Then, she stares at his erection, licking her lips. Once the man starts to fuck her in earnest, she begs the observer to fuck her mouth. He holds back, making her so desperate, then finally gives in and comes down her throat while the other man comes inside of her.

As predicted, her response arrives in exactly five minutes and six seconds. How did I know it would take that long? Because the video is five minutes and six seconds long.

Red: Fuck, that was hot.

Me: I thought so too.

Red: That was a great start to my day, thank you.

Me: You're going to have a great end to your day, so I thought it made sense that you have a good start.

Red: What if it doesn't work out with Tobias?

Me: Meh. Then I'll take you to my place. We can put some of these videos on the big screen TV in my living room and have a Tumblr session together.

Red: I like the sound of that.

Me: I'm headed to the airport.

Red: Okay, see you at 9?

Me: That's the plan, but keep your phone on you...

Red: ?

Me: You'll see.

Nine PM seems like an eternity from now, but by the time my plane lands, it's already noon. I have to stop at the office to give my boss an update on my trip, and on the way, I send Quinn the next video I saved. This one has the woman on her knees with two men standing in front of her. She holds both cocks, taking turns licking and sucking them, until the men get impatient. When she has the first one in her mouth, the second man pulls her face away, her saliva leaving a wet trail hanging from the tip of his dick to her face. He stuffs her full of his erection until the other man returns the favor, pulling her mouth back to him. She goes back and forth between them until they shift closer together so their dicks are almost touching and she can lick both of them simultaneously. When she attempts to wrap her lips around them both at the same time, they groan and come together on her pretty lips.

Red: I'm in a perpetual state of horniness, thanks to you.

Me: Ditto.

Finally, after I leave my office, I head home. Traveling is always so draining, and I want to take a catnap so I can be fresh for tonight. Before I collapse on my bed, I send the third video on my list to Quinn.

This one crosses a line I haven't crossed with Quinn yet—anal sex—but I want to go there. In the video, one man devours the woman's pussy with his mouth while the other man fucks her ass. The woman has a look of pure bliss, drunk on pleasure. They make her come several times before coming themselves.

Red: Do you want my pussy rubbed raw before tonight?

Me: Did you make yourself come with every video?

Red: Yes.

Me: Are you still horny?

Red: Yes.

Me: I want you so horny you can't think straight.

Red: Mission accomplished.

Quinn

C harlie has been torturing me with these videos all day. I need to ask him about Sunday. I'm sure he'll come with me if he's available, but I need to get this request out of the way so we don't have to talk about it tonight.

Me: Okay, time-out from the naughty videos for one minute. I have a favor to ask you.

Charlie: What's up?

Me: My family is having a get-together on Sunday, and they invited my ex-husband.

Charlie: Seriously? Want me to come with?

Me: Can you?

Charlie: No problem. This Sunday?

Me: Yes.

Charlie: I'm free.

Me: Thank you, I'll owe you one.

Charlie: You can pay me back with orgasms.

Me: Deal.

Charlie: See you soon. I'll be there at nine.

Me: I'll be ready.

An eternity later—or only four hours—after I finish the work I had planned for today, shower, primp, and change, I hear a knock at the door. My heart races and my stomach flutters with nervous anticipation. I want Charlie and Tobias to get along. I think they will, as they're both fun, laid-back guys, but I'm worried Charlie will be surprised that Tobias is bisexual. I haven't told him on purpose, because I don't want to freak him out—not that I think Charlie is homophobic or anything. I just don't want him to think Tobias is going to try to get in Charlie's pants instead of mine.

That said, the thought of Tobias getting into Charlie's pants shoots a thrill of excitement through my nervous system. Watching gay porn is my guilty pleasure. The sight of masculine bodies, rough hands tugging at hard cocks, watching cum land on stubble…*unf.* Let's just say I won't complain if the boys want to play with each other, too.

But, first things first, I have to get the door. I find Charlie leaning up against the doorjamb. He scans me from head to toe, a slow smile curving his lips.

"Red." His eyes gleam as he takes in my obvious excitement.

"Charlie." I bite my lip in an effort to play it cool, but it's no use. My smile slips through, and at the sight of it, his dimples appear. *Those dimples.*

He leans forward and wraps his arms around me in a bear hug. I realize this is the first time I've seen him since the night he told me about Anna, and I'm so glad he's back to his normal self. I melt into his embrace, breathing him in, holding on a couple beats longer than I usually do.

"Any cold feet? It's not too late to change your mind." His expression grows serious with concern, and I love that he wants to make sure I'm comfortable.

"My feet are nice and toasty, what about yours?"

"Also toasty. You ready?"

"All set." I slip into my jacket and grab my purse then lock the door.

Charlie takes my hand as we walk to his car, *and* he opens the door for me. There are those date-like manners again. *What an odd date this is*—he's taking me out to watch another man give me orgasms.

A giggle erupts from my throat at the thought.

"What's so funny?" He grins over at me as he starts up the car and pulls out into the street.

"Just…this. I can't believe I'm doing this. I never thought I was this kind of woman."

He narrows his eyes at me. "What kind of woman?"

"The…you know…threesome kind, or whatever this is." I wave my hand in front of me.

"The kind of woman that likes to explore her sexuality? The kind of woman that likes to try new things? The kind of woman that doesn't let society dictate the way she leads her life?"

Hmm. I don't mind being *that* kind of woman. I feel his stare at the stoplight.

"Quinn."

My mirth dies and my smile fades at his serious tone. I meet his blue eyes and raise my eyebrows in question.

"You listen to me: I think you're fucking amazing—strong, beautiful, talented, sexy as fuck. If doing this is going to change your opinion of yourself, let's not."

My chest squeezes at his sincerity and I feel so much better about tonight. Despite my excitement, a small part of me wondered what he'll think of me after tonight; if his opinion of me would change. Now he's worried about what I'll think of *myself*, and that alone makes me square my shoulders, raise my chin, and reassure him.

"I want this, Charlie, *really* want it. I promise I won't regret it later."

He leans forward, smiling, and places a soft kiss on my lips. "That's more like it."

The light turns green and at the blast of the horn behind us, Charlie steps on the gas and focuses on the road.

"So tell me more about Tobias," he requests.

"Let's see…I told you the basics. He works at the gallery with me and he's so talented. His pieces always sell out because they're so different."

"And you guys used to hook up?"

I'm looking for jealousy, but Charlie just looks curious. *Do I want him to be jealous?* I don't know the answer to that question. "Yes. After my divorce, he took me out for a drink and showed me how much fun it can be to be single and unattached."

"You ever want more with him?"

"No." I haven't wanted more with anyone since Reid. "I wouldn't even consider Tobias a close friend. He's a sexy acquaintance that is always up for a good time, nothing more, nothing less. I know he's trustworthy because I work with him, but it's not like we talk on the phone or hang out frequently," I explain. I don't want Charlie to think he's walking into some kind of unrequited love situation.

"Well, okay then," he says as he parks the car and turns off the ignition. "Let's go meet him."

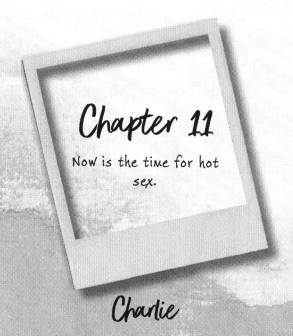

Chapter 11

Now is the time for hot sex.

Charlie

I take Quinn's hand in mine as we navigate the lobby of Hamilton House, a swanky hotel downtown. Friday night means it's busy, and as people bump into us, I pull her into my side and wrap my arm around her waist. Sapphire is a popular bar connected to the hotel, and as the name suggests, all the lights are blue, casting its occupants in an azure haze. We stop at the coat check then claim a newly abandoned high-top table by the front window.

I'm assuming Tobias isn't here yet, though I wouldn't know if he was.

A server approaches the table as Quinn looks around. "What can I get you to drink?" he asks, indicating the laminated list of specials in the middle of the table.

A laugh bubbles out of her at the first name on the list. "I'll take a voyeur, please."

"I'll have a Maker's Mark on the rocks, please."

The server smiles politely, nods, and then retreats to place our order at the bar.

"So tell me about your trip," she suggests.

"Really? We're going to try to talk

about something right now?" I'm so distracted, I'm not sure normal conversation is possible. The semi in my pants twitches, threatening to become a full-blown erection with the direction my thoughts are headed.

"What do you suggest? We just sit here and stare at each other while we wait?"

I sigh. She has a point. "Okay. Tell me something I don't know about you, something weird."

She thinks for a moment then her eyes light up. "I can tie a cherry stem in a knot with my tongue."

"No way! I need to see that."

"You don't believe my tongue is talented?" She blinks innocently.

"Oh, I know your tongue is talented, I've just never seen someone do that before."

"When the server comes back with our drinks, we'll ask him for a cherry and I'll show you." She smirks sexily, totally confident she'll be able to do it. "Okay, your turn."

"Hmm, let me think…I've never broken a bone before. Both Dom and Tabby broke bones when we were kids, but I never did. I wanted to, though."

She laughs. "You wanted to break a bone?"

"Yeah. They got to miss school to get their casts then all their friends signed the casts. I was jealous."

"Well, let me tell you, I broke my arm when I was 12 while I was skiing, and it sucked, so consider yourself lucky."

"I guess." I shrug.

The server comes back to our table with our drinks, and conveniently enough, Quinn's drink is topped with two cherries.

"Ready to watch my talented tongue?"

"Fuck yes, show me." I lean forward, following her every move. She holds the cherry in front of her mouth, giving me a wicked grin, and plucks the cherry off the stem with her teeth. She chews and swallows quickly, then puts the two-inch stem in her mouth. Her lips are closed, but her jaw works, opening and wiggling from side to side. I wish I could see what is happening inside her mouth. There's no way she can tie that thing into a knot with just her tongue.

Less than a minute passes before she holds it up for me to see.

"Holy shit! You did it!" The stem now has a loose knot in the middle. "Do it again."

She laughs and grabs the second cherry, repeating the act, and then holds that one up proudly, too.

"That's amazing! How can you do that?"

She grins. "Oh, just a result of being bored and drunk a lot in college."

"Well, I was already impressed with your tongue, but now I'm extra impressed." I lean forward to kiss her, needing to touch her tongue with mine. Her mouth is sweet, like the cherries she just ate, and I can't get enough of her taste. I deepen the kiss, rubbing my tongue against hers, and hold her face in my hands, keeping her head right where I want it—until I sense someone standing right next to Quinn. We pull apart and I find a tall man with long black hair, bright green eyes, and an amused grin.

"You guys decide to start without me?" he asks.

"Tobias, there you are!" Quinn turns to him but doesn't move out of my hold, and I realize my hands are still on her face. I drop them but lower one arm to the small of her back and she does the same, crossing her arm over mine so her hand is on my back, too. "Tobias, meet Charlie. Charlie, this is Tobias."

He sets his beer on the table. "Nice to meet you, Charlie." He smiles and shakes my hand. It's a good handshake—firm, but not challenging.

"You too."

"Thanks for inviting me out tonight, you guys."

"I'm glad you could make it," Quinn says as she leans into him to give him a side hug. I watch closely, testing myself to see if I have any feelings of jealousy, but her arm stays linked over mine, and while I can see a flush in her cheeks from either excitement or anxiety, her eyes don't light up when she greets him like they do when she sees me.

There's a moment of silence that could push thing into an awkward, uncomfortable vibe, but that's the last thing I want.

"So, Tobias, did you know Quinn can tie a cherry stem into a knot with her tongue?" I ask him.

He chuckles, eyes widening with surprise. "Really?" He looks at her for confirmation. She holds up the two knotted cherry stems as proof, smiling proudly. "I knew your tongue was talented."

"That's what I said, too."

"We were just sharing weird things about ourselves. You want to take a turn?"

He scratches the dark stubble on his face and thinks. "Weird facts, huh? Let me see." His fingers drum on the table as he tries to come up with something to share. "I'm incredibly flexible. I don't know why—it isn't something I've worked on or anything—but when I was 15 and masturbating three times a day, I decided to test out how flexible I was." He smiles devilishly. "By sucking myself off."

I choke mid-sip and start laughing. "Did you succeed?"

"Yep. I was just getting into the groove when my mom barged in with clean laundry."

"No way!" Quinn splutters.

"Oh shit! You didn't lock the door?" I ask him.

"I thought I *had* locked the door, but evidently it didn't catch. She was so startled, she dropped the laundry basket and screamed, which prompted me to jerk out of the precarious position I was in and fall off my bed."

"Oh my God!" Quinn laughs. "I can't believe that happened to you."

"To make matters worse, I knocked over my nightstand in the process and broke my toe."

"Your toe? Do you get a cast for a broken toe?"

"Depends on the break, but mine didn't need one, it just got wrapped to the toe next to it for a few weeks. But, it was enough to take me out of track for a month, and everyone kept asking me how I broke my toe."

"Oh man, that's quite a story," I say, chuckling. "What did you tell everyone?"

"The truth—that I broke it while masturbating." He shrugs. "No one believed me."

"I bet not," Quinn busts up. "But that is quite a nifty trick. Can you still do it?" Her eyes dance with amusement.

Tobias's lips twist in a crooked grin. "Last I tried, I could still do it."

"Charlie was able to get this one girl to lick her own nipples. I wish I could do that."

"Sounds pretty hot. Were you there?"

Quinn looks over at me with heat in her expression. "I was."

Tobias bites his lower lip and gives us a sexy grin. "And tonight you want to watch, is that right?" he asks me.

I look between the two, trying to imagine what it would look like to see him touch her, to watch Quinn touch him. My dick swells in my pants, twitching at the thought. Holding Quinn's gaze, I nod slowly. "I do."

"Quinn?" he asks her.

"Yes," she answers, a little breathless.

"Well then, I'm in." His eyes linger on Quinn's lips.

I drain the rest of my drink then lean forward to kiss her, hard and hot. Then I lean to whisper in her ear, "I'm going to get us a room for the night. I'll go on up and text you the room number. Join me in 10 minutes?"

She pulls back to look at me. "You don't want to go up together?" Concern wrinkles her forehead.

"No, I want you to double check with Tobias that he still wants to do this." I kiss her forehead. "I'll be waiting."

Quinn

Tobias and I watch Charlie's retreating form as he leaves Sapphire to go into the hotel lobby. The view of his back is almost as appealing as his front—the way his clothes hang off his broad shoulders, the way his waist tapers in, his effortless grace and sexy swagger. More than a few heads turn to watch him go, both male and female.

"You forgot to mention that Charlie is hot as fuck," Tobias says, still staring.

"Did I?"

"I bet he has a gorgeous cock."

"Oh yes, he sure does," I confirm with a sigh.

"Is there any chance he'd let me play with it?" His green eyes sparkle and he bites his lower lip.

A laugh erupts out of me. "I don't know, but you'll likely get to see it tonight."

"I can't tell you how excited I am that you invited me to join you guys, but I'm calling you on your bullshit."

"What bullshit?" My eyebrows lift in confusion.

"You and Charlie, you said you're just friends."

"We are," I protest.

He rolls his eyes. "Sure you are. You guys can't take your eyes off each other, and the chemistry—holy fuck. I thought I might burn up just from standing this close while he kissed you."

"Good chemistry doesn't equal a relationship."

"Okay, it's not my business, but trust me, I feel something more between you than chemistry, and it's a *good* thing, Quinn, not a bad thing. Don't fight it just because you don't like the label."

I consider his words. Charlie and I have gotten pretty close lately, so close that he's often my first and last thought of the day, but a *relationship*? Neither one of us wants that. Is it the word? I shake my head because now

109

is not the time to figure this out.

Now is the time for hot sex.

"Tobias."

He meets my gaze. "Yes."

"Are you still in?" I take in his sexily tousled hair, the dark stubble dotting his square jaw, and his pink lips, which are wet from the last sip of his beer.

"Yes."

My cell vibrates in my hand, making my heart rate jump as well.

Charlie: Room 1102

Me: Okay. Be right up.

Charlie: Door's unlocked.

"Is he in the room?"

"Yes, let's go."

Tobias doesn't take my hand or so much as touch me on the way to the elevator. He seems to sense that this night is about the three of us, and that I don't want to get started unless Charlie's with us.

The room is open, as expected. My palms are sweaty and I try to discreetly rub them against the fabric of my black dress. It's a standard hotel room: king-sized bed in the middle with a desk and TV directly across from it and a side chair between the bed and the window wall. Soft, sultry music is playing from somewhere, and the lamp is turned to the lowest setting, bathing the room in ambient light.

Charlie is sitting on the chair, fully dressed, one leg crossed over the other with his ankle resting on his knee. My eyes are drawn to his and I watch as he looks between me and Tobias, noting that we aren't touching. His eyes blaze at me, and it just takes that one look for my nipples to stiffen. He notices my body's reaction to him and smirks at me.

That smirk relaxes me. It's still just me and Charlie.

And Tobias.

How do we start?

Charlie must read the question in my expression because he stands and walks around the bed until he's right in front of me.

"You doing okay?"

I nod slowly. I think I'm okay.

He places his hands on my shoulders and leans in to kiss me. His tongue is hot and demanding, and I lose my breath as he tugs me in so our bodies connect from chest to hip. He's hard; I can feel his erection against my belly.

"Tobias," he says as he breaks our kiss.

"Yes."

"I think Quinn has too many clothes on, don't you?"

Tobias grins at him and nods in agreement. "Way too many."

"Can Tobias undress you, Red?"

I nod my head jerkily as Charlie sits on the bed and pulls my hips to position me so I'm facing him. Tobias comes up behind me and brushes my hair over one shoulder so he can locate the zipper on my dress. I know it's coming but the sound of the zipper still startles me, and goose bumps surface on my skin as his warm hands slide the straps over my shoulders until the dress falls to my feet. Charlie leans down to help and I brace my hands on his shoulders as I step out of it.

I'm now in my bra, panties, and heels. Though the thought of staying in my heels is sexy, my legs are wobbling enough with my anticipation, so I kick them off.

That's better.

Charlie looks over my shoulder and nods at Tobias. This silent exchange between them makes my blood burn hotter and then I feel fingers at the back of my bra, undoing the clasp. My breasts sag and sway at the loss of support, and Tobias again pulls the straps over my shoulders and down my arms, handing it off to Charlie, who then drapes it over my dress. My nipples pebble as the cool air hits my overheated skin, and this time, Tobias's hands smooth down my back, under my arms, and then rest just under my breasts. My nipples tingle and my breasts feel achy, swollen with the need to be touched.

Charlie follows Tobias's hands, tracking his movements. I can't stop watching his face, how his pupils dilate and his cheeks flush with arousal.

Tobias's fingers make gentle circles on my skin, and just when I think he's going to put me out of my misery and touch my nipples, his hands sweep over my abdomen toward the elastic of my underwear. His touch is firm, making my soft, supple curves yield to the pressure. Five or ten years ago I may have been embarrassed by the softness of my belly and hips, but I've learned to love my body. Besides, with the way Charlie is looking at me right now, I can't feel anything but desired.

Tobias slides his fingers under the fabric of my panties and frees me of my last article of clothing. Standing here, naked, in between two incredibly gorgeous, *fully clothed* men, is such a rush. Both of their attention is fixed solely on me.

Any hesitation I felt earlier leaves.

"You like what you see?" I smirk at Charlie. He looks up, expression softening, and gives me that wide, dimple-popping, panty-dropping grin.

"Very much."

"I'm thinking you guys are overdressed," I point out.

"What are you going to do about that?" he asks, nodding his chin to Tobias.

I look over my shoulder and find Tobias staring at me. His green eyes are heavy-lidded with lust and his black wavy hair is tousled from running his fingers through it. It's the first time I've truly looked at Tobias since we entered the room and it's abundantly clear from the tent in his pants that he is enjoying this little game.

"I think I'm going to start with you," I tell him with a saucy smile. I tug his shirt up over his stomach and shoulders until he helps me pull it off, tossing it to the side of the room. Tobias is leaner than Charlie, but he's toned, with not an ounce of fat anywhere on his body. His chest is covered with a smattering of dark hair, lessening in density over his abdomen then gathering together in a dark happy trail.

Leaning forward, I unbuckle the waistband of his pants, surprised that he is actually wearing something other than holey jeans. Unzipping is tricky work, what with the raging hard-on trapped under there. Very carefully, I finish my task, discovering that Tobias is commando. His uncut cock springs forward, as if happy to be free from its prison. I drop the pants and he shuffles out of his shoes then leans down to remove his socks.

Now two of us are naked...

"Tobias, want to play a game?" Charlie asks, his voice rough with lust.

Tobias smirks at him. "I thought we were playing."

"It's a game called *Would You Rather*," Charlie clarifies.

"I like the sound of that."

"Thought so. Would you rather eat Quinn's pussy or have her suck your cock?"

Fuck. Yes please.

I look between the two men, both with hot eyes on me.

"I'd rather eat her pussy."

Said pussy clenches at those words, at the way they're discussing me as if I'm not here.

"Excellent choice. Quinn's pussy is delicious."

"I know." There's that reminder that Tobias and I have done this before.

My eyes fly to Charlie to gauge his reaction, but surprisingly, he doesn't seem jealous. He stands up, making room for me to get on the bed.

"Show me." Charlie is calling the shots.

"What about what I want?" I pout.

"Do you want him to eat your pussy?" Charlie asks me.

I can't deny that I do. "Yes."

"Then lie back and spread your legs. Show us your gorgeous pussy."

Fuck. I lie back on the bed, propped up on my elbows, and slowly stretch my legs, widening them as far as I can with my knees bent and feet flat on the mattress. I look up and the view is…magnificent. Two men stand in front of me, staring right in between my legs. Charlie is still fully clothed in his long-sleeved blue shirt and charcoal slacks. The blue of his shirt brings out the blue of his irises, and that ocean blue gaze glitters at me. Next to him, almost shoulder to shoulder, Tobias stands naked, hand stroking his swollen erection, licking his lips as he stares at my pussy.

"Fuck, she's wet," Tobias groans.

Being the center of their attention is heady, and my body is ready for the touching to begin. I feel so exposed, so naughty.

As if reading my mind, Tobias kneels in front of the bed and runs his hands up my thighs, spreading them wider apart and pinning them open. I look at Charlie while he watches Tobias.

The first lick is heaven, hot and wet, right up my center, ending with a flick to my clit. I can't stop my eyes from closing or the moan from slipping out. Tobias delivers lick after lick, paying attention to everything but my clit. He grunts as he eats me, and I feel the puff of air against my wet, heated skin.

Charlie's gaze doesn't leave my pussy. He watches Tobias's ministrations closely, as if studying for a test. I don't know why this makes everything feel so much better, but it does.

My hips begin to move, searching for friction where I need it most, but Tobias is good at evading me. My nipples are tingling from the lack of attention and I give in to the desire to touch them myself, lying all the way back and pinching the sensitive tips.

"Fuck, Red, look at you," Charlie says gruffly. Our eyes connect and it's like he's in awe of me. He stares at me with such naked lust. "Does it feel good to have Tobias eat you?"

"God, yes."

He palms his erection, rubbing it over his pants. I stare at the outline of his dick and lick my lips, wishing I could suck him right now. To my relief, Charlie unbuckles his belt, unbuttons his pants, and frees his rigid erection from the confines of his pants. He sighs as he wraps a hand around it and gives it a squeeze.

"Do you want Tobias to fuck you while I watch?"

Do I want Tobias to fuck me? The excitement I see in Charlie's face tells me *he* wants this, and the thought of those shining blue eyes watching me get fucked by another man while he strokes his cock lazily ratchets up my arousal to epic proportions.

"Yes," I moan, gasping in surprise as Tobias's tongue swipes over my puckered hole.

"What did he do?" He looks at Tobias to see what gave me that reaction.

"He licked my asshole," I tell him, my voice catching as Tobias does it again.

"Fuck. Show me, Tobias. Let me see that dirty hole."

Tobias moves back a bit, and Charlie leans over his shoulder to look at me, open and exposed. My asshole clenches at their attention.

"*Fuuuuck.* Have you fucked her there before?" Charlie asks him.

"I haven't, have you?"

"Not yet."

Not yet… My hole clenches again then I feel a finger rubbing the wrinkled skin. *Who's touching me?* Looking between my legs, I see two gorgeous heads gathered close together, both arms forward, hands out of my line of sight. There's another swipe, this time swirling into my pussy to collect my arousal then back over my pucker to wet it. A finger pushes gently, but my muscles involuntarily clench up.

"It needs to be wetter," Charlie tells Tobias before he leans closer and spits. The saliva lands on right on my hole with a splat, the sound so lewd. Tobias chuckles, then a finger runs over the spittle, spreading the wetness around.

"More please," Tobias requests, his voice a low rumble.

Another spit lands on its intended target, and *fuck me*, the sound is so obscene I just might come.

"See how she likes that? Her pussy is getting wetter."

It's like they're having a casual conversation while I'm burning up, desperate for release. There's that gentle pressure on my asshole again, but this time, the fingertip is slippery and I feel the tip make forward progress, slipping inside just a bit.

"Fuck, she's tight," Tobias tells Charlie.

I hear Charlie inhale then watch as he leans forward, almost as if he can't help himself, and licks my pussy, sucking my clit into his mouth and letting go with a pop.

"Mmmm," I moan, my hips trying to follow his mouth for more friction. Firm hands hold my legs in place and looking down, I see it's Charlie's hand on my right leg and Tobias's hand on my left. I love the fact that they're both touching me at the same time.

Then Tobias leans forward, making me see stars with a swipe of his tongue, starting by the finger in my asshole then licking all the way up my center but evading my clit. I groan my complaint, and Charlie chuckles darkly, leaning forward to do the same.

Fuck. They take turns licking me with wet, hungry tongues, then I lose track of who is doing what, only Tobias's stubble giving me a clue about which tongue is his as I'm unable to keep my eyes open anymore. All I experience is their touch and the resulting sensations. I'm drunk with lust and when I look, I see both heads in between my legs, both tongues devouring me. Somehow, the finger has wedged farther into my ass and is pumping in and out with short, shallow strokes.

I need to come, and all other thoughts fade to the background of my consciousness. I'm writhing against their mouths, desperate for more. It's only these two men, their wonderful appendages, and the need to come. I reach down with both hands, my right hand threading through the short strands of Charlie's blond hair, my left tangling into Tobias's long, black hair. I cradle their heads, pulling them into my body, trying to direct their attention.

"Charlie, Tobias," I say as I pant. "I need more."

"What do you need, Red?" Charlie mumbles in between licks and sucks.

"I need you guys to fill me up." I want to be stuffed full of them.

"Can you be more specific?"

"I need one of you to fuck my pussy and the other one to fuck my mouth." There, I said it. That is exactly what I want and I have no idea when the opportunity will present itself again.

"Well, isn't she demanding?" he says to Tobias.

"You said specific," I point out.

"Shall we play *Would You Rather* again?" Tobias asks.

"I'd rather watch you fuck her."

"I'd rather fuck her."

"Win-win."

"Fuck, hurry up!" I complain.

They stand up, and Tobias digs in his discarded pants for a condom while Charlie finally sheds his clothing. He crawls onto the bed, kneeling alongside me, tugging on his shaft with his masculine hand. I love the way it looks when he strokes himself. The piercing glints at me, and my mouth waters at the sight. Grabbing a pillow, he motions for me to lift my hips up and slides the pillow under my ass to prop me up a bit higher.

Tobias rips open the condom, rolls it on, and joins us on the bed. We all do a little shuffle until he fits between my legs, then I wrap them around his hips, pulling him closer to me. His pale skin and dark hair are a striking contrast to Charlie's golden skin and sparse hair.

Charlie's eyes are everywhere, watching my face, watching Tobias, watching Tobias's cock as he rubs it up and down my slit, getting it wet with my arousal. It feels so good, I can't stop my hips from thrusting forward, seeking more. Tobias moves closer, the coarse hairs on his legs tickling my skin, and the head of his cock lines up at my entrance. I check Charlie's face, needing to see that he's watching this, that he's okay with this. He hasn't missed a thing, and he squeezes his cock as he stares while Tobias sinks into me.

We all groan at that first slide inside.

Charlie starts to jerk in earnest as Tobias gets to work, fucking me with deep, powerful thrusts. My breasts sway with each one, my body bouncing as I absorb the impact. I need to hold on to something and my hands fist the sheets, struggling for purchase, but that's not enough. I reach out to Charlie, needing to touch him.

"Look at you, Red. You're taking his cock so deep. You hungry for more?"

"Yes, I want more. I want you in my mouth."

"You dirty, dirty girl." He moves closer to me, but as I lean forward with an open mouth, he keeps himself just out of my reach. I reach forward with my hands, planning to grab a hold of his erection, but he catches my hands and pins them to the bed above me with one swift move. He keeps one hand pinning my wrists together firmly, and the new position arches my back.

"Fuck," Tobias mutters. "She's so tight. I'm not going to last."

"Charlie," I whimper, opening my mouth like a baby bird waiting for a feeding. I stare up at him, letting him see my desperation.

"You know what I want to hear."

He wants me to beg. *Bossy man.*

"Please, Charlie, I need you in my mouth. I want you to come down my throat."

"Fuck yes." With a grunt of satisfaction, he kneels closer and allows me to wrap my lips around his engorged cockhead.

"Mmm," I moan with my mouth full of him. He's still holding my hands, so I have no control, no leverage. I can only take what he gives me.

I feel so dirty, stuffed full of two men.

I feel...*alive.*

Sexy.

And despite being on my back with my hands pinned above my head, I feel powerful. These two men are losing control, all because of how much they want me.

I suck and lick Charlie, breathing through my nose as he starts to fuck my mouth. Soon there is a chorus of groans and grunts and curses as coordination gives way to the chase of release. I feel fingers pluck at my clit—I don't know whose fingers at this point, but it's just what I need.

My orgasm is ripped out of me, burning hot pleasure so intense it causes me to jerk and tremble, to whimper and groan around the cock in my mouth. Tobias pounds into me, muttering, "I'm so close, fuck I'm coming." He slams in one more time then stills, and I actually feel the pulse of his dick as he finds his release.

Charlie is the last to find his orgasm, as if he needed to watch both of us fall apart before he allowed himself to come. He shouts that masculine shout that borders on pain then fills my mouth with his pleasure. I try not to gag, but there's so much hot fluid, it takes me by surprise. My eyes burn as I swallow as fast as I can, and tears fall down the sides of my face as I lick him clean.

As my brain slowly reboots, the boys chuckle. It's a sound of relief, a happy, incredulous sound. Tobias eases out of me and I open my eyes, smiling up at both of them.

Charlie's cobalt orbs smolder at me as he wipes my face clean and kisses my lips. "That was amazing."

It really was.

Chapter 12

It's like a dream.

Charlie

I wake up slowly, registering a warm, soft body in my arms and Quinn's wild hair tickling my skin. We're tangled up in each other as we usually are when we sleep together—her head on my chest, my arm across her waist, our legs intertwined—and it's so comfortable. Blinking my eyes open, I see that Quinn is still sleeping peacefully, and we're both naked.

As I smooth my hands up and down her back and arms, tracing those freckles I'm so addicted to, my mind flits back to last night. Though I was excited at the thought of what would happen, I wasn't sure how I would feel. Would I be jealous? Turned on? Turned off? Would I not want to see another guy's hands on her? Another guy's cock inside her?

The reality was so much better than the fantasy.

Not only was I turned on by the entire thing, I feel closer to Quinn somehow. Sharing her with Tobias made her feel… like she's mine.

I know that's stupid—another man fucked her, and she *isn't* mine.

She doesn't *want to be* mine.

I don't *want* a relationship.

But I realize none of that matters anymore.

The only reason it was so hot last night is because we were there together. I don't know if I would have gotten that worked up if I was watching some other random woman. My body reacted so strongly because it was Quinn—the way she watched to make sure I was looking, the way she was so desperate for me to touch her, her gasps and moans and sassy mouth.

Fuck.

She shifts in my arms, and my morning wood is all too happy when it ends up lodged right in between her legs. Her slit is hot on my dick and my hips push forward, seeking more friction.

"Mmm," she mumbles sleepily, pushing her hips forward to meet mine.

Fuck yes. I shift so we're on our sides and she slides her leg up over my hip, opening herself up to me, rocking forward against my cock. Her eyes are still closed so I can't be sure she's awake. Am I an asshole if I want to bury myself inside of her when she's asleep?

Her head is buried in my neck, her breaths still deep and even. Though it would only take the slightest forward movement to slip inside her, I hold back. I just can't take advantage of her. Trying to rein in my lust, I release a breath I hadn't realized I was holding and continue to trail my fingertips over her soft skin.

She sighs sweetly and presses her fingertips against my skin. Slowly, her free hand trails along my stomach, lingering over my abs, then through my happy trail until she reaches my swollen cock. I grunt as she wraps her hand around my shaft and rubs my cockhead over her clit.

"Mmm," she moans again, sounding half-asleep, but her hand is very much awake when she pulls my dick forward and bucks her hips in just the right way for me to end up inside her slick heat. *Okay then.*

Knowing she wants me, I surge forward, seating myself inside her until I'm as deep as I can get. We both groan in pleasure, and I begin to fuck her slow and sleepy, all the while holding her close to me and touching her everywhere—her shoulder that curves so sexily, her hip that flares out from her slim waist, the back of her knee that has the softest skin I've ever felt.

It's slow and unhurried.

It's like a dream.

Closing my eyes, I immerse myself in this feeling of bliss.

Quinn's sounds are a symphony of sex, soft whimpers and gasps that turn into moans and grunts. I follow those sounds with my body, trying to get her to make more.

Soon the slow pace isn't enough and I roll on top of her, needing more control. She opens her eyes in surprise, those whiskey brown orbs locking onto mine, and I hold her gaze while I settle into this new position. Her legs wrap around my waist and I link my fingers with hers, bringing our joined hands above her head. I need to get deeper, and even though I know logically that isn't possible, I try anyway, my hips bucking and thrusting into her wet heat.

Her face has me hypnotized, her sounds have me frantic, and I'm lost—lost in this moment, lost in this woman.

Quinn's hands squeeze mine and she thrusts her pelvis up to match my movements. I can tell she's getting close from her pants and whimpers and moans. I need to look into her eyes as she falls apart. I grind into her pelvis with every thrust, trying to stimulate her clit, and she gasps, causing my balls to draw up tight at the sound.

Fuck. I'm close. I can feel my orgasm starting at the base of my spine, pleasure zinging down all of my nerve endings, but I need her to come first. Sweat breaks out on my forehead and back as I try to hold off my orgasm.

Then I feel it, the way her pussy flutters as she's about to come. *Yes.* I stare into her eyes, so full of lust, and I see the pleasure course into her. Her eyes open wide, her mouth forming a pretty O, then her brow furrows, almost as if she's in pain. She crests to that razor-sharp edge of pleasure and pain, of feeling so good it hurts, and it's stunning. Her body begins to tremble and jerk, and when her pussy clamps on my dick, I stop holding back and let my orgasm take me. When it hits, I pour so much more than just my cum into her—I think I leave some of my soul inside her.

Spent, I lean my forehead to hers and catch my breath, not yet ready to leave the warmth of her body. Her legs wrap around my waist and her arms snake around my neck, holding me to her.

"Well that's quite a way to wake up. At first, I thought I was dreaming." Her voice is low and sultry, raspy with sleep.

"I think I'm still dreaming," I tell her quietly. My body collapses onto hers. *That was intense.* "I can't get enough of you." It's true. Even right now, I'm still inside her, and I don't want to move.

Unable to resist, I kiss her. Her lips meet mine in a sweet, almost reverent kiss. I try to tell her my feelings are changing with this kiss, as I don't know if I can find the words. We've been so clear with each other from the beginning that neither one of us wants a relationship, so how can I go back on that now?

Does her soft sigh mean she understands?

Does her lingering kiss mean she feels the same?

I can't tell, but I do know that after last night with Tobias and this morning, I feel closer to her than ever before.

Reluctantly, I pull out. "Come on, let's shower and have some breakfast before we have to leave."

"What did you think about last night?" I ask Quinn as we dig into our breakfast. It's Saturday morning and the restaurant in Hamilton House is packed, but the service is fast and the food is delicious. The aroma of bacon fills my nose and I bite into the crispy piece, relishing the flavor as it practically melts in my mouth.

"Are we really going to do this? Talk about it?" Quinn's face flushes and I love the color on her cheeks.

"Don't get shy on me now. I know you had fun. Was it better than you thought it would be?"

A small, sexy smile tugs at her lips as she loses focus, remembering what we did with Tobias. Her eyes meet mine with a naughty twinkle. "Yes, I had a lot of fun. Did you?" She looks at me curiously.

I think back to watching Tobias fuck her. "Fuck yes I did. You don't even know how hot you are."

"I'm glad you had fun, too."

"What's the verdict? Is it something you'd like to do again, or was that a one-time deal?"

"I guess it depends." She cuts up her Belgian waffle into neat little squares, making sure there is a bit of strawberry and whipped cream on every piece, stalling for time.

"On?" I ask her. I'd do it again in a heartbeat.

"On who. I know you and Tobias, I trust you guys and feel safe. I can't imagine feeling safe enough to be comfortable with someone random."

The thought of Quinn having a threesome without me makes my stomach clench. "I can appreciate that." Women are so much more vulnerable than men. "What if I was there?" I swallow. "Would you do it again if I was with you?"

She stares at me a moment, her whiskey brown eyes boring into mine. Can she tell I need more of her? That I'd do pretty much anything to make her fantasies come true? The words are on the tip of my tongue, but she nods slowly before I can get them out.

"Yes, Charlie. I'd do it again if you were with me."

I feel my dimples tug my cheeks, my smile is so big. I drag my tongue over my teeth, biting my lower lip as I stare at her pretty flushed cheeks.

"Sounds good, Red."

The server stops by to top off our drinks, breaking our attention.

"So, give me some background on your family and the douchebag ex. What am I in for tomorrow?"

Quinn bites into her waffle and moans. "Must you ruin a good breakfast with this topic?"

I eat another morsel of bacon and let out a satisfied sigh. "Hey, we don't have to talk at all. I can just listen to you moan and add to my spank bank."

"You're such a pervert."

"Takes one to know one." I smirk at her.

She moans around the last bite of her decadent food and my dick swells at the sound.

"Be careful. You'll give all the guys in this place a boner moaning like that."

"Oh, please. No one can hear me." She rolls her eyes at me.

I look around and sure enough, the man at the table next to us is dining with a woman, but he keeps glancing at Quinn.

"Three o'clock."

"What?"

"Check your three o'clock."

Quinn glances to her right and catches the guy adjusting his pants. Better yet, he glances her way and flushes when he catches her looking at him.

Quinn's eyes widen as she realizes I was right.

"Told you. You better stop moaning and tell me about tomorrow before all the guys surrounding us get in trouble with their dates."

She shoots me a grin that tells me she's all too pleased with herself. "Okay, okay. What do you want to know?"

"Just give me a basic rundown. Who's going to be there? Why is your ex going to be there? What do I have to know?" I ask her as I take a sip of my coffee.

"My parents, Liam and Nora, are hardcore Catholics who don't believe in divorce. They didn't approve when I divorced Reid." She spits his name.

"If you don't mind my asking, what happened with you guys? Why did you get divorced?"

Quinn sighs, resigned to the topic. "It's a great story," she says flatly. "I walked in on him fucking his secretary in our bed." She looks away, not meeting my eyes as she tells me this. Is she embarrassed?

"Asshole. And your parents still invite him over for family functions? Don't they know what he did?" I don't understand how hardcore Catholics could see past adultery.

"My sentiments exactly!" She slaps her hand on the table, making the silverware jump. A few heads turn in our direction at her outburst. She holds up her hands in apology. "Sorry."

"Do you have any brothers or sisters?"

"I have a sister, Shannon. She's your age, actually." She taps her finger to her mouth, lost in thought. I never think much about our age difference and up until right now, I never thought Quinn did either.

"Are you close with Shannon?"

"We get along, but I wouldn't call us friends. She's a musician and spends all her free time focusing on her career."

"Wow, so two artists in the family. What do your parents do?"

"My dad is the principal of the local Catholic grade school and my mom is the secretary at the local Catholic high school."

"Okay, so do I need to…tone myself down?" This is going to be a repeat of my family get-togethers all over again.

"No, Charlie. I like you just fine the way you are. I don't want you to change a thing. My family has a hard time accepting my choices in career and life, but I am who I am. I'm tired of trying to please everyone—it never made anyone happy anyway. Now I just want to live for me."

"I like that motto. And for the record, I like who you are, Quinn Fitzpatrick," I say. When she meets my eyes, I can't stop the smile that stretches my lips.

Quinn

Charlie's ocean blue eyes sparkle at me in a new way today, and it's as if our bodies are connected by an invisible thread. He can't keep his hands off me and strangely enough…I like it. I don't feel claustrophobic at his attention. I don't feel suffocated by his touch. In fact, my fingers itch to touch him, too—his firm, strong, body…his smooth, golden skin.

I haven't felt this close to someone since Reid, *before* everything went to shit.

Ugh, why did I have to think of him?

"What's that frown for?" Charlie asks, smoothing out the wrinkle I get in my forehead when I scowl.

He takes my hand as we walk out of the hotel toward his car. It's a warm spring day for April in Columbus, and the sun feels good on my skin.

"Oh nothing, just remembered I have to see fuckface tomorrow."

"Don't think about him. We're going to make him so jealous he won't know what hit him. What do you have going on today?"

I like the idea of making Reid jealous, not because I want him back, but because I don't understand why he continues to come to my family gatherings. I want to make him feel uncomfortable because he makes me feel uncomfortable. I think about my schedule for today and come up with nothing.

"I don't have much going on, what about you?"

"Want to spend the day with me?"

I glance sideways at him. We've spent all night together and will be together tomorrow afternoon, yet he wants to spend the day together today too?

At my hesitation, he starts to backtrack. "You know what? Forget I asked. I should probably get unpacked from my trip—"

"No, I'd love to spend the day with you."

He turns to face me, a hint of vulnerability shining in his expression. "Really?"

"On one condition."

"What's the condition?"

"You paint with me again."

He looks dubious. "That didn't go so well last time."

"It went awesomely last time. Did I tell you I brought your piece to my gallery?"

"No way." His eyes widen in surprise.

"Yes way. My manager loves it. It will be for sale in the next viewing."

"Ugh. Why did you tell me that? I'm sure no one will buy it."

"I'm not so sure about that." I squeeze his hand when he tries to move away from me. "My manager asked me to get more work out of you."

He casts another doubtful look my way. "You don't have to stroke my ego, you know. You can stroke something else if you like." He wiggles his eyebrows suggestively.

"I'm not stroking your ego. Come on, paint with me. You can pick an activity, too. I'll do anything you want."

"Anything?"

The way he says it, his face bright like a little kid on Christmas, makes me worried about what he'll choose. "Don't make me regret it."

"This will be fun. My activity is first."

30 minutes later, I find myself at the zoo, watching a gigantic manatee float around. It's a perfect day for the zoo, as the weather is not too hot and not too cold. The animals are all out in their exhibits, enjoying the sunshine as much as we are.

"How can manatees get this big eating just lettuce?" I ask Charlie as he snaps a couple shots on his camera.

He shrugs. "Beats me. They must eat a lot of lettuce." He takes a couple more pictures then grabs my hand to tug me to the sea turtles. "This is my favorite exhibit."

There is a bench in front of this exhibit, and we take a seat to enjoy the view. I watch the turtles as they lazily swim around their aquarium then look over at Charlie. A small smile of wonder tugs at his mouth while he stares intently at the turtles and the look on his face is so endearing, I stealthily take out my cell and snap a picture of him.

The shutter sound snaps him out of his reverie, and I try to pocket my phone nonchalantly, but I'm not fast enough. "See something you like, Red?" He smirks.

"I couldn't help myself, you look like a little boy in here. It's cute."

"Cute?" He spits the word, scowling. "I'm not cute. I'm hot, sexy—badass, even, but not cute."

I laugh at his outrage at being called cute. "Well, hate to break it to you, *badass*, but just then you looked pretty damn cute."

"Whatever," he mutters, holding his camera up to his face to take a few pictures of the sea turtles.

We walk around the zoo, stopping at various exhibits. Columbus has an amazing zoo and I'm embarrassed to admit I've never been here before. The animals are interesting, but I have to say that my favorite part is watching Charlie and his reaction to the animals. Hours pass easily as we stroll hand in hand, joking and laughing.

"Hey, are you hungry?" he asks as we pass the food court.

"Yep. Want to eat here before we go?"

"Sure."

We choose pizza and grab a table outside.

"Let's play a game," he suggests.

"What game?" I ask as I take a bite of the cheesy goodness.

"When I was younger, Dom, Tabby, and I used to love to people watch. We'd always try to guess what they do for a living."

"You'd guess their profession just by looking at them?"

"Yes." He chuckles. "It involves a lot of stereotypes and assumptions, but it's fun."

"I think I'm going to suck, but okay, let's do it. You first."

He scans the tables and zeroes in on a young woman dressed in khaki pants and a white polo shirt, her brown hair combed neatly back into a high ponytail. She's smiling brightly at the older woman next to her and exudes a friendly disposition. "Her." He nods. "She's a schoolteacher. She just graduated and teaches kindergarten."

"Not bad, hotshot. I can totally see that."

"Your turn," he says as he takes a bite of his slice of pizza.

I look at the surrounding people, trying to guess at what they might do for a living. Nothing strikes me as obvious until I land on a muscular man wearing gym shorts, tennis shoes, and a baseball hat with a picture of a dumbbell on the front of it.

"Him." I nod in Muscle Man's direction. "He's a personal trainer."

Charlie nods and smiles at me. "You're getting it."

"What do you say we create a different version of this game?" I give him a naughty smile.

"What do you have going on in that dirty mind of yours?"

"Well, guessing professions is kind of fun, but what about if we guessed what they're like in bed?"

"You mean during sex?" Charlie raises his eyebrows in interest.

"Yes. Let's take your kindergarten teacher, for example. I bet she's a dominatrix."

He laughs so hard he snorts. "Her?"

"You laugh all you want, but it's the quiet ones that often surprise you. I bet she's into hardcore BDSM."

"What about Mister Muscles?"

I study the handsome, well-built guy. "I bet he could be her submissive."

We both look at the two people across the room from each other and bust up laughing.

"I don't know if I believe you, but I like your version of this game better."

"I'm full of good ideas."

"Yes, you are," Charlie agrees.

"Speaking of good ideas, I think it's time to go paint."

"You want to go paint, huh?" Charlie pouts.

The sight of those lips pursed so prettily makes me want to lean forward and kiss him.

So, I do.

I lean forward in the middle of the food court at the zoo, and I kiss his lips.

It's a soft peck at first, but then Charlie puts his hand behind my neck and brings me back for a second kiss. This one's longer, his tongue slipping into my mouth to tangle with mine, and I can't help but melt into him, inhaling in his scent, relishing in his touch.

Charlie smiles into my mouth and mumbles, "Okay, you convinced me. Let's go paint."

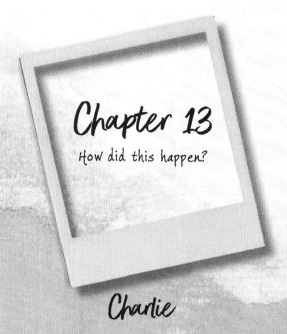

Chapter 13

How did this happen?

Charlie

Checking myself over in the mirror one last time, I deem myself worthy of meeting Quinn's family and the assface ex-husband. I opted for what my parents would call "country club casual" attire—khaki pants with a navy button-down—so I won't be underdressed or overdressed. I know Quinn said to just be myself, but I can be myself and look good at the same time.

I must admit, I'm curious about her family and where she comes from. I never would've dreamed that her parents are ultraconservative and disapproved of her divorcing her cheating ex-husband.

Me: I'm on my way, be there in 15.

Red: Sounds good, see you then.

When I pull up in her driveway, I don't remember driving here—I was so lost in thought that autopilot took over. Quinn opens the door wearing a powder blue sweater and a long navy skirt that swishes over the tops of her feet. The sweater is so soft, I can't help but reach out and touch her, petting her shoulder and upper arm.

"Mmm, you wore this on purpose, didn't you?"

"On purpose?" she asks, confusion making that adorable wrinkle on her forehead pop out.

"So I'd keep touching you. Don't you know you don't need a soft sweater for that? I already can't keep my hands off you, now it's just going to be worse," I mock complain, leaning forward to gather her body close to mine and kiss her. "Did you miss me?"

She chuckles. "Oh, absolutely I did. For the whole two hours since I saw you last, I missed you terribly." She's joking, of course.

What's pathetic is that I actually did miss her. Even after spending the day together yesterday, first at the zoo and then at her house. Even after spending the night inside of her. Even after waking up with her and showering with her and eating breakfast with her.

Even though we were only apart for two measly hours.

I still missed her.

Fucking hell. What is happening to me?

"You ready?" I ask her, trying to regain some control over my train of thought.

"Yes, let's do this."

Quinn gives me directions to her parents' house and we're there sooner than I expected. She looks at the front door with a scowl on her face, like she's no more excited to be here than I am.

"You're going to pay me for this in orgasms, right?" I leer at her, trying to distract her from her thoughts.

She turns to me with a playful smile. "Seriously? I didn't give you enough orgasms over the last couple of days?"

I chuckle. "Nope. I want more."

"Yes, Charlie, sex fiend that you are, I'll owe you more orgasms after this."

"Sounds good." I reach over the center console for her hand. "I got your back, Quinn. You ready to go in there?"

She takes a deep breath, squares her shoulders, and then nods.

We make our way to the front door and she rings the doorbell. An older version of Quinn—minus the red hair—answers the door. She has the same brown eyes, the same freckles dotting her skin, and the same frame as her daughter. They're very similar, but her eyes don't shine with mischief, her smile isn't playful, and her hair is dark, almost black.

She looks from Quinn to me, a frown on her face. Did Quinn not tell her she was bringing me? I flash her my most charming smile, hoping to start off on the right foot. Moms usually love me.

Though I haven't met many girlfriends' moms, Anna's mom loved me all those years ago, and Max's mom and Logan's mom love me.

"Hi Mom, this is my friend, Charlie. Remember I told you I was bringing a date?"

Manners force her to shake my hand. "Hi there, Mrs. Fitzpatrick. Nice to meet you."

"Charlie, is it? Hi, I'm Nora." She gives me a small smile then focuses her attention back on her daughter.

"Quinn, you know Reid is here. This might make him uncomfortable."

What the actual fuck?

Quinn stiffens beside me. "Seriously, Mom? You make *me* uncomfortable by inviting my ex-husband. Charlie is with me today. Do you want us to come in or not?"

Good girl. I wrap my arm around her waist, letting her know I'm right here, ready to stay or go, whatever she wants to do.

Her mom's frown deepens and she wrings her hands together. "Come in, of course." She opens the door and steps aside to let us pass.

Their house is modest with dated furniture and wood paneling on the walls, but the food smells amazing and my stomach rumbles at the aroma.

"Your father made pot roast with potatoes and carrots. I hope you like that, Charlie."

"It smells amazing," I tell her honestly.

I get the first genuine smile from Quinn's mom, albeit small and brief.

People are talking in the next room. As we round the corner, I see a middle-aged man with dark hair, a thick beard, and fair skin talking with a very pretty girl and some other guy who I assume are Quinn's sister and the douchebag. Quinn's sister looks just like their mom, too, and the douchebag looks just as smarmy as I thought he would. He's tall and skinny with brown hair slicked back (who the fuck wears their hair that way, anyway?) and brown eyes that laser in on Quinn and track her movements, lingering on our joint hands.

He totally wants her back.

"Hey everyone." Quinn waves to the room with one hand while the other is still linked with mine. "This is Charlie. Charlie, this is my sister, Shannon, my dad, Liam, and my *ex*-husband, Reid."

I shake everyone's hand, squeezing Reid's a tad more forcefully than necessary. He smiles pleasantly enough when he shakes my hand, but his eyes narrow in on me, as if warning me to stay away from his girl. *Ha! I was balls deep in her just this morning.*

After the introductions are over, I turn to Quinn. "You mean to tell me you are the only one in your family with red hair?" I touch her wild, curly locks, loving how soft her hair is.

"Ugh, tell me about it." She rolls her eyes, as if she's disgusted with her hair.

"She gets it from our grandmother," Shannon informs me.

"It's beautiful," I tell her. Her expression softens at my compliment and I take the opportunity to make smarmy-pants jealous by pulling her into my side and kissing her temple. I linger, burrowing my nose in her hair and taking a sniff. She smells of something I can't quite place but it makes me salivate all the same. Quinn wraps her arm around my waist, melting into me and holding on tight.

I check our audience. Reid is glaring at us—me in particular—and disapproval tugs Mr. Fitzpatrick's mouth into a grimace, gaze bouncing from us to Reid with worry. Shannon looks at us with a small smile on her face. Seems about right.

"Well, is everyone hungry? The food is ready," Quinn's dad grumbles, motioning to the dining room.

Everyone murmurs their agreement and makes their way into the dining room while Quinn's mom brings the food in from the kitchen. I keep Quinn by my side as the room empties and when we're finally alone, I kiss her. Her mouth is delicious and it makes me forget this tense atmosphere. I'm used to feeling like an outcast at my family functions, but I want to distract her from her family drama. I take the kiss from respectable to porn-worthy, tilting her head with my hands so my tongue can reach inside. *Mmm.*

"Hey," I say quietly, "you know what I've been thinking about?"

"What's that?" She looks up at me.

I put my lips right at the shell of her ear. "Fucking your ass."

"Charlie!" she exclaims, eyes darting around us to see if anyone could hear me.

"Calm your tits, Red. No one can hear. But after we leave here, we're going to my place and I'm going to take your ass."

"What if I don't want to?" she whispers, smirking up at me.

"Trust me, once my tongue and fingers are done with that tight little hole, you'll be begging for my cock."

Her pupils dilate, her cheeks flush, and her nipples pebble with desire. She may sass me back, but she likes my dirty talk.

"Now come on, let's get through this shit show. When it gets tense in there, just think about what your reward is when we leave." Without waiting for a response, I tug her into the dining room and we take our places.

An awkward silence stretches while everyone fills their plates with food. It does smell delicious, and my stomach rumbles despite our company.

"So, how long have you guys known each other?" Shannon asks, a friendly smile on her face.

I turn to Quinn, trying to calculate the time.

"About eight months," she answers.

Has it been that long? My eyebrows go up at the realization. "Yeah, I guess you're right. We met before Max's accident."

"Max?" Mrs. Fitzpatrick asks.

"Yeah, Monica's boyfriend, Max. Remember when he was hit while riding his bike?" Quinn reminds her.

"Fiancé, now," I correct.

"That's right, I keep forgetting they're engaged."

"Monica's getting married?" Shannon asks.

"Yep. Max is my best friend, and we met through Max and Monica," I explain.

"Oh, how wonderful for Monica that she found someone to spend the rest of her life with," Mrs. Fitzpatrick says, looking at Quinn meaningfully. She just glares back at her mother.

"I'm really happy for them. Max is *devoted* to her," I say pointedly, looking at Reid.

"And what is it that you do for a living?" Reid asks, looking at me like I'm a bug he'd like to smash with his shoe.

"I'm a photographer," I answer easily.

"Charlie works at Picture This. He's one of the most requested photographers on their team," Quinn tells everyone. Warmth blossoms in my belly at the pride in her voice—or is she just trying to stick it to Reid? Either way, I'm not accustomed to anyone bragging about my career other than Max and Logan, and it feels good to hear someone talk about my job in a positive light instead of a negative one.

"Oh, I've heard of Picture This," Shannon chimes in. "How cool that you're both artists. Have you seen Quinn's studio?"

"Studio?" Reid asks.

"Yeah, she doesn't need to rent a studio anymore, she has one in her place," Shannon explains to him.

It's then that I realize the place Quinn lives in now is the place she got after her divorce, so Reid has likely never been to her condo. I like the fact that I've fucked her in almost every room but he hasn't even seen it.

"I've seen her studio, it's amazing," I say, looking over at Quinn, remembering how just last night we painted together again. In the same way that Quinn put a sexy spin on my *guess stranger's profession* game at the zoo, I put a sexy spin on painting. My rule was that we had to paint naked, and it was very…inspiring. My thoughts drift further back to the very first time we painted together and I used a paintbrush on her pussy. *Fuck, that was hot.*

She holds my gaze and her cheeks flush, telling me she remembers exactly what I'm remembering.

"Charlie's a talented painter, too. Suzanne's going to sell his pieces at Art Redefined."

"I don't know about that…we have yet to see if anyone will buy my first piece," I protest.

"It'll sell. Suzanne was sure of it."

"And how old are you, if you don't mind my asking?" Mrs. Fitzpatrick asks me.

"26," I report.

"Me, too," Shannon tells me. "When is your birthday?"

"November 8th."

"Mine is November 25th! We were both born in November, how about that?"

"So you're six years younger than Quinn," Reid helpfully points out. Give the man a cookie for being able to do basic math.

Quinn's parents keep looking from me to Quinn with a frown. *Not this age thing again.*

"How's work going at the studio?" Reid asks her. It's the first time he's addressed Quinn directly.

"Fine," she says with hostility while glaring at him. "Not like you ever cared before," she mutters.

"Are you making more money than you used to?" Reid asks.

Quinn stiffens beside me, as do I. *What the fuck?* That was way out of line. I don't know exactly how much Quinn makes, but I know she does well for herself and lives comfortably selling her art. I'm waiting for her parents or sister to defend her, but Quinn doesn't wait for anyone to jump to her aid.

"My income is none of your concern." Her tone is ice.

"Just making sure you don't need any help." Condescension is in his every word, yet Quinn's parents seem pleased by his comment, giving him a small smile. My fists clench and I hope I get to talk to this asswipe without any company at some point.

"Nope." Her lips pop the P sound.

"So Shannon, Quinn tells me you're a musician?" I attempt to redirect the conversation. Shannon smiles at me and excitedly tells the table all about her recent gigs and studio time. Quinn relaxes next to me and I give her a pointed look, trying to remind her about our previous conversation. Having finished my food, my hand drops to her thigh and I squeeze her leg, hoping my touch will help to distract her.

Quinn

Charlie's presence shouldn't feel so comforting. The way he stiffened at my parents' and Reid's inappropriate comments shouldn't make me feel like he's on my team. The way he changed the subject when I was about to launch myself at Reid and claw his eyes out when he asked me about my income shouldn't have made me relax. His ill-timed promise to fuck my ass when we leave definitely shouldn't have lit me up inside, distracting me from my fucked-up family.

But...

Having Charlie here does all of the above.

My parents are NOT on my team, not even a little bit, and Shannon means well, but she hates confrontation, so she tends to get quiet instead of coming to my defense.

Charlie, though, hates Reid on principle. I could tell he was irritated with my mother's comment at the front door when she said his presence would make Reid uncomfortable, and when Reid asked if I was making more money than I used to, I saw his fists clench as if he was ready to tackle him to the ground and beat him to a bloody pulp. He could, too—I bet Charlie outweighs him by 50 pounds of muscle.

It makes me feel better, knowing he's on my side.

And...I can't stop thinking about the promise of his mouth, fingers, and cock in my ass. His ploy to distract me is working.

I put my silverware on my plate even though I'm not done with my meal. My appetite is gone and I wonder what the hell we're still doing here.

Once Shannon is done telling Charlie about her new guitar, I start to make our goodbyes. "Mom, Dad, thanks for having us, but I think we're going to get going."

"Oh wait, you can't go yet," Shannon pleads. "I made your favorite dessert. I just need to pop it in the oven so the marshmallows can get warm and gooey."

The look in her eyes makes me hesitate. "You made the cookie s'mores?" My sister loves to bake and when I visited home during college, she would make me desserts to try to get me to stay longer. One of her concoctions is a layered dessert with cookie dough on the bottom, a layer of Hershey's milk chocolate bars, a layer of marshmallows, topped off with another layer of cookie dough, chocolate chips, and graham cracker crust on top. When you cut into it, it's an explosion of s'mores and chocolate chip cookies in your mouth.

I look over at Charlie and he nods, telling me it's okay if I want to stay a bit longer.

"Okay, we'll stay for dessert, but we have to get going after that."

"I'll go warm it up now," Shannon says as she picks up her plate and takes it into the kitchen. I do the same and motion for Charlie to get his plate and follow me. I don't want to leave him alone with my parents and Reid—who knows what they'd say to him, or what he'd say to them.

In the kitchen, I find Shannon sliding a glass pan into the oven. I collect the dishes, put them in the sink, and start to wash them. Surprisingly, Charlie gets a hand towel and starts to dry them.

Shannon leans on the counter next to us. "So how are you, honestly?" she asks me. I wish I were closer to my sister, and I'm glad we have a moment to talk.

"I'm good," I tell her. "I just wish they'd stop inviting Reid here. It's been two years since the divorce."

"I know, when are they going to give it up already?" she agrees.

I shrug and roll my eyes in frustration. "What about you? Seeing anyone?"

Her face pinks. She may not have red hair like I do, but she does have the pale skin that tends to show every emotion in different shades of pink. "No, not really."

Her words say no, but that blush says yes. "You are seeing someone!"

She looks back to Charlie and bites her lip.

"Don't let me stop you." Charlie chuckles. "I have to go to the bathroom anyway. Which way is it?" he asks me, drying the last plate and wiping his hands off on the towel.

"Down that hall, first door to your right." Once he's out of earshot, I turn back to Shannon. "Now spill."

She smiles tentatively at me, hesitant to start.

"Come on! When's the last time we had girl talk?" I prod.

"It's not serious, but his name is Guy and he's a singer."

"Ooooh, a singer? How sexy. Would I have heard any of his songs?"

"No, he's just starting out, but his voice…it's so amazing. We met at the studio—he had time booked right before mine. When I showed up early for my session, I got to hear him sing. Then we started chatting after and have been out a few times, but I know neither one of us has time to dedicate to a relationship."

"Then just have fun. Why does all dating need to equate to a serious relationship?"

"Is that what you're doing with Charlie? Having fun? Or is it serious?"

Damn, this shouldn't be a difficult question. Charlie and I are having fun.

We're having fun in bed.

But…

I think of painting in my studio with Charlie.

Him crying in my arms after telling me about the baby.

The way he fucked me so reverently after the threesome with Tobias.

Strolling through the zoo yesterday, seeing him so cute with his camera and love of animals.

It's on the tip of my tongue to say we're not serious, that we're just friends who like to fuck, but my heart squeezes in my chest and my stomach churns at the thought.

Fucking hell. How did this happen?

"That look on your face is answer enough." She gives me a knowing smile. "I know you haven't wanted a relationship since Reid fucked you over, but don't miss something amazing because you're so focused on Reid. Charlie isn't Reid. It's not fair to him to treat him that way, and it's not fair to yourself."

I sigh dramatically, not having any words. I know she's right, and I know Charlie and I should talk about what's happening, but I kind of just want to stick my head in the sand for a little while longer.

The aroma of Shannon's dessert fills the kitchen, giving me the subject change I need. "This smells divine! Is it ready to eat yet?"

Shannon opens the oven door just a bit to peek inside. "Looks ready to me. Let me take it out." As she reaches for the oven mitt, I hear Charlie's voice rising.

Charlie is not an angry person. Aside from his encounter with Anna, I've never seen him get mad, but I know Reid pissed him off earlier. As my thoughts race to figure out what's going on, I meet Shannon's worried face then dart from the kitchen to find out.

"Don't you fucking talk about her like that!" I hear Charlie growl as I walk into the hallway.

"She didn't tell you the whole story yet, did she?" Reid asks.

Oh no. My stomach drops and anxiety seeps into every cell in my body. *No, no, no, no.*

"Fuck off, you piece of shit. I may not know all of the details, but I know you cheated on your *wife*," Charlie fires back. "What the fuck are you even doing here at her parents' house? You didn't do enough damage by fucking up your marriage? You have to show up at family dinners and make her uncomfortable too?"

"I was invited, unlike you."

"Quinn invited me. You know coming around is not going to make her take you back. You should've cherished what you had with her when you had it, because she's done with you, asswipe. You're never getting her back."

"Because of you?"

"No, because of *you*."

I reach Charlie and put my hand on his arm. His muscles are tense, coiled and ready to strike. He turns at my touch and I see his cheeks are flushed in anger.

"Hey, you," I whisper to him, wrapping my hand around his waist. He leans into me and wraps his arm around me protectively.

"What the fuck, Reid?" I glare at him.

He raises his hands up in surrender. "Fine, fine."

"How is Bambi, anyway?"

He raises his eyebrows at the mention of his secretary, the one I found him fucking in our bed.

"Barbara and I are no longer together."

"Did you cheat on her, too?"

"I told you, sleeping with Barbara was a mistake, just something I had to get out of my system."

A laugh jumps out of my throat, sounding more like a bark than anything. "Well, I'm so glad you got that out of your system. Why do you keep coming here? Why keep in touch with my parents?"

He eyes Charlie with disdain. "You're my wife, Quinn."

"*Ex*-wife." He sounds like my parents—maybe they've brainwashed him. "I was your wife up until I found out you were fucking everyone else but me."

"And why was that?" *Oh, that asshole. He is not going to blame his affair on me.*

"Because you made a choice, Reid. Don't you dare put this one me. Your dick didn't accidentally land in her cunt IN OUR BED," I screech.

My body tenses, my blood pressure rising to a boiling point, and I'm about two seconds from losing my shit. This time, it's Charlie soothing me.

"Okay, I think it's time for us to go," Charlie announces firmly.

"That sounds like the best idea ever." We make our way to the kitchen and Shannon jumps from the entryway, totally eavesdropping, I'm sure. I would have, too, if I were in her position.

"Sorry, Shannon, but I'm going to pass on dessert."

"No worries." We hug briefly and head to the living room where my parents usually sit and relax after dinner. They definitely heard the entire exchange from here.

"Mom, Dad, we're going to get going."

"Thanks for having me, Mr. and Mrs. Fitzpatrick," Charlie says, nodding to them politely.

I don't wait for them to stand up or respond. They'd probably say something in Reid's defense, or tell me to watch my mouth. Their loyalty to a man who cheated on their daughter makes me sick. What kind of parents do that? Choose to side with an adulterer over their own flesh and blood?

I'm disappointed in their behavior tonight.

I'm also disappointed in myself for being disappointed, because it means I had expectations.

I take a deep breath as Charlie guides me outside, my hand secure in his.

As soon as we're outside, he turns on me, pressing me up against the front door and kissing me soundly. It's so unexpected, I stiffen up at first, but I don't resist for long. He kisses me so hard my lips sting.

"You ready for your reward?"

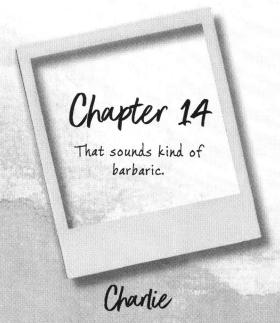

Chapter 14

That sounds kind of barbaric.

Charlie

I'm so ramped up from my altercation with that twatface. When he started talking shit about Quinn, my vision turned red and every ounce of my being went into defense mode.

I wanted to punch him.

Almost did, too. If Quinn hadn't touched me, it would have been over.

Seeing Quinn's family and how little support she has doesn't make me feel pity for her. This feeling is more like…awe of how she can be so strong and independent *despite* the lack of support. A weaker woman might crumble in the face of parents pushing her to stay in a marriage without trust, but not Quinn. She calls them on their shit and walked away from the man who broke his promise to her. She's so fucking amazing.

I want Quinn.

I want my tongue in her mouth.

I want to rub my dick all over her body. On her sassy mouth that speaks her mind even when it isn't easy. In her gorgeous fiery red hair. On the countless freckles that dot her body.

I want to come on her skin and rub it in so my essence stays with her all day.

I want to mark her as *mine*—mine to fuck, mine to share, mine to pleasure.

These feelings of possession are undeniable, and I don't want to hold them back anymore. But first, I'm going to make good on my promise to take her ass. Not every woman likes anal, but I know she has done this before, just not with me.

Not yet, anyway.

We stumble into my place, our hands all over each other, panting with desperation. As soon as we manage to close the door, I tear her clothes off of her, pulling clumsily at the fabric. My desire has robbed me of finesse, but Quinn doesn't seem to mind, as she's taking my clothes off just as frantically. Once we're both naked, I pick her up, her hot pussy against my stomach, legs wrapped around my waist, and I carry her into my bedroom. I'm going to need my lube for this, or else I would've just fucked her in the foyer.

In my bedroom, I put her down on the bed, unable to stop looking at the perfection that is this woman. Her eyes meet mine and I try to convey all I'm feeling for her.

"Are you ready?" I ask her.

In response, she rolls over onto her stomach, grabs a pillow for her head, and tucks her knees under her abdomen, effectively raising her ass in the air for me.

My cock jumps at the sight. *I guess that's a yes.* I reach into my nightstand drawer for the lube, put it beside her, then crawl onto the bed and bury my face in that amazing spot between her legs. The scent of her pussy fills my nose and I inhale deeply, loving the fact that she's all worked up because of me.

I spread her cheeks apart, giving me easier access to her pussy, licking, nipping, rubbing my face up and down her sensitive flesh. From this angle, having my mouth on her pussy means my nose rubs against her pucker. I feel the wrinkled skin as I dive my tongue into her wet heat, as deep as I can get it. Her arousal mixed with my saliva makes her slippery, and I plan to put that slipperiness to good use.

She moans and groans her pleasure as I work her, the sounds muffled by the pillow. I want to make her come once before I start working on her ass; she needs to be loose and relaxed.

Pulling her clit into my mouth, I suck on it, loving the way her thighs tremble. With Quinn, I know too much attention to her clit can drive her orgasm away, so I let it go and slide my index finger into her, teasing her with little flicks and licks.

My cock wants in on this action, but I ignore it, inserting a second finger into her pussy, pushing them in and out while I torment her clit.

She's moving her pelvis now, as best she can from this angle, widening her legs and pushing into my face. I'm completely smothered by her, my face covered in her wetness, but I don't care. I could live here, between Quinn's legs.

Her sounds start to escalate and I feel the flutters inside of her, so I work my fingers faster and leave her clit completely alone.

"Fuck, Charlie!" she complains.

"You know what I want to hear, Red."

"Fuck you."

I chuckle, slowing the pace of my fingers. She curses, gets up on her hands and knees, and starts rocking her body, fucking herself on my fingers.

Fuck, that's hot.

She's chasing her orgasm herself, trying to avoid begging me—but I'm a selfish prick and I want her to beg me.

So, I take my fingers out slowly.

"Charlie Nelson, I need you to make me come, you bastard!"

"Now, that isn't very nice, calling me names." I kiss her left cheek then get closer to her, kissing the spot right in between her asshole and pussy. I can't help but give her a long swipe with my tongue.

"Please, Charlie, please make me come," she says, flopping her upper body back down on the pillow in supplication.

Fuck yes. I insert three fingers this time, then suck her clit into my mouth, hard. Three pumps later, she comes, trembling around my fingers. Her screams echo in my head, music to my ears.

Before she has a chance to come down from her orgasm, I'm pulling my fingers from her cunt and dragging the arousal up to her pucker. My fingers are slippery and I rub that tightly clenched hole, feeling the texture of the sensitive skin there.

"Mmmm," she moans.

I lick her pussy again, relishing the way it spasms around my tongue one last time, and then I trail my tongue up to her asshole. I let my saliva pool in my mouth and let myself drool all over her tiny hole, thinking about how tight she's going to be. I kiss the creased skin then explore the surface with my tongue. I lick up and down, around and around, then dip down to her pussy, nipping her sensitive clit to give her a jolt of sensation every now and then.

"Fuck, Red. This hole is so tight. I'm going to stretch it real good to get it ready for my cock."

She groans in response.

Flexing my tongue to make it firm, I probe the hole, trying to breach it, but she clenches up in response.

"Hold your cheeks open for me."

Surprisingly, she obeys with no objections, resting her face on the pillow sideways and reaching her hands back to hold herself open for me. Now that's better. I look at her, pussy dripping wet, asshole clenched tight.

"Relax that hole for me."

"I am relaxed," she argues.

"I can see how tight it is. Relax for me baby. Let me in."

She takes a deep breath and lets it out slowly, and I can see her muscles relax ever so slightly. Once again, I lick her, groaning in pleasure at touching this forbidden spot. Then I flex my tongue and try to enter. This time, I slip in, not very far, but enough to feel that tight ring of muscle, just inside her opening. *Fuck yes.* I work my tongue all around, using my fingers on her clit to keep her distracted.

Quinn wiggles against me, moaning loudly. I slide my finger into her pussy to get it nice and wet then bring it up to her anus, right beside my tongue. I push to gain entrance and she clenches, the hole puckering up around my fingertip.

"Breathe baby, nice and steady. It's just my fingertip." I pet her hip and thigh, soothing her while I apply more pressure and my finger gains entrance to the first knuckle. "Good girl," I praise.

I alternate like this, with my tongue and finger, until my entire index finger is inside her. It's hot and tight inside Quinn.

"Fuck, I wish you could see this," I tell her.

I grab the lube on the bed, withdraw my finger, and apply an abundant amount around and into her hole as it gapes slightly open. I insert my finger again, and it slides inside so much easier now.

I work that hole open until three fingers are buried in her ass, and the sight of it makes me want to come. A light sheen of sweat covers Quinn's back.

"You're doing so good, taking three of my fingers."

"Charlie," she moans.

"What, baby? What do you need?" I can't see much of her face, but she sounds blissed out.

"More," she whimpers.

"More fingers?"

"No, more of you. I need your cock. I'm ready for it."

I gently remove my fingers, kiss her puckered entrance one last time, and then sit back on my haunches.

"Roll over and my cock is yours."

Quinn

My world is reduced to the feel of Charlie, his tongue and his fingers. He has taken his time to prep me, giving me an orgasm and stretching me open. That first finger felt enormous, but I got used to it after a while.

Now I need his cock.

I roll over, not arguing at his command. We position the pillow under my hips and I pull my knees back, giving him better access. He strokes his cock while he admires the view, and I notice he is so hard it must be painful. The tip is purple and I swear I see it jump in his hand. He pours a generous amount of lube then strokes it again for good measure. As he moves up the bed to kneel in between my legs, I admire this man in front of me. He's beyond gorgeous.

I feared his reaction when we left my parents' place. I thought I'd see pity in his expression, but when he pinned me against the front door and kissed me with that brutal kiss, it was like he knew exactly what I needed from him.

He positions his cock, nudging my hole, and stares into my eyes.

"Relax, Red. Give me a deep breath, and let it out nice and slow."

This is not my first rodeo with anal, but I love the care he's taking to make it good for me.

I nod, taking a deep breath and trying to remain as relaxed as I can.

The pressure is intense, his dick so much bigger than his fingers. I inhale sharply when I feel him pop through that ring of muscle.

"God, Quinn, you're so fucking tight." Sweat beads up on his forehead and upper lip and he grimaces, as if it's all he can do to stay still right now—but I don't want him to stay still. I want him to sink the rest of that gorgeous cock into me. I tilt up my pelvis, relaxing my asshole as much as I can.

"More, Charlie. Give it to me."

He opens his eyes, trying to gauge my expression, and what he sees must convince him I'm ready for more.

He drizzles more lube around his cock for good measure, pulling back and forth in shallow strokes to get his erection as slippery as possible. Then he wedges it in, pushing forward forcefully, holding my gaze as he buries himself in me until I can feel his pubic hair against my skin.

Holy fuckity fuck.

"Ahhh," I cry out, unable to keep it in.

Concern takes over Charlie's face. "Are you okay?"

I take a deep breath and try to acclimate to the intrusion. "Fuck, your cock is big."

He begins to back out and I stop him, wrapping my legs around his waist. "Don't you dare. I just needed a second. I've never had a cock as big as yours up my ass."

He stills. "You sure? I don't want to hurt you."

"I'm not fragile, I promise. I want you to fuck me. Fuck my ass like it's never been fucked before."

He relaxes and smiles at me, giving me that sexy, panty-dropping smile.

"That I can do." He removes my legs from around his waist and motions for me to hold my knees back like I was before. "I need to play with your sweet pussy. I want to feel you come while I'm buried in your ass."

Yesss. Typically, the only way I come from anal is with a vibrator against my clit, but we're at his house—no toys here. However, Charlie is well versed in how to make me come.

He holds my thighs open wide and slides in and out of my ass, keeping his movements smooth and controlled, allowing me a moment to get used to the feel of him burrowing into me then pulling almost all the way out. He watches the spot where we're connected and I wish I could see too.

Then he moves his hands in toward my center and swipes a finger up my slit, flicking at my clit.

"Yesss," I moan, closing my eyes as I take in all the different sensations.

A sudden smack to my pussy has my eyes flying back open.

"Did you just slap me?" I ask, incensed.

His response is another slap, this time landing right on my clit. The pain surprises me initially but then morphs somehow into pleasure. A deep moan escapes me without permission and he chuckles.

"You like it."

"No I don't," I huff.

Slap.

"Fuck!"

"Is that why you're so wet? Because you don't like it?" His finger pumps into my cunt, and the pressure of his cock in my ass makes my pussy tighter and his finger feel so much bigger than ever before, not to mention the sensation of his piercing rubbing up and down my sensitive flesh.

His cock is pumping faster now, and his finger matches the rhythm. I feel my orgasm start to build.

"Your pussy doesn't lie, Red. You like my cock in your ass, and you like when I slap your clit. Are you going to come? Give. It. To. Me." The last words are punctuated not only with his thrusts, but also with a slap to my clit.

"God," I sob, trying not to let go of my legs. My body is bouncing with the force of his thrusts and I'm hanging right on the edge. I look up to Charlie, desperation in my face. "Please," I whisper.

He holds my gaze as he snaps his hips and pinches my clit all at once. The two sensations at once push me into bliss and I scream out, falling apart with blinding pleasure. I feel my pussy spasm around his finger, and I also feel my ass clench around his cock.

Then he shouts and follows me, his cock pulsing inside me.

Maybe it takes minutes to come down from my orgasm, maybe hours, but when I'm conscious again, I register that Charlie is wiping me clean with a warm washcloth. I hear the water running in the bathroom as he washes his hands then a warm body cocoons mine and I drift off to sleep.

I wake up to the sensation of being watched, like a tickle on the back of my neck. Sure enough, when I open my eyes, cobalt blue eyes are staring at me.

"Hey sleepy." Charlie smiles.

"Hey sexy. Sorry I conked out. How long have I been asleep?" I stretch languidly, feeling a twinge in my nether regions.

"Not long, maybe a half hour or so."

"You couldn't sleep?" He seems so serious right now.

"Just thinking."

"About?" I prod.

"Us." *Oh fuck. Are we going to talk about us? What if he doesn't feel the same things I'm feeling? What if he tells me we need to back off?* My heart rate kicks up a notch and I'm instantly wide awake.

"What about us?" I swallow, needing more spit in my mouth.

He looks at me warily. "I know we started this thing not wanting anything serious."

"We did." I nod and hold my breath.

"It seems like we've gotten a bit carried away."

What does that mean? Is that a good thing or a bad thing?

"You're probably right."

He takes a deep breath, preparing to say something else, and my lungs all but freeze up. "The thing is, you've gotten under my skin, Quinn. I can't stop thinking about you." His expression is so sincere.

"I can't stop thinking about you either," I tell him, blowing out the breath I was holding.

"I want you to be mine." Vulnerability shines in his eyes, and I immediately want to soothe it.

My smile is hard to contain, but I try. "Yours? That sounds kind of barbaric."

"Yes, *mine*—mine to fuck, mine to talk to, mine to protect." He kisses my lips so sweetly I could cry. "And I'll be yours."

"Mine?" I like the sound of that.

He nods.

"Mine to fuck and talk to and protect?"

"If you want." He studies me, looking from one eye to the other, trying to gauge my reaction. "You're killing me here, Red. What do you think about this? About us?"

"I…" *How do I explain this?* "I'm not sure I ever want to get married again, Charlie."

"Whoa, whoa." He chuckles. "That was not a proposal."

"I'm just saying, I was married before and the contract did nothing. Saying vows in front of a judge or a priest, it doesn't mean anything other than making it a very expensive breakup. A relationship has to be a commitment between two people. If you want to get married someday, I'm not the one for you."

"I don't need a promise of marriage, Quinn."

"What do you need a promise of then?"

"What if…" He ponders this for a second. "What if we make up our own rules?"

I raise my eyebrows in question. "What?"

"What I'm saying is that I want us to be together. I want you to be mine and I want to be yours, but we can define our own relationship, Quinn. If we're both on the same page, we can do whatever we want."

His gorgeous blue eyes pin me with their intensity. I can't look away, but I'm not sure how I feel about what he's saying.

"We can decide if we want to play with someone else. As long as we both want it and no one is getting hurt, I don't see what's wrong with that."

"I was cheated on once before, and I don't think I can go through that again," I tell him.

"I don't want to have sex with anyone else unless you're there—unless you want to play with someone else *together*. Do you consider what we did with Tobias cheating?"

"Well, no..." I drift off, trying to gather my thoughts. "You want to be like...swingers?"

"I don't know what the definition of swingers is, but I think that's more like swapping partners, and I don't want to swap. I want you all the time. I only want to include someone else if we both want to."

"But, what if you want to have sex with someone else and I'm not there?"

"I haven't had sex with anyone else since that night at Club Bailar with Miss Double D when you watched me—if you call that sex. I haven't wanted to. When I went to New York for my work trip, someone tried to pick me up at the bar and you know what I did?"

Oh no. My stomach drops at the thought of him fucking someone else while he was away. "No, what?"

"I blew her off to text you."

The knot in my belly loosens. "You did?"

"I did. When's the last time you had sex with someone else?"

"Well, Tobias." That was just the other night.

"I mean without me there."

I think about this. "Not since before that night at Club Bailar either."

He raises only his right eyebrow as if to say I made his point.

"So let me get this straight: you want to be in a relationship with me, but we can decide to have sex with other people and as long as we're both there, it's okay?" I'm skeptical. "What if I don't ever want to have sex with a third person?"

"Then we won't. The only reason I would want to have sex with someone else would be to have you watch me, if it turned you on to see me, or to play together. If you weren't there, I'd rather just be with you." He shrugs as if this is the simplest thing and I'm being a dunce for not getting it.

"And you're okay with me having sex with another guy as long as you're there?"

"I'm saying that we talk about it, as a couple, and decide if we want to play with someone else. If I don't like the guy or you don't like the girl—or vice versa—then we don't play, no questions."

"That sounds a bit...*unconventional*."

"Yes. Be unconventional with me, Quinn." His eyes plead with me to take this chance with him.

I waver, unsure if I want to give Charlie the power to hurt me.

He sees my indecision and pulls me into his arms. "If you don't want this, just tell me. I know I just sort of sprang this on you. I'm going to go take a shower and give you some time to think, okay?" He kisses my forehead, a sad, resigned smile on his face, and starts to get out of bed.

My heart jumps into my throat at the thought of him leaving right now, thinking I don't want him. "Wait." I grab his arm, tugging him back to me. Hope seeps into his eyes, but he's hesitant, and I can see I have the power to hurt him, too. "Don't go. I'm afraid of the whole third person thing, afraid there's a thin line between playing and cheating, but I'm willing to try."

"I promise we'll only do it if we both want to. If you don't want to share, my cock is all yours. I won't ever cheat on you, Quinn. I know that's a big deal."

"Okay. And I promise I won't ever lie to you, Charlie. I know that's a deal breaker for you."

His smile breaks across his face, as bright as the sun. I think mine must match his, because my cheeks hurt.

"So, we're going to do this? You're mine?"

I laugh out loud at his boyish excitement. "And you're mine. What shall I do with you?"

"I can think of a few things." He wiggles his eyebrows.

"So can I."

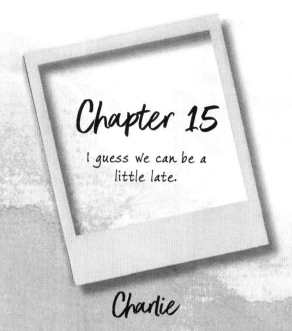

Chapter 15

I guess we can be a little late.

Charlie

Having a girlfriend is…amazing, but I think it's only because the girlfriend is Quinn. Friday arrives in a flash and I realize we've seen each other almost every day this week. If we don't see each other during the day, we end up in each other's bed, and sex with her just keeps getting better and better.

I love that she isn't clingy; she has her career and understands that I have mine. I love that she creates amazing art. Last night, she told me she was going to try to get some work done before I got there and left the door unlocked for me. When I arrived, I found her in the studio, wearing a paint-splattered shirt with the music blaring and a look of pure focus and concentration on her face. I must've taken 30 pictures of her while she was painting before she noticed I was there. I'm going to edit the photos and see if she wants to put them up on her website. Hell, maybe I'll even put them up on mine.

Tonight is happy hour with the boys and Max asked if the ladies could join us. This used to be annoying, but ironically,

I'm glad he asked. I've seen Quinn all week long, but I can't wait to see her again. This will be the first night we're around our friends as a couple and I know Max and Logan are going to give me shit about it.

In fact, I'd rather get this over with now than wait until later.

Me: Okay boys, I have news.

Logan: You jack off again? That's not news.

Max: What's your news?

Me: Fuck off Logan. Like you don't jack off.

Logan: Tate takes good care of me. You jack off less when you have regular amazing sex, but you wouldn't know about that.

Me: Actually, I would.

Max: ??? Are you saying you have a girlfriend?

Me: Yes, that's what I'm saying.

Logan: Are you kidding?

Me: I never kid about sex.

Max: Who is she? Are you bringing her tonight?

Logan: Yeah, I have to see it to believe it.

Me: It's Quinn.

Two beats go by with no response. No jumping dots indicating that someone is writing a message, nothing, and I know it's about to start. So, I set my phone down and return some emails while they get their reactions out of their systems. Then I pick it back up and scroll through their responses.

Logan: I fucking told you, Max! You owe me $50.

Max: Quinn? Monica swears she isn't the relationship type.

Logan: I called it.

Max: Quinn Fitzpatrick?

Logan: Mr. I don't need a girlfriend when I can fuck a different girl every

night.

Max: I can't believe Monica didn't tell me.

Logan: Charlie! Where the fuck did you go?

Max: He's ignoring us.

Logan: Maybe he's making it up.

Max: Nah, he isn't making it up. Why would he?

Max: Besides, this is awesome. The girls all get along. It would have sucked if he started dating someone like Candi.

Logan: Oh God, that laugh.

Max: Quinn is perfect for Charlie. She'll keep him on his toes.

Me: You guys done yet?

Max: She coming tonight?

Me: Yes, she'll be there.

Logan: This I have to see.

I chuckle as I pocket my cell. Moments later, I hear a knock at my door.

"Come in."

My boss, Jason, peeks his head through my door. "Got a sec?"

"Of course, what's up?"

He opens the door up all the way and takes a seat on the other side of my desk. Jason is a heavyset man with salt and pepper hair. Laugh lines are carved into his face, framing his mouth with parenthesis, and his brown eyes are kind.

"Just wanted to touch base about New York. Roger emailed me that he was so pleased with your last meeting. Thanks so much for taking care of him."

"That's what I'm here for." I smile at him. Jason is a fair boss and has given me such support since I started working here. "I'm working on some design concepts for his marketing campaign now. I'll send them to you when I'm done."

"You've handled this new acquisition well, Charlie. There may be a spot in management coming up, and your name is at the top of my list to fill that spot. I'll recommend you for the job if you think it's something you want."

My eyebrows shoot up in surprise. "A spot in management?" I've never wanted to go into management, but I'm thrilled he has me in mind for a promotion.

"I think you'd make a great manager. The staff all respect your talent and you can make people do things while making them laugh."

I chuckle. "I appreciate you letting me know."

He stands up and heads toward the door. "I'll keep you posted on the opening, and I look forward to seeing your concept. You'll be going back to New York next week to finalize plans with Roger, right?"

"You got it."

"Have a good weekend, Charlie."

"You too, Jason," I say as he shuts my office door.

Huh. I'm still in shock. He thinks I'm management material.

Managers don't take pictures though, and I don't know how I'd survive without taking pictures. I know there are photographers in the company that start in my position and work their way up to management, but I could see myself keeping the job I have forever. I like working on projects, coming up with concepts, taking the pictures, and putting together the ads.

Still, it's flattering to hear that Jason thinks I could be a manager if I want to be.

The clock tells me it's time to leave, so I power down my computer, grab my cell, and head out. My mind is still reeling from that brief talk with Jason. As I exit the door, I find it's raining outside. Spring is in the air and though it's wet, I stop, tilt my head up to the sky, and close my eyes. I love the smell of spring. The frigid chill of winter is gone, replaced by a warm, fresh scent full of spring blossoms and new beginnings. Most of the people around me are dashing around, trying not to get wet, but I take my time, relishing the feel of the raindrops on my skin.

Just as soon as I sit down in my car, my cell lights up with a call from my mom. I'm in too good a mood for her to spoil it, so I wipe the raindrops off my hands and face and answer cheerfully.

"Hi there, my beautiful mother," I chirp, hoping my good mood is contagious.

"Charlie? Is that you?"

"Of course it's me, you called my phone, remember?" I chuckle.

"What has gotten into you?"

"Nothing, Mom. I'm just in a good mood. What's up?" I ask, smiling at the thought of seeing Quinn soon.

"Well, I was talking to Patricia, my friend from Green Briars, and she mentioned that she's going to the open house at Art Redefined next Sunday. Isn't that where your friend works? The girl you brought to Green Briars?"

"Quinn? Yes, it's where she sells her pieces. Are you going?"

"Well, apparently, it's exclusive to members only, but Patricia was raving about it. Maybe you could talk to Quinn and see if you could get a pair of tickets for me and your father?"

I'll be damned. My pieces are going to be for sale at this event, and my mother wants to go to it because her prissy friend bragged about an exclusive members-only open house and she doesn't want to be outdone.

"Sure, I'll be seeing Quinn soon, I'll ask her about it."

"Marvelous. I was afraid you were going to tell me you no longer talked to her."

"No, actually, Quinn is my girlfriend."

"Really?"

I'm not sure I like her tone. "Yes."

"Well, that's something. You usually flit from girl to girl, since Anna anyway. I never thought I'd see you settle down with one girl."

"Quinn and I just…click. She's amazing."

"Too bad she doesn't have a better job."

My smile is long gone now. "Quinn has an amazing job. She's very talented, as you'll be able to see if you go to her open house, and if you're referring to her income, she makes quite a good living off of her talent."

"I heard she's divorced."

I wonder how she heard that. "So what?"

"So nothing. I'd have liked to see you settle down with someone a bit more…refined, someone more like Anna."

That name again, twice in one conversation. I grit my teeth to try to rein in my anger. "Anna and I have been over a long time, Mom, and Quinn is divorced, but that doesn't change the fact that she's an amazing woman."

"Okay, don't get all prickly on me, Charles," she reprimands.

"Well it's difficult not to when you call me to get tickets to an art gallery that you've never wanted to go to before, mention my ex-girlfriend twice in one conversation, and insult my current girlfriend." I grip the steering wheel so hard my knuckles turn white.

155

"I did not insult your girlfriend."

"Yes, you did." Maybe other people let her bullshit slide, but I'm going to call her on it. "It shouldn't matter what job or income someone I date has, Mom. I can't help but think your response to Quinn might be different if she were a lawyer."

"Of course it would."

"My point exactly."

"And what is that supposed to mean?" There's that haughty tone again; it grates on my nerves.

"It means that not everyone is a lawyer, and that's okay, yet you have this attitude that anyone who isn't a lawyer isn't as good as you are."

Silence. Maybe she huffs, I can't tell, but I'm on a roll now.

"*I'm* not a lawyer. I know you're disappointed about that, but it's just not in me. I love what I do, and I'm good at it—so good, in fact, that my boss just told me he wants me to move up to management when a position opens up—yet you and Dad never care about my accomplishments." The words are ripped out of me and I'm panting from the exertion it took to say them out loud.

"Maybe that's because I don't understand your world."

"Maybe you could show some interest," I bite back. "You know what, Mom? Never mind. I have to go." I swipe to end the call and grip the phone so hard in my hand that I almost *want* to hear it crack. Then I remember it's my phone and I'll just have to buy a new one if it breaks. I blow out a breath, run my hands over my face and through my damp hair, and force my tense muscles to relax.

I need to face the facts.

My mom is a selfish snob.

My dad is not that much better.

Dom and Tabby are okay, but I still end up feeling like an outcast every time we get together.

Then my thoughts drift to Max and Logan. Those guys accept me for who I am, even if I do act like a goofball 99% of the time. Too bad they aren't my brothers.

You know what, fuck that.

They're more like family than my actual family is, and Quinn—being with her makes me so damn happy. When she praises me for my talent, it makes me feel like I'm a king, like I could do anything.

Time to go see my people.

Quinn

Humid air fills the bathroom as I step out of the shower. The towel is warm when I go to grab it and I hold it over my skin to chase the goose bumps away. That towel heater was so worth it, my latest favorite gadget. I finish drying off then slip into my favorite purple robe and stare at myself in the mirror. Even now, after working all day and fresh from the shower, I look happy.

My cheeks are flushed; maybe it's due to the heat of my shower, or maybe it's due to the naughty thoughts I keep having about Charlie.

My skin, fair as ever, shows what can only be a hickey on my neck. He accidentally gave me one last night during sex. He latched on to my neck while pounding into me and I loved the feel of his mouth on me, the sharp sting when he sucked on my skin. Afterward, when he saw the mark he left, he loved it so much he decided to give me a few more. I open my robe and find several dark blue and purple spots that stand out on my pale skin. One is on the swell of my right breast, one just under my left breast, one on either side of my pubic hair, and one on the inside of my right thigh, near the juncture of where my leg connects to my body. I'm decorated with bruises, but it feels like more, like I'm decorated with his mark, his *brand*.

There is no hiding the hickey on my neck, but the others are easily concealed with clothes.

Unless…

Unless we play with someone else. They'd see the marks Charlie left on my body.

Why do I like that idea so much?

All week long we've been so consumed with each other and our new-found status, I've had no time to think about the concept of us being a couple exclusive to each other except when we decide we want to play with a third. He hasn't brought it up once, and neither have I.

But I'm thinking about it now, and strangely…I *like* the idea. As my imagination runs away with possibilities of what we could do, my cell beeps, notifying me of waiting text messages.

Yikes, there are a LOT of text messages. Scrolling through, I find several from Charlie and Monica. I click on Charlie's first.

Charlie: Hey babe, I told Max and Logan about us. Figured I'd break it to them before tonight. FYI

Charlie: I can't stop thinking about the trail of hickeys I left all over your

body. Hope they're still there.

I smile and hit reply.

Me: Yes, they're still there. I look like I've been abused with all these bruises.

Charlie: More like worshiped. I like my mark on you.

Me: I kind of like it, too.

Charlie: And now my dick is hard. I'm on my way to pick you up, think we have time for a quickie?

Me: I just got out of the shower and I'm getting ready.

Charlie: Perfect. I can dirty you back up again.

Me: We'll see.

I protest, but I'm aching for his cock. It's like I've become addicted, and there's no cure.

I click on Monica's messages next and scroll up to the first new one.

Monica: Holy shit.

Monica: You're dating Charlie?

Monica: I mean, I knew you guys were sleeping together, but are you ACTUALLY dating?

Monica: Max said Charlie said you are.

Monica: Okay, I realize that sounded grade schoolish, but QUINN!

Monica: I need details. Spill.

I smile as I read her texts. I knew she was going to bombard me with questions, and that's kind of why I didn't tell her sooner. I needed time to let this soak in before I had to explain it to anyone else.

Me: Hey, can you talk?

The explanation will go much faster if we can talk instead of text, and not two seconds later, my cell rings in my hand with Monica's pretty face flashing on the screen.

"Hey you!"

"Oh my goodness! I'm so glad you pulled your head out of your ass! I always knew there was something more between you and Charlie. Tell me everything!"

I laugh at her exuberance. "I hate to burst your bubble, but there was only just sex between us for a while, but ever since that one night at Club Bailar, things just…got intense. We started seeing each other more and more, and it just feels like I can be myself with him, you know?"

"That's amazing, Quinn! I'm so happy for you!"

"Thanks babe. I know you wanted us to get together."

"Well, yeah! He's Max's best friend—it makes it pretty convenient for me."

I laugh. "Listen, he's on his way to pick me up now. See you at O'Malley's soon."

"Sounds good. Bye."

I opt to let my hair air dry, running a brush and some product through it to tame my wild mane, but it's no use—the curls twist this way and that, having a mind of their own. My makeup routine is not long: a bit of concealer under my eyes, powder on my nose and cheeks, cherry red lipstick, and mascara. I don't have a strong enough concealer to hide the hickey, but I don't care. A dark part of me wants people to see it, and I have a feeling Charlie would hate it if I covered it up with makeup.

Just as I'm about to go into my closet and get dressed, I hear a knock at the front door. Knowing it's Charlie, I fasten my robe and look through the peephole. Sure enough, a gorgeous male specimen with blond hair and dimples stands on my stoop. Unlocking and opening the door, I smile wide to greet him.

"Hey, hotstuff."

"Hey." He smiles back, lips turning up in a small smile, but it doesn't quite reach his eyes and my favorite dimples remain hidden. I study his face some more as he walks into my space.

"What happened?"

"Nothing." I can tell he's trying to shake it off, but something is bothering my usually happy man.

I touch his face, his smooth skin and square jawline. My fingers run over his sensual bottom lip. "You know, a perk of having a girlfriend is that you get to unload on me. I'm a good listener."

"I know you are." He stares down at me and I know we're both thinking about the night he told me about Anna and the baby.

"So spill. I know something is bothering you. What happened? Bad day at work?" My hands travel up his shoulders and wrap around his neck as I hold him to me, pulling him into a hug. His muscular arms wrap around my back, cocooning me with his warm body. His nose digs into my hair and sniffs.

"You smell good."

"You're deflecting." I bring him to the couch and force him to sit then straddle him. He finally notices I'm wearing a robe and his eyes travel down my form, lingering on my nipples.

"Are you naked under there?"

"If you tell me what's bothering you, I'll show you," I taunt.

"Or, I could just open your robe right now." He grabs the knot in the middle and starts to undo it, but I grab his wrists.

"Charlie." My quiet voice stills his movements.

He meets my gaze and blows out a breath. "It's nothing—nothing new anyway. I actually had a great day at work. Jason, my boss, told me there might be a management job opening up and he thinks I'd be a good fit."

"That's great, but would you still be designing if you were in management?" I know he loves the creative part of his job.

"That's the thing, designing wouldn't be a part of the job. I'd be in charge of projects and approving or declining other designers' concepts, but still, it's nice to be recognized, you know?"

"Absolutely, that had to feel good. I know you'd be an amazing manager, but I hope you choose what makes you happy." I rest my hands on his chest, waiting for him to tell me the bad part.

"Then my mom called."

"Ah." Now I understand his mood completely. Talking to my mom always reminds me how much we don't get along. I'm fine with this, for the most part, but some conversations with her pour salt on a wound I thought had healed up, making me feel a bit raw and grumpy.

"She wants tickets to the open house at Art Redefined, by the way." He rolls his eyes at this.

"She does? She never mentioned that she likes to go there at that dinner I went to with you." I'm sure Charlie mentioned the name of the gallery then.

"That's because she isn't a fan of art. She just wants to go because her friend from the country club goes and she wants to show her up."

"I see," I mutter. Fake people piss me off. "Well, I *can* get tickets for her if you want me to, or you can tell her we're sold out—whatever makes you feel better."

Charlie shrugs and looks away. "I ended up telling her off," he says quietly.

I turn his face back toward mine. "Good for you."

"I just told off my mother. That does not feel good."

"I know it doesn't feel good, but maybe she had it coming. I'm sure you've held it back a million times before now. But if you stood up for yourself, I'm proud of you," I say emphatically. Dealing with my own parents has taught me how difficult it can be to choose a job they don't approve of, and even worse, to choose a path in life they don't approve of.

He wraps his arms around my waist and buries his head in my chest. I cradle him to me, my fingers digging into his hair and petting him. "So, since your pieces will be on display at that open house, do you want to go with me?"

He tilts his head up, looking up at me from where he's comfortably resting. "Do you usually go?"

"Not every month, but I've been a few times. It might be fun for you to watch how people react to your so-called *garbage*."

"I want to go to see *your* pieces."

"Okay." I smile down at him.

"Do I get to see what's under this robe now?"

I crane my neck to check the clock. "We should get going…"

"Come on, I held up my end of the deal, and I want to check on my marks, see if any need freshening up." He unties my robe and I let him. The sides fall open, cold air hitting my naked skin. My nipples pebble under his gaze and he licks his lips.

"Are you planning to keep me marked forever?" I breathe, loving the way his hands smooth over my skin, finding each bruise and inspecting his work.

"Maybe. I didn't expect to like it so much, but my inner caveman wants everyone to know you're mine."

I didn't think I'd like the gleam of possessiveness in his eyes so much, but his inner caveman is hot as fuck.

His hands slide up to my breasts, weighing them, holding them, pinching the stiff peaks. I arch into his touch, giving him all the access he needs. I'm sitting right over his crotch and I feel his dick harden. I groan when he leans forward to suck my right nipple into his mouth, like he wants to eat me, and my pelvis rotates, pushing down into his erection.

"I need to be inside you, Red."

"I guess we can be a little late."

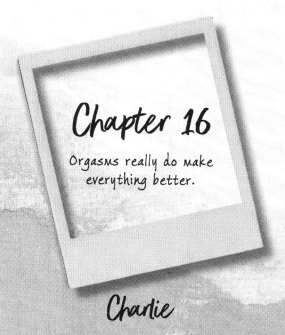

Chapter 16

Orgasms really do make everything better.

Charlie

Orgasms really do make everything better. Quinn rode me with her pretty tits bouncing in my face until I came so hard I saw stars. Now, feeling better after talking to my girlfriend about my problems and emptying my balls into her, my mood has improved drastically.

I squeeze Quinn's hand as we make our way through O'Malley's to our regular table in the back. Predictably, Max, Monica, Logan, and Tate are already here, laughing with each other as they pick at some nachos on the table.

"Well look who decided to show up! We figured you bailed on us." Logan stands to greet me and Quinn.

"And miss all the fun and gossip? Never!" I pat Logan on the back and turn to Tate. "Hey gorgeous!" I pick her up, twirl her tiny frame around then set her back down. Next up is Monica, who gets the same treatment. She laughs as I pick her up to squeeze her. "How're you, beautiful?"

"I'm good, Charlie." She smiles at me, then leans to whisper in my ear. "Take good care of my girl. She may seem tough as nails, but she's been hurt." She pins me with her hazel eyes, concern etched all over her pretty face.

I nod solemnly. "I'll take good care of her, and I'll give her lots of orgasms, too."

"Charlie!" Monica turns red and splutters. I laugh at her reaction and turn to see Max picking Quinn up and twirling her around, much like I just did to both Tate and Monica.

Without thinking, I move forward. "All right, all right, enough groping my woman." I yank Quinn out of his arms and hold her to my side protectively.

Max and Logan crack up. "Seriously?" Max asks, wheezing with laughter. "I can't believe this."

"That's rich coming from you," Logan says as he cackles.

Whatever. I scowl at them, which makes them erupt in a second round of laughter. I look down at Quinn and she's smiling up at me, trying to suppress a giggle. I raise my eyebrows at her as if to say, *You're laughing at me, too?*

"It *is* pretty funny," she whispers.

Everyone sits back down while I get drinks from the bar. When I take my seat next to Quinn, I notice everyone looking at us, as if waiting for us to do something.

"Hey, you guys want to see what Quinn can do with her tongue?"

Max and Logan grimace while Monica and Tate let out a scolding chorus of "Charlie!" and Quinn jabs me, her elbow digging into my side painfully.

"Ouch! I meant your cherry trick, Red. What'd you think I meant?"

She laughs. "Oh!"

I rub my side, pouting. "That hurt. You have some sharp elbows, woman."

"Sorry babe."

I look to the table to clarify. "You guys were staring at us, as if waiting for us to perform a trick. Did you know Quinn can tie a cherry stem in a knot with her tongue? It's a pretty cool trick."

"Hey, I remember that!" Monica says. "I probably tried a thousand times, but could never get it."

Tate has a cherry in her drink and hands it over. After eating the cherry, Quinn pops the stem in her mouth, taking only a moment to manipulate it with her tongue, and then presents the stem to the table. Everyone is sufficiently impressed, ooo-ing and aaah-ing.

"What is *that*? Are you hurt?" Monica questions, pointing to Quinn's neck.

"Oh, this?" Quinn covers the hickey I gave her with her hand and looks up at me for help, face flushing at the attention.

"My fault. I got a little overzealous last night." My dick twitches remembering all the other hickeys I put on her body.

"A hickey? Really, Charlie?" Max asks. "I don't think I've given a hickey since I was in high school."

"I haven't either, but I remembered how much fun they are." I wiggle my eyebrows suggestively.

"Why don't you just pee on her?" Logan asks.

"Because that would be gross. Maybe you guys are into golden showers, but that's a no-go for me."

"Ewwww, golden showers? That sounds horrifying. Do people actually do that?" Tate asks, face contorted, showing exactly how grossed out she is.

"Anyway," I say, drawing out the word, trying to veer the topic away from the hickey on Quinn's neck. "What's going on with you guys? How was your week?" I ask no one in specific. We all chat for a bit, catching up. Logan and Tate tell us how their dog, Sparky just chewed up all of Tate's shoes.

"The horror!" I mock gasp.

"Hey, he ruined over $800 worth of shoes!" Tate exclaims.

My eyes widen. "You have over $800 worth of shoes? Wow."

"I know," Logan agrees. "Someone has a shoe addiction."

"*Someone* has a computer addiction. How much have you spent on computers and tablets this year alone?" Tate huffs, crossing her arms over her chest and looking at Logan.

He raises his hands up. "That's different. Computers are my job! I have to be up on all the technology."

"By personally buying them yourself?"

"Hey, I bet you could deduct that in your taxes, if it truly is for work purposes," Quinn pipes up. "Since I have a studio in my home, I've learned a lot about tax deductions."

"Hey, good call. I'll talk to my accountant about it."

This mollifies Tate, and the subject moves to Max and Monica. Monica tells us she's stepping down as director of the ER.

"Oh no! Does that mean you won't be Max's boss anymore?"

"I suppose you're right," Monica confirms, and they look at each other as if they just realized that fact right now.

"Man, your sex life is probably ruined now. No more naughty boss role playing."

"That's okay, they still have naughty nurse fantasies," Quinn points out.

Usually, the mention of a naughty nurse makes my cock twitch, but the naughty nurse in this scenario is Max. I cringe. "I think you just spoiled naughty nurse fantasies for me forever."

"That's too bad, I have a naughty nurse Halloween costume," Quinn says with a smirk.

I raise my eyebrows in interest. "Reeeaaaallly?"

She smiles up at me, those whiskey brown eyes full of warmth and mischief. "Uh-huh."

"Okay, you fixed it. I can now fantasize about my very own naughty nurse. I think I'm coming down with a cold, want to go home so you can take care of me?" I sniffle.

"Maybe later." She pats my thigh and turns back to Monica. "But why are you stepping down? Did something happen at the hospital?"

"No, no big drama. It's just a lot of stress and I think I'm going to be spending more time at Safe Zone." Safe Zone is a women's shelter where Tate works as a social worker. and Monica has been working there on the weekends, or something like that.

"That's awesome!" Quinn says, seeing Monica's smile.

"How are the wedding plans coming?" Tate asks.

"Well, we're actually thinking of getting married soon. Maybe in June?" Monica looks to Max for confirmation. He nods, eyes softening when he looks at her. Anyone can clearly see the affection he has for her.

"Wow, isn't that fast? I mean, I've never been married, but don't engagements usually last years?" I ask.

"They can, but we don't want to wait that long. Besides, we're keeping it simple. Some people make it about the wedding, we just want it to be about us." I swear she actually glows when she talks about marrying Max.

"Well, you know what that means."

Everyone looks up at me, clueless.

"That means I need to get started with planning the bachelor party! I thought I had more time than this! But don't worry, I think I can manage."

Everyone chuckles, but I'm serious.

"Yeah," Quinn agrees. "And as maid of honor, I need to plan the bridal shower *and* bachelorette party." A wrinkle forms in her forehead and I realize she actually does look worried.

"Oh, Quinn, I don't need anything like that," Monica protests.

"Shut it, chica, you're happy as fuck and we need to celebrate the end of your singledom with a proper party."

"But please keep it simple—and no strippers."

"Pft. You get no say in the matter," Quinn tells her, and Max starts to frown at the thought of Monica watching strippers.

"I can help with the bridal shower," Tate offers.

"That would be great."

"Why don't we have a combined bachelor/bachelorette party?" Max suggests.

"Spoken like a true, pussy-whipped man." *Joint bachelor/bachelorette party.* I shake my head at the ridiculous notion.

"Fuck. Off." Max flips me the bird.

I laugh and flip him off right back.

As the girls talk more about bridal parties and registering and all that shit, I sit back and take a sip of my beer. This is exactly what I needed. This feels like family.

As we head out from O'Malley's, I lean into Quinn, loving the way she feels against my side. Everyone else headed home, but I don't want the night to end yet.

"What do you want to do now?" I ask her, burying my face in her curls and breathing in her scent.

"You want to get something to eat?"

"No, I'm still full from the burger—unless you're hungry?"

"No, I'm still full, too."

We walk slowly to my car, both trying to come up with a plan. All the talk of strippers and bachelor parties is in the back of my brain.

"Hey, I have an idea—do you want to go to some strip clubs with me?"

"Really?"

"Yes. I was serious about wanting to plan a cool bachelor party for Max. I haven't been to one in a while and some of them do cool shows for bachelor parties."

"Couldn't you just call and get that information?"

"Now where's the fun in that?"

"And you want *me* to go with you to watch naked women dance?"

"Yes." She starts to pull away from me, but I hold her close. "Have you ever been to a strip club before?"

"To watch men strip, not women."

"You'd be surprised at how many women go. Come on, Red. It'll be fun, I promise."

"I'll go on one condition."

"What's that?"

"If I go with you to check out the female strip clubs, then you go with me to check out the male strip clubs."

I mull this over, not quite sure how to get out of it without seeming like a hypocrite.

I shrug. "Okay."

She beams at me. "Okay."

Quinn

The first two clubs we went to were awful, so tacky and seedy I thought I might catch an STD by sitting down. We walked around and left fairly quickly.

This third one, however, is way classier than the others. From the outside, Allure doesn't look like much—no lit sign, no flashing lights boasting *adult entertainment* or *gentlemen's club*. In fact, I think I've driven by this place a million times without knowing what it is.

After the security guard checks our IDs, he informs us that it's ladies night. How convenient for me. For Charlie, however, there is a steep cover. Charlie explains to him that we're checking the place out for a potential bachelor party, the man uses his walkie talkie to notify the manager to come talk with us, and he lets both of us in for free. "No alcohol and no touching the girls," he reminds us.

Once we step through the hallway, the corridor opens into a huge room with a center stage and several catwalks that branch out into the audience. Seating consists of half tables, so no one has to sit with their back to the stage. Several tables have a pole going through the middle to the ceiling, and everything is decorated in rich tones of purple. The walls look like they're made of purple satin, the bar tops are glowing a deep eggplant color, and everything gleams and shines, looking clean, classy, and luxurious. I feel a bit underdressed in my sweater dress and heeled boots.

It looks like we're in between acts as no one is on the stage at the moment, so I relax and absorb the feel of the place. Sultry music wraps around me and I check out the other occupants. There are no rowdy college kids here, no inappropriate hollering or catcalls. All the men look pretty normal, and Charlie was right—I do see a few other couples here.

"Why no alcohol?" I ask.

He pulls my chair closer to his and wraps an arm around my back. "Clubs that have full nudity don't allow alcohol."

"Ah, so the girls take it all off here?"

"I'd assume so."

"Makes sense I guess. Minimize stupidity by minimizing drunk guests."

"Exactly."

A man dressed in a charcoal grey suit approaches the table. "Are you the guests inquiring about a bachelor party?"

"That's us," Charlie confirms.

"I'm Matt Williams, the manager here at Allure." He shakes our hands firmly. "Come with me."

We both raise our eyebrows and stand to follow him. He takes us to his office and motions for us to sit at the table in front of his desk.

"Thanks for considering Allure for your friend's celebration."

Charlie nods. "Thanks for taking the time to talk to us."

"We pride ourselves on delivering a good time while still maintaining class and taste. We have several party rooms that are completely separate from the rest of the patrons and several different packages to choose from."

He goes through the list and I must admit, I'm impressed. They chat about cost and availability.

"Our main act is just about to start and you'll be able to see several of the most popular dancers. Why don't you watch that and see who you might like to book, then I'll arrange a private show for you."

Charlie looks at me cautiously. "Okay. We'll watch the act then follow up with you."

As we make our way back to the main room, I yearn for another drink. I'm about to watch several women strip down to nothing, right next to Charlie. I take a deep breath and examine my thoughts. I could give in to the jealous feelings that simmer in the background at the thought of Charlie getting turned on by naked strangers, but I remember that he wanted me here with him, that he hasn't stopped touching me for one second, and that he was inside me just a few hours ago. He's given me no reason to be jealous.

"You want to stay for a private show?" I ask Charlie.

"Up to you, Red. Let's just stay for a bit and see how this goes. We can leave any time you want."

"Okay." I push all jealous feelings aside and decide to have fun and enjoy the show. Maybe I'll learn a few new tricks.

The lights dim, leaving on only the lights illuminating the walkways. When the music starts, it's a slow, rhythmic, almost tribal beat. I can't quite place the style, but it sounds Middle Eastern. Six women walk onto the stage, forming a long line, and they are dressed in traditional belly dancing costumes. I've always loved watching belly dancers, wishing I were coordinated enough to get my hips to move like theirs.

I lean forward, genuinely excited to watch them dance. I hope they put on an actual show, not just strip to the music.

Charlie's hand is warm on my back, rubbing my shoulders then sliding down, letting me know his attention is still on me.

Spotlights follow each woman in her path and I squint to get a good look at the girls. It seems like they try to make their show diverse as they range in skin tone, curviness, and height. Their costumes are the same, but all a different color.

I wonder which one appeals to Charlie the most.

There's a pause in the music and all of them strike a pose, arms stretched gracefully out to their sides, and then it begins. They start a perfectly synchronized belly dance. Little bells decorate their skirts and tinkle when their hips move. They're absolutely stunning. They change positions, twining through each other while never missing a beat of their coordinated movements.

They're all very good, but I'm drawn to the dark-skinned, Middle Eastern woman. She has jet-black hair, so shiny and long. Her skin is gorgeous, like coffee with cream, and her eyes are dark and lined with kohl, making her look mysterious and exotic. More than anything, what draws my eye to her is the expression on her face and the way she moves her body.

While all the women on stage are doing the same movements, her hips seem to sway just a little bit more, and she's looking into the crowd with a coy smile, as if she loves what she's doing right now. She looks powerful and so damn sexy.

"You should see your face right now," Charlie whispers in my ear.

"They're so good," I tell him, impressed once again.

"Yeah, they are," he agrees. "Which one do you like the best?"

"The one in the blue." I point out my favorite dancer.

"Huh, me too. She's owning that stage."

"I wish I could move like that."

"I like the way you move just fine."

"Uh-huh."

We quiet down to continue watching. So far no one has removed any clothing. With that thought, the music changes a bit, gets a tad more sultry, and the women start to walk down the catwalk. They pass tables, smiling down at the patrons as they sashay their hips while walking. I wait for my favorite one to pass, watching only her, and as she approaches our table, she locks eyes with me. I'm a bit gobsmacked by how gorgeous she is. She smiles sexily at me, looking over to Charlie and noticing his arm on my back. I smile up at her, trying to tell her with my gaze how impressed I am with her. Once the women make their way to the end of the walkway, they turn around and start hopping onto tables.

Wow.

When my favorite woman approaches us, she hops off and lands gracefully on our table.

I look at Charlie and mouth, *It's her,* feeling lucky that she chose us. He smiles warmly at me and pulls me closer to his side, his body heat seeping into me.

The music pauses, giving them some signal to all clap twice rapidly, then it changes tempo again. The women have all spread out into the audience, spotlights on them, and they resume their choreographed dance, but this time, they start to shed their clothes.

I can't look away from the woman on our table; I'm going to call her Blue, for the color of her costume, which contrasts perfectly with her skin. First, she removes a piece of the skirt that was longer, leaving behind a miniskirt with decorative silver chains draping on her hips. Then come the sleeves on her arms, which apparently were not attached to the short top. One by one, all timed to certain parts of the music, every piece of fabric is removed, leaving only the decorative chains on her hips.

I'm completely mesmerized by her gorgeous body. Her boobs are full, tipped with large brown nipples, hard from the cold air. Her skin is flawless and dusted with shimmering lotion, making it look like she's glowing in the light. Her pubic hair is shaved completely, making it easy to see her clit peeking at us.

My hand squeezes Charlie's thigh and sweat breaks out on my skin.

Holy fuck, it's hot in here.

Once the women are naked, I assume the dance will end, but it doesn't.

They gyrate their hips for us, going through all the belly dancing movements again, this time, much more provocatively.

Blue turns and looks at me, gaze intense while she bucks her pelvis up into the air, as if fucking some imaginary person.

Fuck, that's hot.

I start to squirm in my seat, clenching my thighs together.

She moves her hands up her hips and cups her breasts, pinching her nipples. I can see her eyes close in pleasure, as if she isn't just performing for us, but enjoying her own touch.

Either she's a good actress, or she is actually enjoying this.

She toys with her nipples a bit more, licking her lips while staring at my mouth, then she turns so she's facing away from us and bends over to clasp her ankles, giving us an unobstructed view of her pussy and ass.

Wow.

I'm not sure why I wasn't expecting that. I mean, it's a classic stripper move, but she's completely exposed, and I can see…*everything*—including the fact that she's wet. Her slit is shiny with arousal, there's no doubt about it. Her hands glide up her inner thighs and I urge them to go farther, wanting her to touch herself but thinking there's no way she will.

But she does.

One finger runs up and down her slit, rubbing wetness around her clit.

Holy fuck.

My eyes are unblinking, wide open so I don't miss a thing. I might also be panting, my own nipples and pussy tingling.

In between her legs, I can see her face. She's looking directly at me, eyelids heavy with lust. Then she looks at Charlie, giving him a sexy wink. Her finger lingers on her clit, as if wanting to play with herself some more, and I'm surprisingly disappointed when it moves away and she finishes the dance on cue with the rest of the women.

I'm so hot, I'm ready to combust.

I clap with the rest of the patrons and Charlie retrieves his wallet, handing over a tip. *Tips!* How could I forget! Blue definitely deserves a tip.

She kneels on the table as the music stops and the lights turn up a bit.

"Thank you," she says as she takes the money from Charlie.

Her eyes flit to me and she gives me a warm smile.

"Thank you, that was incredible," I tell her.

"I'm glad you enjoyed it. Could I interest you in a private dance?" She directs this question right at me.

The manager did say we could have a private dance, though at the time

I didn't anticipate taking him up on it.

Right now, though, the thought of watching her dance some more sounds like fun.

I look over at Charlie and he shrugs, indicating that it's all up to me. "Can we?" I smile up at him.

His smile is slow and naughty. "Yes we can."

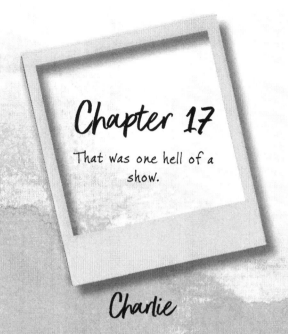

Chapter 17

That was one hell of a show.

Charlie

I was taking a chance, asking Quinn to come check out strip clubs with me, but I have to say, I've had more fun with her than I would have had with Max and Logan. I loved watching her transition from nervous to jealous to relaxed. I knew she would realize there was nothing to be jealous about—I meant it when I said I'm hers.

The best part, though, was watching her get turned on, transfixed by the show. The dancers were amazing, putting on a performance that was skilled and synchronized, undoubtedly sexy. Allure outclasses the other strip clubs we checked out tonight by far.

Currently, Quinn and I are seated on a love seat in a small private room. The lighting is dim, soft music playing in the background and the scent of vanilla making me feel warm, relaxed, and slightly hungry. After the dance, we tracked Matt down and told him we'd like a private show from the dancer in blue. Tallah is her name. He escorted us back here and said she'd be in shortly.

Quinn is all hot and bothered, which makes me all hot and bothered, too. When

Tallah bent over on our table and fingered her wet slit, I thought Quinn might come on the spot, she was so mesmerized by her pussy.

I drape her legs over mine, arranging us more comfortably on the couch. "So, on a scale of one to ten, how close are you to coming right now?"

She laughs. "Probably like an eight," she admits.

I rub my hand up her leg, to her inner thigh. "Want me to make you come right now?" I raise an eyebrow. I'm dying to see how wet she is. I bet her clit is swollen, too, the way it gets when she's incredibly turned on.

She wavers, eyeing the door, not wanting to push my hand away, but not sure if it's a good idea. I move my hand up farther and she lets me, widening her legs a bit. My fingers brush against her panties, which are soaked, and she gasps. I lean closer, swallowing her gasps with a hungry kiss, and I move her panties to the side, sinking my index finger inside of her. She moans into my mouth, and I swear, my cock is so hard I might come in my pants. She's wet, and I waste no time, teasing her clit with my thumb while pumping my finger in and out. She grasps my arm with one hand and my neck with the other, straining to reach her climax. Grunting in frustration, she straddles me, giving me better access to her hot, needy cunt.

I spread her arousal up and over her clit, giving her the slippery friction I know she needs. Her kisses grow more frantic as she works her hips, fucking herself on my fingers. *Fuck yes.* She's so sexy like this, lost in the chase of pleasure.

I flick her clit and bite her lower lip as she sinks down, pussy clamping on my finger, legs trembling, fingers digging into my shoulders. She shudders and groans and I hold her close, kissing her while she goes to bliss and back.

I fix her underwear, straightening the crotch, and she watches while I lick my fingers clean.

"Fuck, Charlie."

"I know." My cock is weeping in my pants, dying to come out and play.

Just as Quinn gets up to rearrange her dress, the door opens, making Quinn jump in surprise.

Tallah walks in with a new outfit on. She sees how disheveled we are and shoots us a knowing grin. Quinn straightens out her clothes as best she can and sits down next to me. I pull her close and shrug.

"Sorry, we had an urgent matter to tend to."

Tallah smiles and nods as if this is commonplace. It probably is—I mean, we are in a private room inside a strip club. People come here looking for pleasure, looking to get lost in arousal.

"I'm glad you liked the show," she tells Quinn. I have a theory that Tallah is either bisexual or a lesbian, what with the way she keeps eyeing Quinn.

"I absolutely did. I've always wanted to belly dance, but I'm just not that coordinated."

Tallah's eyes light up. "Oh nonsense. Anyone can learn. Maybe I could teach you a few moves and we could both dance for…" She looks to me.

"Oh, that's Charlie, and I'm Quinn."

She smiles kindly. "What do you say, Quinn, would you like to dance for Charlie?"

Sweet baby Jesus, I've just died and gone to heaven. *Please say yes.*

Quinn looks at me, taking note of my reaction. She grins and nods.

"Okay, but fair warning, I'm definitely not as coordinated as you are."

Tallah goes to a panel in the wall and hits some controls, changing the music to something tribal and sultry, similar to the tune that was playing earlier during the show. Then she motions for me to sit in a chair in the middle of the room and pulls Quinn to stand with her.

"We're going to ignore Charlie for a moment," she says to Quinn. "What I want you to do for me is close your eyes and feel the music."

Quinn obeys, closing her eyes. Tallah stands behind her and puts her hands on Quinn's hips.

Quinn's eyes pop open at the contact. "I thought we weren't allowed to touch you?"

"Men aren't allowed to touch the dancers, but the dancers are allowed to touch, if you don't mind."

"I don't mind." Quinn looks over at me and smirks when she sees me watching them intently.

"Okay, close your eyes again."

When Quinn's eyes are closed again, Tallah steps up right behind her, pressing her front to Quinn's back and clasping Quinn's hips with her hands.

"Move with me," she whispers to Quinn as she starts swaying, ever so gently at first. It's a simple movement, side to side, but exaggerating the hip movement a bit more. At this slow pace, Quinn matches her, and the two of them move together in sync.

"Good, you're getting it. Now we're going to try to snap it up on the right side." She starts the new rhythm, and though it takes Quinn a couple of tries, she ends up getting it.

"You're doing so well, isn't she, Charlie?"

"Red, I'm loving this. You're doing fantastic," I praise.

She smiles mischievously at me, her whiskey brown eyes twinkling. I smile back at her and try to suppress a groan when Tallah's hands wander up and down Quinn's curves.

What I want to do is free my dick from the confines of my pants and start stroking it, but I'm not sure if that's allowed, and I don't want this show to stop. I have two beautiful women dancing for me, and you better believe this whole night is going in the spank bank for later.

Quinn

I feel like I'm drunk, or maybe like I'm having an out-of-body experience. I never thought I'd be standing in the private room of a strip club, learning to belly dance with a stripper.

She's standing so close, her soft curves pressed up against mine, her light perfume surrounding me. I'm hot, so worked up from Charlie's attention and now Tallah's body heat. My dress is a lightweight sweater, trapping my body heat and making me even hotter.

"I think it's time to take this off," Tallah whispers in my ear, fingering the neckline of my dress. *Holy fuck, she wants me to strip, too?* My eyes widen at her suggestion, and I miss one of the movements she's guiding me through. My heart rate speeds up, pulse hammering. Do I want to take my clothes off right now?

Charlie and Tallah are the only two in here, but I eye the door warily.

"The door is locked, and no one will come in unless I hit the button we reserve for problems," she whispers, figuring out what I'm thinking. "I'm going to take my clothes off, too. Join me." She says this like it's a normal thing to do—which, for her, I guess it is.

I look at Charlie, his gaze hot on me, watching my every move, a prominent bulge in his crotch. I've never felt more sexy or desired, even with a gorgeous stripper standing next to me. His eyes are only for me.

I want to dance for him.

I want to strip for him.

I nod, deciding to be crazy. She sees my decision and fingers the zipper at my neck. "May I?"

I nod again, steeling myself. She brushes my hair to the side and over my shoulder then unzips my dress. It falls off my shoulders, but not completely down. She steps around to the front of me and pulls it the rest of the way off, helping me step out of it. I stand there, in my tall black boots and my red bra and panties, proud that I'm at least wearing a matching set.

Charlie's eyelids are heavy with arousal, his cheeks taut, jaw clenching at the sight of me. Fuck, he's so damn sexy.

Tallah turns around, showing me her back, and gathers her hair up and out of the way. "Help me with my top?"

It's a halter top, tied at the back of her neck. I reach up and tug on one of the ends, loosening it. The strings fall down, exposing her breasts to Charlie. She turns around to face me and I can't help but stare at her chest, comparing her rack to mine. Her brown nipples are bigger than mine, but my breasts are fuller.

Leaning into me, naked breasts and all, she reaches behind me to undo my bra. I feel it loosen then fall to the floor in front of us, and our breasts are suddenly about an inch away from touching.

"Sweet baby Jesus," Charlie curses under his breath. I look at him. He's pretty tense, his upper lip sweating. My poor Charlie, his cock is probably so hard right now.

I don't feel too bad for him though.

Tallah lowers her miniskirt, taking whatever was under there—if anything—off along with it. She nods for me to do the same. At this point, I'm in for a penny, in for a pound. I take off my underwear then take off my boots. We stand together, completely naked. She looks at my body with interest and then I remember the hickeys that decorate my skin. Instead of making me want to cover up, they embolden me, making me stand tall for her to see Charlie's marks on me.

"Come, let's get closer to Charlie," she suggests.

I smile at her. "His cock is probably miserable. Is he allowed to take off his clothes too?" I ask her sweetly.

"I think that's an excellent idea."

We go to Charlie and I tug him up to standing. He complies, eyes glittering at me with need. "Hey, hotstuff."

"Red," he growls.

"Why don't we get you out of these clothes?"

He looks to Tallah for confirmation, and she nods with a smile.

"Thank Christ." He takes off his shirt while I unbuckle his pants. His cock springs free, hard as stone, wetness gathered at the tip. He shuffles awkwardly while trying to toe off his shoes and kick away his pants. I watch Tallah, wanting to see what she thinks of Charlie's naked body. He is perfection. She takes him in, gaze roving over his sculpted muscles, broad shoulders, six-pack abs, tapered waist, and muscular thighs, and once her eyes land on his cock, they widen.

Charlie's cock is truly gorgeous, and that piercing makes it all the more amazing.

He sits back down on the chair, cock pointing toward the ceiling, and blows out a deep breath. Part of me wants to sink to my knees and swallow as much of his cock as I can, but the other part of me wants to make this night truly unforgettable for him.

I look to Tallah and she comes closer to me. "Let's dance some more," I say.

She smiles at me and nods in agreement. She positions herself behind me again, and though I know she's naked, the feel of her nipples and soft breasts on my back takes me by surprise. Her pelvis cradles my ass and her hands rest on my hips. "Ready?" she breathes into my ear. I shiver and nod. We start to move again, me following her movements. This time, my eyes are wide open, staring into Charlie's. Those blue orbs burn me with his gaze, watching my breasts sway, watching my hips move, watching Tallah's hands on me.

"Look how much he wants you," she whispers.

His desire is apparent in every cell of his being. Here I am, standing naked with a stripper, but it isn't Tallah he's watching—it's me.

She guides me closer to him until he has to widen his legs so we can stand in between them.

He groans as if in pain. "Fuuuck, Red, you're killing me."

I exaggerate my hip movements more, loving the way his cock jumps at the sight. "You poor thing. Should we stop?"

"No, please don't stop."

Tallah changes the direction of our movements, and instead of swaying side to side, we start moving front to back. This makes me feel like we're fucking some invisible person.

Charlies stares right at my pussy, which is right in front of him.

His expression turns a bit desperate. Hell, I'm a bit desperate for him, too. My legs widen with Tallah's prodding and cool air hits my wet pussy, making me pulse with need.

Unable to take it anymore, Charlie grabs the base of his cock and squeezes, groaning in agony. "Tallah, tell me what's allowed here. I'm dying."

"Do you want him?" she asks me.

"God yes."

"Then take him."

I crane my neck look at her, surprised at her suggestion that we fuck here, but I find her gaze locked on Charlie's cock, a look of hunger on her face. Seeing how much she wants him makes my heart race and my pussy wet.

"Do you want…" I try to find the right way to phrase my question. "Do you want to play with us? See what that cock feels like? See what he tastes like?" This is no doubt against the rules of Allure, but I know she is not faking her desire.

Her brown eyes snap to mine, wide with surprise, curiosity, and desire.

"But you're together, aren't you? I don't want to cause trouble."

I look at Charlie—he can most definitely hear us. He meets my gaze and nods, telling me it's okay with him if it's okay with me, reassuring me that we make the rules. Thinking for a moment, I try to search my feelings for jealousy, but there's none to be found. I'm just so damn turned on and I can't deny that Tallah is part of the reason for that.

"We're together, but we like to…" I trail off, looking to Charlie for help.

"What Quinn is trying to say is that we'd love for you to join us, as long as it doesn't get you in trouble with your employer or with your significant other. We could always take this to a different location."

She absorbs this, looking from Charlie to me.

Unable to resist any longer, I sink to my knees and wrap my hand around the magnificent cock in front of me. I stroke him up and down and he hisses at my touch. I look up at Tallah, who's watching me with wide eyes, and lick his cock from base to tip, moaning my pleasure. Charlie curses and touches my face, his breaths speeding up.

"Do you want to help me, Tallah?" I point Charlie's erection toward her, stroking up and down the hard shaft. My display seems to have convinced her, as she doesn't hesitate before kneeling down between Charlie's legs, facing me. I lick the tip, flicking my tongue on the underside by the piercing, and watch as she licks her lips.

Again, I point Charlie's erection toward her and she looks up at Charlie, as if asking for permission. He smiles down at her, sweat beading on his upper lip, and nods. She leans forward, moving into my space as I am kneeling between Charlie's legs, too, and our shoulders touch. I'm hypnotized by the sight of her wet tongue reaching out to touch the piercing. I think of how that metal ball feels against my tongue, cold and hard, in contrast with the surrounding skin, warm and pliant. She gives it an experimental flick and smiles when Charlie's cock pulses in my hand. I look up to see Charlie's reaction, but instead of watching Tallah, he's watching me, eyes hot and intense.

My pussy clenches at the ferocity of his desire and I reach down to press my fingers against my clit. It throbs against my hand, needing friction.

Charlie's eyes widen at my movement. "Are you touching yourself, Red?"

A moan escapes my lips and I nod. "I can't help it."

"Are you wet?"

"So wet."

"What about you, Tallah?" he asks her while she's licking the head of his dick like a lollipop. "Are you wet?"

She looks directly at me. "Would you like to feel how wet I am?"

Holy fuck. I have never touched a woman sexually before, nor have I ever wanted to. I thought this would be all about Charlie, that maybe he would touch her and she would touch him, but he curses at the suggestion, so I know he likes the idea of me touching her.

I scan Tallah's body, seeing her erect nipples, flat stomach, and bare pussy. Her clit is peeking out at me. Would it feel like mine? I adjust my position, angling myself more so we're facing each other right in between Charlie's splayed legs.

She sees me looking at her pussy and in between licks she says, "Please."

Heart hammering, I let go of Charlie's cock and reach forward. My palm lands on her flat stomach, and I smooth down her soft skin to the juncture between her legs. She widens her thighs, giving me better access, and tilts her pelvis up, pressing into my hand, as if asking me to keep going.

As I cup her sex, she angles Charlie's cock toward my mouth, giving me a turn. Instead of licking, I suck him into my mouth as far as I can and just hold him there. Saliva pools around his cockhead and I move my tongue back and forth on the underside, feeling that metal ball warm up.

With Charlie in my mouth, I feel her slit with my index finger. It's hot and slippery with her arousal. The warmth seeps into my skin and I trail my finger up and down, almost shyly, comparing what she feels like to what my pussy feels like. It's kind of the same, yet different. She's entirely hairless, the skin soft and smooth. Her lips are smaller than mine, and it seems to make her clit more accessible. She gasps when I circle the hard nub, spreading her wetness around to make her slippery. I like slippery friction, so I thought maybe she'd like it too.

"Is she wet, Red?"

My lips pop off of Charlie's cock and I angle it back to Tallah. Looking up at him, I say, "She's soaked."

"*Fuuuuck.*" He stands up, squeezing the base of his cock again. Tallah and I kneel up, raising our butts off the ground, to follow his movement. I keep my finger where it is, exploring, while she inches closer to me. Charlie's dick is in our faces, right in between our mouths. Tallah opens her mouth and Charlie glides in slowly, forcing her to open her mouth wider. Fuck, her lips are stretched around him.

"Tallah, I want you to touch Quinn. Show me how wet she is." My eyes fly up to his. He nods again, telling me he wants this so much, that he wants to see her touch me, too. Tallah watches me, her mouth stuffed full of that thick cock, and she touches my hips with her hands. I startle slightly, and she smooths her hands back and forth, petting me. Then she reaches my breasts, weighing them and pulling them so I have to move my body forward, and lines my nipples up with hers. She closes her eyes, slurping softly around Charlie's cock, and sways her upper body so our nipples touch and catch, moving them back and forth.

Fuck, that feels good. Charlie's hand is on my face, fingers tangling in my hair, and he pulls out of Tallah's mouth and pushes into mine. I stare up at him, licking and sucking while my finger is on another woman's cunt, and feel her glide one hand down to my pussy. She hesitates right on the verge of cupping me then skips over to touch my inner thigh. My pussy clenches, aching to be touched, to be filled, anything that might get me closer to an orgasm.

I look at Tallah, pleading with her to touch me, and pinch her clit.

"Ah," she gasps, and Charlie takes the opportunity to slip back into her mouth.

I feel her fingers hover over my sex again, so I widen my legs and tilt my pelvis up like she did. Then I feel it, her fingers touching my lips, spreading them apart to touch my entrance and collect my arousal. *Mmm.* Her touch is bolder than mine.

She rubs her fingers up and down, coating them in my arousal, then holds them up to Charlie.

The scent of sex fills the air.

"God, Red, you're completely soaked. I think you should clean up Tallah's fingers."

Lick my own juices off her finger?

It's like he can hear my question because he nods. "That's right, open your mouth and lick her fingers clean."

So, I do, and my pussy throbs as I taste myself, musky and salty.

She puts them back on me as soon as I'm done, circling my clit and rubbing my slit. I mimic her movements, feeling my orgasm start to approach.

Charlie pulls out of Tallah's mouth and leaves his dick in between us then gently nudges our faces together so my mouth is touching one side of his shaft and Tallah's is touching the opposite side. I can see where he's going with this, so I open my mouth wide, as does Tallah, and he starts to thrust between us, using both of our mouths at the same time. He curses and mutters about how perfect we are, how good this feels, how lucky he is. We slurp around him, coating his dick with our saliva so he can glide between our lips easily.

I moan, feeling drunk with arousal. Maybe I feel Tallah's tongue and lips touch mine, but I could care less at this point.

She starts rocking into my hand, and when I start to do the same, grinding my pussy on her finger, she pushes two fingers inside me and flicks my clit with her thumb. My eyes widen, and I'm unable to control the sounds that escape me now. I do the same to her, feeling her heat surround my fingers as I push them in and out.

It all becomes too much—Charlie's cock sliding between our lips, Tallah's nipples nudging mine, her fingers deep inside me, scissoring and stroking, her thumb on my clit, teasing me, my fingers inside of her, making her gasp and moan.

Charlie starts to grunt louder and I can feel his cock pulse and jump against my lips. That precipice of pleasure nears, and I strain, reaching for it, desperate to come.

Tallah finds her orgasm first, her pussy fluttering around my fingers, her soft cries filling my ears.

"Fuuuuck, I'm going to come. I need your mouth, Red. Swallow me."

I open wide, too uncoordinated to do anything but let him thrust in and out of my mouth while Tallah continues to work my pussy.

Intense pleasure consumes me, stealing my vision and making me scream. The sound is muffled by the cock coming in my mouth as hot jets of semen flood me, making me gag and tear up, which somehow intensifies my orgasm.

I tremble and shake while gentle fingers pet my clit, soothing and milking every last spasm.

When I can open my eyes again, Charlie is kneeling with us, grinning at me. We all look at each other and laugh, content and sated.

"That was one hell of a show," he tells Tallah.

We fall into a big heap on the floor, limbs tangled as our heart rates normalize.

I close my eyes and smile. We had a threesome as a couple and if anything, I feel closer to Charlie than ever. Never once did he make me feel like he wanted Tallah more than he wanted me.

Maybe we really can do this.

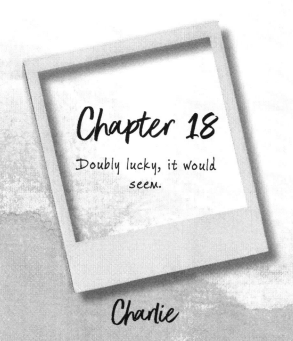

Chapter 18

Doubly lucky, it would seem.

Charlie

What is that? I contemplate as I stare at an abstract piece of art. I see swirls and patterns, but mostly it just looks like a two-year-old made it. I check the price tag and grimace. $1500? Sheesh. What a rip-off.

Quinn and I are at the open house at Art Redefined. She had to take care of something in the back, so I'm wandering the gallery, champagne glass in hand. Jazz music plays in the background and servers circle the room with trays full of fancy finger food and cocktails.

The art on display is an eclectic mix of different styles and different media. I can pick Quinn's pieces out from all the rest, my eye in tune with her style. Now that I've watched her work so many times, seeing her pieces makes me think of what she looks like when she's painting.

A sculpture in the center of the room catches my eye. *Wow.* It's a tree with different branches intertwining together and breaking off into smaller ones. It's large and imposing, probably twice as tall as I am. As I get closer, I notice all the detail carved

into it. It's impressive, so much so that my fingers itch for my camera to capture its beauty. I check out the tag and find the name *Tobias Renolds*. My eyebrows rise in surprise. I knew Tobias sold pieces here, too, but I had completely forgotten until this very moment.

"What do you think?" a deep voice rumbles beside me. Speak of the devil. I turn to find Tobias in a sharp navy blue suit, cocktail in hand.

"It's amazing," I tell him honestly.

His green eyes take me in. "This old thing." He smirks.

"How long did it take you?"

"Six months."

"Holy shit." My response is louder than I wanted it to be, causing a couple people to turn around and look at me. I hold up my hand in apology.

Tobias chuckles. "Can't take you anywhere."

I tug at the collar of my dress shirt. "I'm not a shirt-and-tie kind of guy."

"Me either," he agrees. We stand in comfortable silence, assessing the crowd. My family should be here any minute. When Quinn told Suzanne I was coming with her, she gave us a few extra tickets. Feeling poorly about my last conversation with my mom, I thought this might be a nice olive branch.

"So you and Quinn?" He raises his eyebrows in question.

I smile and nod. "Me and Quinn."

"I knew it," he says, eyes twinkling at me, lips smiling. "She kept trying to tell me there was nothing more between you guys, but I could feel it. Even when I was inside her that night, I could tell she was yours."

"We both tried to fight it, but after that night, I didn't want to stop it from happening anymore. It just feels, right. I feel like she gets me, and I get her." I shrug, not quite sure why I'm explaining this to Tobias.

"I'm happy for you guys, but I can't say I'm not disappointed."

"Why's that?"

"Completely selfish reasons, of course. That night gave me a lot of material to jerk off to."

I chuckle. "Me too," I admit. "It was a lot of fun." I choose not to tell him that Quinn and I still partake in threesomes. Not because I don't want to have a repeat of that first night with Tobias, but because I want it to be up to Quinn. If she wants to invite him to play with us again, I'd love it, but not if she doesn't want it too. It's like my desire is directly proportional to hers.

He flashes me a wolfish grin, showing me his straight, white teeth. "It most definitely was. You're a lucky man."

"I am." I still can't believe I get to call her mine.

"There you are, sorry it took me so long." Quinn's arms wrap around my waist from behind, then I pull her to my side, admiring the view of her all dressed up in an emerald green dress. The shiny satin fabric reflects the light and contrasts beautifully with her pale skin and red hair. The back is my favorite, as there isn't much to it, plunging down to her lower back, putting her beautiful skin on display. I can't stop touching her, laying a hand on her bare back.

"Hey Quinn." Tobias nods to her.

"Tobias." She smiles at him with a nod of her own.

My mind flashes back to that night, to Tobias pounding into her while she sucked my cock, and now we're just standing here, talking like causal friends. I look for a trace of awkwardness, but all I find is arousal.

Quinn turns to me. "Did you see this piece?" She nods to the tree we're standing in front of.

"Kind of hard to miss," I joke.

"It's Tobias's show-off piece. I mean, seriously? Do you have to be so talented?" she complains.

"Oh fuck off. You have more pieces in here than any other artist. When do you find the time to make all of them?" he asks her.

"Well, when you don't spend six months of your life dedicated to only one piece, you have the time to make more." She chuckles. "Hey, did Charlie tell you about his pieces?"

Surprised green eyes meet mine. "You paint?"

I grimace, uncomfortable with the attention. "No, not really. Quinn just convinced me to try it. I'm sure they'll end up in the garbage at the end of the night."

"Ha! Have you talked to Suzanne yet?" Quinn smiles up at me knowingly.

"No."

"There seems to be a bit of a bidding war going on with your work."

"What? I don't believe you." No way does anyone want my art, let alone more than one person. "You must be mistaken."

She beams up at me. "I'm not. I told you they would sell. Let's go talk to her, she's dying to meet you." She tugs on my hand, pulling me behind her. I wave to Tobias and reluctantly follow Quinn. We stop next to a pretty woman with an asymmetric haircut, bold makeup, and chunky jewelry.

"Suzanne, this is Charlie."

"Hey there, Charlie!" She holds out her hand and shakes mine vigorously.

"Nice to meet you, Suzanne."

"I'm so excited you decided to come tonight. Your pieces are garnering the most attention of any new artist on display."

I laugh. "I find that hard to believe."

"Well, maybe you'll believe me when I pay you. Speaking of which, I need you to fill out a form with your bank information before you go."

"No problem."

"Now, tell me you'll make more." She bats her eyelashes, smiling wide.

"Honestly, I'm not much of a painter. My passion is photography. I don't see any photographs for sale here, though."

She taps her finger against her lip. "The owner isn't crazy about photography, but I've been trying to convince him otherwise. Why don't you email me five of your favorite images and I'll matte them, frame them, and put them on display at our next open house? We can test the waters with our customers, see if they sell."

"That I can do."

"Excellent." She beams at me. "I have to go greet some more guests, but don't forget to stop and see me about that paperwork before you go."

"Okay."

"That went well." I smile down at Quinn. "I never thought of selling photography outside of my job."

"Suzanne is wonderful to work with. I have a great feeling about this."

I think of the pictures I took of her while she was painting in her studio, and an idea forms in the back of my mind; I'll have to talk with Suzanne about it later. "Me too." I pull her in close, smoothing my hands down her back again, breathing her in.

"Charles, is that you?" I hear my mom's voice ring out. Quinn tries to move away, but I hold on tight, keeping her at my side. This could either go really well or really poorly. I take a deep breath for fortification and Quinn squeezes my hand.

"Hi Mom, Dad." I nod to my parents. "You remember Quinn."

"Mr. and Mrs. Nelson, I'm so glad you could make it."

"Thank you for the tickets, Quinn." My mom smiles stiffly at us.

"You're welcome. My boss, Suzanne, may approach you about becoming members, just be warned. She's quite the saleswoman," Quinn says, folding her hands together awkwardly.

"Have you had a chance to look around?" I ask them.

"No, we just got here," my dad tells us.

"I'm going to go look for Patricia." My mom excuses herself.

"Dom and Tabby are on their way."

"I'm glad they're coming, too."

My dad stares at me a beat, hesitating. Quinn must be able to tell because she excuses herself, stating that she needs to check on something.

I stare back at my dad, waiting for him to rip into me.

"Your mother told me about your conversation."

I nod and look away. "Figured she would."

"Well I just want to say that I'm sorry."

What? I look at him in surprise. "Come again?"

"I'm sorry you feel like we're disappointed in you, Charlie. I admit that I wished you would've become a lawyer when you were younger, but I'm happy you're doing something that makes you happy. I just don't know how to talk about much else."

Shock fills me—and doubt.

"I know I've done a poor job of showing you, but hearing the way you feel...it made me realize what a bad father I've been."

I clench my jaw. "You and Mom haven't been very inclusive."

"Valid point. Duly noted." He still sounds like a lawyer, but I guess it's because he *is* a lawyer. "Will you give me a chance to do better?"

My face heats and my mouth gapes, unsure how to respond. Maybe I could say it's too little too late, tell him to fuck off, tell him he *has* been a bad father by always making me feel like I was never good enough.

But what good would that do? Staring into his blue eyes, so much like my own, I see sincerity and regret.

"I'd like that, but I want to make this clear: Quinn is important to me. Please tell Mom to treat her with respect."

His eyes widen and he nods slowly, knowing I've never told him a woman is important to me—not since Anna anyway. "She suits you, I think."

This makes me smile. "She does."

Quinn

B
abe, you ready yet?" Charlie shouts from the living room. Max and Monica's bridal shower is today, but instead of having an elaborate fancy affair at a party center, we turned it into an informal cookout at my place. Oh, and men are invited, too.

"Be right out!" I holler back at him. Everyone is due to arrive in 20 minutes and I still need to set out the appetizers and drinks on the bar. I stare at my reflection, making sure I haven't forgotten anything major. Sundress on with strapless bra—check. Teeth brushed, makeup on, hair wrangled into a somewhat presentable style—check, check, check.

Then I meet my eyes and take a deep breath. This is a happy day. Monica is my best friend, and I'm beyond thrilled that she found Max. I will not think of my own bridal shower. *No.* I don't know why it lingers in the back of my mind, anyway. I'm happy I divorced that cheating prick, and I'm happy with Charlie.

Really happy, like start-daydreaming-in-the-middle-of-getting-food-out-of-the-refrigerator kind of happy.

He gets me. He makes me feel more alive and desired and cherished than I ever have before, and things are still going strong two months in. We practically live together at this point, always ending up at each other's place every night, and I've had more orgasms in the last two months than most people have in their lifetime.

So, I'm not jealous or upset that my friend is getting married. I'm not.

I'm just…a bit nostalgic, I guess. Monica was my maid of honor and threw me a bridal shower, and it's hard not to think about it when I'm now doing the same for her.

I square my shoulders, stick out my chest, lift my chin, and tell myself, "You got this. You are going to have fun and not think about that asswipe for one more second."

"Who are you talking to, Red?" Charlie opens the door and pokes his head inside the bathroom.

I laugh, caught off guard. "No one."

"I heard something." He studies my face with a small smile. "You okay?" He wraps his arms around me and I lean my head against his chest, absorbing his strength.

"I'm perfect," I tell him.

"You definitely *look* perfect. I like this dress, is it new?" He steps back so he can ogle me properly. It's electric blue with straps that crisscross down my back, fun and flirty, and it reminds me of Tallah's belly dancing costume.

"Yeah, I just picked it up. Thank you. You look pretty good yourself." A simple black polo and khakis shouldn't look so good, but they mold to his body in all the right places.

"I have an excellent idea." He grins that panty-dropping smile, his dimples popping. I touch his face, tracing along his dimples with my fingers.

"What's that?"

"I think we should have a quickie." He says it in all seriousness, hands sweeping down my back to cup my ass.

"Charlie, everyone will be here in 20 minutes!"

"Hence the term *quickie*. I can make you come in five." He isn't lying about that.

"And I still have to set up the bar with the appetizers and drinks."

"I already did." His hands smooth down my legs and pull the fabric of my dress up and over my ass.

"You did?"

He nods, pushing his pelvis into me, letting me feel how hard he is already.

"Thank you."

He smiles. "You're welcome." He kisses my nose then my lips, hands roaming all over my backside.

I waiver, knowing I need to push him away. We are hosting a party for crying out loud. We *can't* have sex right now.

He sees me hesitate and slips his hands underneath my underwear, grabbing my ass and pulling my cheeks apart. "You don't even have to get undressed, just let me bend you over this counter and fuck you. I'm so hard, I'll come in two minutes."

"How enticing." He moves my underwear to the side and pinches my clit, causing me to gasp.

"Quinn." He grabs my hand and places it on his crotch—his erection is rock hard. I squeeze it, feeling myself get wet and achy.

"Yes," I say on an exhale.

"Bend over and let me fuck you." He says this sentence slowly, enunciating every word with his deep voice, so full of desire.

His bossy command makes my pussy clench with need.

So, I turn away from him, meet his gaze in the mirror, and bend over, pushing my ass into his pelvis.

His eyes glitter with need. "Good girl."

The party is in full swing. It's a relatively small crowd, 30 of Monica and Max's closest friends and family. I see Monica swaying to the music in the background as she talks to Max's mom, a smile plastered on her face. The food is almost gone—a good sign in my book—and everyone loved Tate's cake. Charlie, Logan, and Max are sitting at the bar in the kitchen, sipping beers and laughing about something.

I call this a success.

Smiling to myself, I begin to tidy up, collecting empty plastic cups and paper plates. I refill the ice bucket and put out a fresh bowl of chips.

"Can we have everyone's attention for a moment?" Max calls out. I turn to find Max and Monica standing side by side in front of the living room, arms wrapped around each other. Charlie comes to stand beside me, holding me into his side like he usually does. I melt into him, grateful for all of his help today. It feels like we did this as a couple.

Everyone quiets down, giving Max their attention.

"We're so grateful that you're all here to celebrate with us. I love Monica so very much, and I can't wait to marry her next month." He leans down to kiss her lips softly, and she beams up at him. Everyone ooohs and aaahs. They stare at each other for a moment, as if communicating some message, and Monica nods once.

"I'm a lucky man. Doubly lucky, it would seem." He smiles at everyone, happiness radiating off of him like the sun. "Because not only has this amazing woman agreed to be my wife, but she's also going to be the mother of my child."

I freeze. Did he just…? Does he mean *someday*? Or is—?

Everyone goes quiet, trying to figure out if he's saying what we think he's saying.

Monica laughs. "You guys! I'm pregnant!"

Cheers erupt all around us and everyone approaches them to give hugs and kisses of congratulations—everyone except for me and Charlie. We stay frozen.

I turn to Charlie to gauge his reaction to this news. He's staring at Max and Monica, wide-eyed and unblinking. He's white as a sheet and sweat has popped out on his forehead and upper lip.

I swallow down my own reaction to this news and focus on him. "Charlie, you okay?" I ask him quietly.

He blinks slowly then rapidly, as if he just zoned out then came back to the present.

"Charlie." I reach up to touch his face and he looks down at me. "You okay?"

Nodding a little too quickly, he says, "Yes. I'm fine." His words are hollow and he looks like he might puke.

"Come outside with me for a second."

He hesitates. "We have to go say something to them."

"We will, but let's just get some fresh air for five minutes. They won't even notice we're gone." I nod to indicate the line of people waiting to hug the happy couple.

He nods and follows me outside to the back deck. I guide him into a seat and he tugs me down so I'm sitting on his lap sideways. My fingers tangle in his hair as he buries his head in my chest and wraps his arms around me. I hold him, heart aching for what he must be feeling. Heart aching for what *I'm* feeling.

We stay entwined for a few minutes, just breathing together, processing this news. Monica and Max are having a baby. It's happy news. They were radiating joy. Despite the likelihood that this was an unplanned pregnancy, they're embracing the news and clearly want to start a family together.

But for those of us who have lost a baby, hearing about someone else's joy can be a painful reminder of the past. My eyes burn with unshed tears and I fight them back, willing them to go away, to just wait until later.

"Hey." I rub Charlie's scalp, nudging him to look up at me.

He slowly raises his head and meets my gaze. His gorgeous blue eyes are swimming in sorrow and regret. He swallows, Adam's apple bobbing, and attempts to school his features, but I can see right through him. He's lost to the ghosts of his past.

"I don't know why I'm…"

"It's okay to be upset, Charlie."

He shakes his head. "But, I'm happy for Max. He's going to be a great dad." His voice breaks on the last word. Chin quivering, he bites his upper lip and takes a deep breath, fighting his emotions.

"They're going to be great parents," I agree.

Tears well in his eyes. "I just can't help but wonder what kind of dad I would have been." His voice is like gravel, like there is an actual lump in his throat preventing the words from coming out. When he blinks, two fat tears drop onto his cheeks. I follow their path down his face.

My heart squeezes with emotion, and my tears fall, too.

I stare at him. "You would've been amazing," I tell him.

He looks away, wiping his face. "Maybe," he mutters.

I pull his face up, forcing him to meet my eyes again. "Charlie Nelson, you listen to me: you are a *good man*. You would have been the best dad you could be, and this right here"—I motion between us and the house—"it's normal to be upset. It doesn't mean you aren't happy for your friend. I have no doubt you will be there to support Max when he needs it."

He nods slowly, gaze locked on mine.

"Thank you," he says softly.

"For what?"

"For believing in me."

I smile softly at him. "You make it easy."

His expression softens, morphing into one of affection.

My heart squeezes yet again, but this time it isn't in pain. This time, it's with love.

I'm *in love* with Charlie Nelson.

He studies my face, and I'm afraid he can see it, my love, as if I wrote it across my forehead. I don't know how to cover it up.

"I love you, Quinn Fitzpatrick."

My heart stops, then gallops into overdrive. My mouth gapes open, unable to contain my surprise. I try to talk, to form a coherent response. *I love you too* is on the tip of my tongue, but I'm flabbergasted.

"I know you love me, too. Don't try to deny it." He smiles, and some of his magnetic charisma colors his expression. It's exactly what I need to stop holding my breath and get my vocal chords working again.

"You're pretty full of yourself," I huff.

"I am," he says confidently. His smile is slow but sure, and it reaches his eyes, chasing the sadness away. The dimples grace me with an appearance. "You make me want to be a better man. I hope one day, in the future, I might get a second chance." He stares at me with hope.

Ice seeps into my veins and dread sinks in my stomach like a brick.

"A second chance?" I croak.

He smiles a self-deprecating smile. "I know I'm doing this all wrong. I've just had a bit of a mental breakdown then told you I love you. I'm going to stop while I'm ahead."

A relieved laugh bubbles out of me.

"You ready to go back in?" he asks.

"Sure, let's go."

I take the short walk back inside to compose myself. The sadness, the pain, the guilt, the regret—I push all those feelings into a box and pack that box tight. I envision sealing it with staples and tape. Then I put the box in a garbage can. I have to get rid of my emotions to make it through the rest of this party. I have a house full of happy people and I will not ruin Monica's bridal shower. That isn't the kind of thing someone forgets, not even when you're on the verge of breaking down.

I just found out the man I'm in love with loves me, too.

I should be elated, but I'm not.

Because I also just found out the man I love wants to have children. He wants *a second chance*. And I can't give that to him.

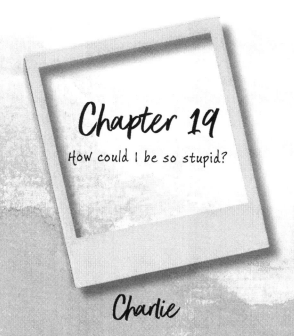

Chapter 19

How could I be so stupid?

Charlie

This week has been crazy. The day after the bridal shower, work took me back to New York to finalize the deal with Roger Diamond. Jason lined up some other clients in the area to meet with while I was there, so I'm just getting back four days later.

Quinn and I have talked every day, but I feel like something has changed. She seems distant; I'm afraid I ran my big mouth and told her I love her too soon.

I know she wasn't looking for anything serious when we started.

But I also know she's falling in love with me, too. I can see it in her eyes, in the way they soften when she looks at me. I can see it in the way she comforts me, how she sticks up for me, even when I'm the one talking badly about myself.

I miss her like crazy. The distance, both physical and emotional, is killing me. I need to see her, kiss her, touch her, make her remember how amazing we are.

But first, I need to wrap up a few things before I leave work and head to happy hour. Max and Logan told me in no uncertain terms that I couldn't ditch them tonight.

I finalize the additions to Quinn's website. She gave me her password weeks ago when I offered to redo it for her, so I uploaded some of the pictures I took of her in her studio as well as some of the pictures of her most recent pieces. What she had before was pretty basic, but she admitted that she didn't get many customers through her website and relied on Art Redefined's site to promote her pieces. I figure it can't hurt to have a better website.

I can't wait for the next open house, either. Suzanne loved my ideas to integrate my photography with Quinn's pieces, so I attach the photos and email them to her. I'm so excited to connect my art with Quinn's—I just hope she feels the same way.

The scary part is that I want to connect more than just my art with Quinn—I've been thinking about us moving in together, too. We sleep together every night (when I'm not out of town anyway) and it makes no sense to keep paying for two places when there's plenty of room at either place for the both of us. But that niggling feeling in the back of my mind tells me not to push this too soon. I don't want to spook her more with talk of moving in together before I have a chance to find out why she's acting off lately.

30 minutes later, I'm shocked to find I'm the first one at O'Malley's. I nurse a beer and take out my cell to text Quinn.

Me: Hey, we still on for tonight?

Red: Yeah, sounds good

Me: I'll be there in a couple of hours. I miss you.

Red: Okay.

I frown at that response. No *I miss you too*. The niggle in the back of my head blossoms into worry. What's wrong? What did I miss? How could I have misread the signs?

"Uh-oh, is there trouble in paradise?" Logan asks me. I'm startled to find him standing over my shoulder, reading my texts.

"Jesus Christ, you scared me. When did you become a ninja?"

"I've always been a ninja." He smirks.

I stand and greet him with a hand clasp and shoulder smack as Max walks up, catching us mid-embrace. "Aww, I need some love, too."

"Fuck off," I say with a smile and yank him in for a real hug, squeezing him extra hard. "I can't believe you're having a baby," I say into his ear.

"I know, I can't believe it either, but I've had some time to get used to the idea. I can't wait."

We sit and Shirley comes over to take our order.

"How was your trip?" Max asks me.

"Work-wise, it was awesome."

"Work-wise?" Logan raises his eyebrows for clarification.

I sigh. "Yeah. I'm killing it at work. My boss even mentioned an opening in management to me."

"Management? I never knew you wanted to go into management," Max says.

"I never did, but the more I think about it, the more the idea is growing on me. It would mean a huge pay raise and less traveling."

"I thought you loved traveling."

"I used to, but lately it just..."

"It takes you away from Quinn." Max hits the nail right on the head.

"Bingo." Logan points to Max. "The look on your face says it all. You are officially pussy-whipped, too. I knew this day would come." Logan and Max smile wide at each other.

"Yeah, yeah. You guys know everything," I mutter.

Max turns to me, all of a sudden serious. "So I wanted to ask you about something."

His somber expression scares me. "What is it? Do you need an organ? You can have anything I have two of."

"No, it's nothing like that. At the party after I made the announcement about the baby, Monica was worried about Quinn for some reason."

I squint, surprised at this. "Why?"

"Not sure, but we couldn't find you guys so we peeked outside and saw you on the back deck. You both looked upset."

My face heats, embarrassed that he saw me having an emotional meltdown. I look away, unsure what to say. How do I explain myself to him? Quinn's words echo in my brain, telling me that sharing what happened might help me grieve. *Let your friends lighten the load you carry.*

"I saw you, too," Logan says quietly. "I've never seen you so upset."

"Is Quinn pregnant?" Max asks.

I blow out a breath. "No."

"Then...what is it?" Max asks gently. "I mean, you don't have to tell us, but...fuck Charlie, if there's anything I can do, just let me know." His bright blue eyes meet mine, full of worry. I look between him and Logan, whose brown eyes shine with concern.

I clench my jaw and swallow down the lump in my throat. *I can do this.* I can tell my best friends in the whole world what happened, but can I do it without crying? I'm not sure, but fuck it. They're my best friends in the whole world.

"There's something I never told you guys," I start.

They both lean closer, attention locked on me, waiting for me to continue.

"Remember when Anna and I broke up?"

They both look a bit thrown at the topic, but they nod.

"I remember being so surprised that she cheated on you. You were torn up for a while after that," Logan comments carefully.

I take a deep, fortifying breath and continue. "Well, she never cheated on me. We broke up for a different reason."

Max's eyes narrow, and I can see the wheels turning in his brain. "Did she get pregnant?" he asks quietly.

I nod, defeated, and proceed to tell them the whole thing—the plans Anna and I made when we were young and in love, the way she hid the pregnancy and the abortion from me until it was done, even the nightmares that still plague me from time to time. Eye contact proves too difficult, so I grab a napkin and start shredding it while I talk.

When I'm done, the only sounds are from the rest of the bar. Neither Max nor Logan has said one word the entire story and now that I'm finished, their silence is killing me. I take a deep, cleansing breath and look up.

Max's fists clenched, facial expression a cross between shock and anger. *Is he mad at me?* Logan looks just as shocked, though less upset.

"Say something. If you're mad at me, just say it already," I tell Max.

"Mad at *you?*" he asks, incredulous. "Why would I be mad at you?"

I shrug. "I don't know, but you look mad right now."

"I'm mad *for you.* I can't believe you went through that. I *hate* that she didn't tell you about it," Max says earnestly.

Relief loosens my muscles and I slump forward, resting my forearms on the table, exhausted from spilling my guts.

"Why didn't you tell us?" Logan asks.

"Fuck, we were 16 years old. I didn't know how to process it myself and the easiest way was to give you a different reason, bury it deep, and start fucking other girls."

"I don't think I'd have been able to fuck anyone else for fear of getting them pregnant," Logan admits.

"I never went without a condom." Not until Quinn, anyway.

"No wonder you were upset last week. I'm sorry I blindsided you with the news. If I had known, I would have told you privately so you could wrap your mind around it without company there."

"It is what it is." I shrug. "You didn't know."

"I'm sorry, Charlie," Logan says.

"It sucks that you had to go through that," Max adds. "But you can talk to us, you know? Sometimes just getting it off your chest makes a difference."

He's right. Having them acknowledge what I went through, it helps. My chest feels lighter, and breathing…it's easier.

I nod, looking at my best friends, and somehow the seriousness of the moment brings out an inappropriate laugh. I just unloaded my painful past on my best friends in the middle of a bar, and we're sitting here, getting all emotional in public. All the emotion of a moment ago turns into levity and I bust up. At first, they gawk at me like I've lost my mind, which only makes me laugh harder, but then Logan joins in, as does Max, and soon the three of us are laughing so hard the people at the bar start looking at us to see what is so funny.

We settle down and I drain my beer, smashing down the pile of shredded napkin in front of me.

"I just have one more question," Max says, eyebrows furrowed.

"Shoot."

"If you guys were outside last week because you got upset, why was Monica worried about Quinn?"

I mull this over. Why would Monica have been worried about Quinn?

"Are you *sure* Quinn isn't pregnant?" Logan asks.

"No, she isn't pregnant. She knows what happened with Anna, she would tell me," I say.

"So you're still using condoms every time?" Max asks.

I hesitate. I haven't been using condoms with Quinn, but I'm sure she's on birth control. I mean, Quinn and I weren't even exclusive when we started going without them; she didn't want kids any more than I did. I just figured she thought it was safe to go without and I trusted her.

"Fuck, Charlie. What birth control is she using?" Max asks.

"I don't know," I admit.

"You didn't ask?"

I shake my head. *How could I be so stupid?*

"When was the last time she had her period?" Max asks.

"How am I supposed to know that?" I bark, anxiety filling my stomach again.

"I assume you're fucking her regularly; it's kind of hard to miss when they're on their period." Logan rolls his eyes.

I rack my brain, trying to remember Quinn having her period, and come up with nothing. We've been sleeping together for months, and not once has she ever turned me down due to her period.

"Well, let's just say she is pregnant, how would you feel about that?" Max asks.

I think about it. Quinn, carrying my child, her belly growing round with our baby…having a little girl with Quinn's wild red hair, or a little boy with my dimples.

My heart starts to beat faster and I smile at the thought of having a family with Quinn. I'm in love with her. I can't imagine having a family with anyone else.

"Oh fuck, you're smiling. I can't believe this, Charlie Nelson. You're smiling at the thought of her pregnant," Logan observes.

"I don't know anything yet, but I'm headed over there tonight after we're done here."

"Well what the fuck are you waiting for? Go ask her!"

I stand, reaching for my wallet. Logan puts up his hand for me to stop. "We got this covered. Just go."

"Thanks!" I call over my shoulder, practically running out the door.

"Text us!" Max shouts.

"I will, bye!"

Maybe that's why she's been distant—she's pregnant but she doesn't know how I'll react. This time I refuse to be kept in the dark.

Quinn

I'm so sorry, Mrs. Campbell," Dr. Stewart, my OB-Gyn says to me, eyes serious and full of concern. "You're bleeding internally. This is because the placenta has invaded into the uterine wall, into the layer of muscle and has started to invade your bladder. We are going to have to do emergency surgery."

"But the baby…I'm only five months pregnant." How can they do surgery on my uterus now without harming Noah?

"We will do everything we can to save the baby, but I have to be completely honest with you, his chances are not good. At 19 weeks gestation, his lungs are not stable enough to breathe on their own."

"Then I don't want the surgery." I cradle my belly, the small baby bump only just starting to show.

"Without the surgery, you'll die. This won't fix itself." I squeeze my eyes shut, hoping this is a nightmare, hoping I'll wake up soon.

"I don't care. I'll take that chance," I tell the doctor.

"Quinn, don't be stupid," Reid says. "We can have other kids."

"I don't want other kids, I want this *one!" I shout, tears spilling in hot rivers down my face.*

Dr. Stewart sighs regretfully, and I know I'm not going to like what he has to say next. "Actually, there is a strong likelihood that we may have to remove your uterus."

"What?" I say, not understanding. Reid squeezes my hand.

"Isn't that a hysterectomy?" Reid asks.

He nods. "It is often difficult to separate the placenta from the uterus and preserve the uterus at the same time. We will make every effort, but you will likely need a hysterectomy."

Numbness seeps into me. This is too much. I can't think.

Noah might not survive. He probably won't.

They'll likely need to remove my uterus, which means I can't ever have kids again.

I won't ever get to feel my child growing in my belly.

I won't ever get to be a mom.

"I'll give you guys a minute, but there is no decision to make here. You need this surgery, Mrs. Campbell."

When I hear the click of the door, the sobs take over. Reid hugs me to him, smoothing my hair and rubbing my back.

"I can't do this."

"It's okay, Quinn. We'll deal with this."

"How?"

"Together. I'll be there every step of the way."

A knock on the door snaps me out of my thoughts. I quickly wipe the tears off my face, amazed that I can still produce them. Footsteps approach the kitchen and I steel myself for what I have to do. *Be strong.*

Charlie comes into view—beautiful Charlie, with his blond hair, blue eyes, and golden skin. *Why does he have to be so beautiful?* It hurts to look at him.

"Hey," he says. *Why does his voice have to sound so good?*

"Hi."

He comes closer and I try not to breathe. This doesn't work, of course, and his scent reaches me before he does, woods and spice wrapping around me like a familiar warm blanket. *Why does he have to smell so good?*

"I missed you," he says warmly. *Why does he have to be so sweet?*

I can't do anything but nod, not wanting to tell him I missed him too, that I haven't washed the sheets on my bed so I could hug his pillow and smell him every night.

"Did you miss me too?" His eyes burn into mine and I know I've done a piss-poor job of hiding the fact that things are going to change, but I couldn't break it off with him while he was away. As difficult as it is, this needed to happen face to face.

I look away and take a deep breath. "We need to talk."

He nods, not surprised.

Heaviness fills me, my limbs weighing a thousand pounds. I open my mouth to rip the bandage off but he interrupts me. "Are you pregnant?"

His question pierces me and I can't stop the sharp intake of breath at the agony I feel. *Oh, how I wish were.*

"No, why would you ask me that?"

"Are you on birth control? I should have asked you after that first time we went without condoms, but I assumed you were on something. I've come inside you a thousand times and I don't remember you having a period. You would tell me if you were pregnant, right?" Vulnerability makes his voice quiet, but I hear his fear. He thinks I'm pulling an Anna, but I'm not.

"I'm—"

"I wouldn't freak out on you, Quinn. I know I'm fucked up from what happened before, but I'd be there for you. I'm *here* for you. We haven't talked much about the future, but nothing would make me happier than having a family with you."

I close my eyes, the pain too much to bear. I can't look at him anymore, the hope in his eyes, the love in his face, the tenderness in his stance, he's too perfect. If I needed any more convincing that what I'm about to do is the right thing, he just gave it to me. Charlie deserves to have a family with someone.

That someone just isn't going to be me.

I clear my throat. "And how would that work? We would get a babysitter when we want to have a threesome?" My voice is strong. *Good job. Keep going.*

His eyes cloud with confusion. "What? I don't understand what you're saying."

"I'm saying I don't think this is going to work out for me anymore, Charlie."

He gawks, rubbing the back of his neck. "Why? Because of the three-somes? I told you, we don't have to do that if you don't want to. It can just be me and you." His eyes pin me, and he begs me to tell him the truth. "Why won't you tell me whether or not you're pregnant?" He's so tense, his shoulders bunch up, and I long to soothe him with my touch.

I meet his gaze and tell him. "I'm not pregnant."

"Are you sure? Why haven't you gotten a period?"

"I'm positive I'm not pregnant. I would tell you if I was," I promise him.

His posture relaxes, but only a fraction.

"Then why are you talking about babysitters and threesomes?"

"I just don't know how our unconventional relationship would be appropriate for the future."

"We make the rules, Quinn—that's what I've said all along. I'd never put sex before our family. I'm sure things would change as our relationship evolves."

"You're missing the point, Charlie."

"Well then tell me what the point is!" His voice is full of frustration.

"I don't want to be in a relationship with you anymore!" I shout.

He flinches as if I've slapped him. "Why?"

"Things are getting too serious. You knew I didn't want a relationship from the start."

"I didn't want one either, but things changed. I'm in love with you, Quinn." He clenches his jaw.

"Well, I'm changing them again."

"I don't understand. We've been inseparable for the last two months. Have I been making it all up in my head? Look at me and tell me you don't have feelings for me."

His eyes are so beautiful, despite being full of pain and confusion. It would be too easy to tell him the truth, but then what? How can we have a happily ever after when his includes a family and my body can't produce one?

It's better this way. He deserves to be happy. He'll find someone else, someone not broken like me. He's young and wonderful. He'll move on.

I meet his gaze and force the words out. "I don't love you, Charlie. I don't want to see you anymore."

His face crumbles, pain etched in his expression. I keep my eyes open, not allowing myself to be a coward. I need to see the pain I'm causing him.

"I don't believe you," he whispers.

I shrug, pretending to be indifferent. "It doesn't matter what you believe."

"Kiss me."

I splutter. No, I can't kiss him. I can't touch him or I'll take everything back and beg him for forgiveness.

"No."

"Just one last kiss and I'll be out of your hair." He walks closer, invading my space.

"No." I back up, keeping distance between us.

"Please, can you give me a kiss goodbye?"

I hit the wall, unable to back up any farther, and he steps closer. My pulse hammers in my throat at his proximity. "Why?"

"Let's call it closure." He leans down, his gorgeous face just inches from mine. My chest rises and falls and I put my hands on his chest to stop him from coming any closer.

It's a mistake, because I feel his heart thudding against his chest. I feel his warmth, his strength, and I long to feel his arms wrap around me.

"Just one kiss and you'll go?" I waiver.

"If you still want me to go, I'll go." Those cobalt orbs beg me.

I nod, wanting to feel his lips one last time.

He kisses me, and it's desperate. His arms wrap around me and pull me into him. My arms snake around his neck and I bury my fingers in his hair. I pour all of my feelings into this kiss. With my body, I tell him I love him, how sorry I am, how much I'll miss him.

I miss him already and he's still here.

His tongue tangles with mine and he lifts me up, bracing my shoulders against the wall. The kiss spirals out of control as my legs wrap around his waist and his pelvis grinds into me.

We can't have sex. I'll never be able to convince him to leave if I feel him inside me again.

It takes monumental effort to tear my lips from his, but I do. "Stop," I whisper.

He smiles down at me, as if he proved his point. "You still want me."

"That's just chemistry."

"You're lying to me."

"You said you'd leave after one kiss. I want you to go."

The light drains out of his eyes and his expression turns blank. He sets me back on my feet and takes a step back, putting distance between us.

"Okay, I'll go. Goodbye Quinn."

Tears threaten to fall. *Don't cry. You can cry when he's gone.*

"Goodbye Charlie."

He stares at me, cataloging my features as if he wants to burn this moment into his memory.

Then he turns around and walks out of my house.

I slide down the wall, hug my knees, and sob.

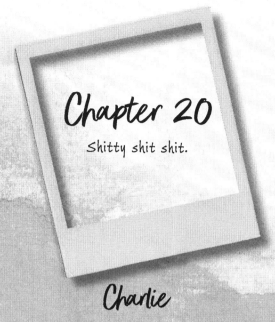

Chapter 20

Shitty shit shit.

Charlie

"Congratulations, Charlie. I'm proud of you, son. You deserve this promotion." My dad's sentiment sounds genuine and I try to bask in his praise, but I still feel hollow, like an organ is missing.

"Thanks Dad."

"Too bad it means you have to relocate. We won't be able to see each other as often."

Now he wants to visit, I think. I've been here for 26 years and he's never wanted to visit much until the last couple of months.

"We'll still see each other. New York is only a short plane ride away."

"True enough. Do you need any help packing?"

"No, Logan and Max are stopping by tomorrow, we have it covered."

"When do you fly out?"

"Monday." Today is Friday, so I have a weekend to pack up my life. Luckily, Picture This is helping me relocate.

"What about Quinn? Will she be moving with you?" I swallow what feels like a piece of shrapnel.

"We broke up."

"You did? That's too bad. I liked her."

"I did too."

"I'm sorry to hear that. Let us know when you get settled in."

"Will do."

We say our goodbyes and hang up.

I turn slowly in my desk chair, assessing the boxes and supplies in my office. My chest aches and I rub it, almost expecting to find a gaping hole. Surprisingly, it feels completely normal on the outside. Isn't that funny, how someone can be hurting so badly on the inside but show no sign of it on the outside?

My cell chirps with a text notification. I want to ignore it, but I know Max and Logan won't leave me alone if I don't text them back.

Max: You're coming out tonight, right? Happy hour?

Me: I'm not feeling it.

Logan: No fucking way, you're coming.

Me: I don't feel like partying tonight.

Max: Do I need to remind you that when I tried to sulk after Monica dumped me, you forced me to come out and threatened to bring strippers to my house?

Me: I'm still not coming.

Logan: Okay, either you're coming out or we'll be there at six PM with strippers. What's the name of that strip club you chose for Max's bachelor party? Allure?

My stomach drops at the thought of Tallah showing up at my place to give me a lap dance.

Me: Don't you dare.

Max: Then just come out. Eat, get drunk, and give us our last happy hour before you move.

It really is our last happy hour. *Fuck.*

Me: Okay. Fine. I'll be there, but I'll be grumpy.

Logan: What else is new? You've been grumpy for the last two weeks.

Max: See you later.

I pocket my phone and sigh heavily. Domenic, Tabby, Max, and Logan have tried to talk me out of this promotion, but I've made my decision. I can't stay here. Everything reminds me of Quinn. Every room in my house has some memory of her in it. Every club or bar I frequent, we visited together. Even my damn camera is ruined with the memories of taking so many pictures of her.

I can't bring myself to delete them, but looking at them hurts.

Especially the sexy ones.

The pain hasn't stopped me from jerking off to them—seems to be the only thing my cock will respond to these days.

What I need is a fresh start, and a new job in a new city will give me that.

From now on, I'm going to avoid relationships. Any dealings with women are going to be about sex alone. Maybe I'll have a new rule: no repeats, one-night stands only. That way, no one can get attached.

My cock laughs at me. He only wants one person.

"So do I," I tell my cock. Then roll my eyes because I'm talking to my cock. Heartbreak will do that to you.

My body aches for Quinn. I want to talk to her. Hug her. Kiss her. Fuck her.

But she made it clear that she doesn't want me.

Quinn

Loud banging on my door jars me out of sleep, and I squint at the alarm clock on my nightstand: 3:30. I struggle to remember if it's morning or afternoon. The drapes are closed, covering the windows completely, so I'm unable to check for daylight.

The pounding continues so I force my body to get up. As I near the door, I hear the shouting.

"Quinn! Come on! I'm not leaving here until you open the door."

It's Monica. I've been dodging her for weeks, ever since the bridal shower, actually. At first, I knew she would want to check with me to make sure I was okay with her news, and I can't begrudge my best friend her happiness. I wanted to give myself more time to get used to the fact that I have to watch her belly grow with this pregnancy.

Then once I broke it off with Charlie, I knew she'd want to talk about it.

I just…couldn't talk about it. It's too painful.

So I've…slept instead.

Not that sleeping helps me forget about Charlie, or my baby. Lately, I dream about them every night, and sometimes Charlie is holding Noah.

"Quinn!" Monica shrieks.

I sigh and open the door a crack.

"Finally!" she exclaims, pushing past me into my house. She's carrying a bag in one hand and a pizza in the other.

"I didn't know you were coming over."

She drops her supplies on the kitchen table and spins to face me, hands on her hips. "How could you know when you haven't answered any of my texts or calls?"

I sigh, knowing she's right.

"It's been weeks!"

"Sorry, Monica, I just…"

Her expression morphs from anger to hurt. "Do you hate me?"

My eyes widen. "What? No! I don't hate you. Why would you ask me that?"

"Oh, you know, because I'm pregnant?"

I wrap my arms around my middle, though it doesn't help me feel any more together. "That's ridiculous."

"I'm sorry, Quinn. I should have told you before the party, but Max and I didn't want to tell anyone until after my first ultrasound—well, actually, he told one of our patients, Mrs. Harvey, but that was only because she basically predicted that I was pregnant the day he found out. I'm totally rambling, I know, but my point is, my ultrasound was Friday and the party was Sunday so we thought it would be a great way to tell everyone at once, but I'm a shit friend because I totally caught you off guard and I never meant for that to happen." She finally stops talking and wrings her hands, nervous and awkward.

"Breathe, Monica, I don't hate you. I'm happy for you." The words sound forced, even to my own ears.

"Well if I were you, I'd hate me."

"Stop it."

She nears me, eyeing me warily. "I'm sorry I'm pregnant."

"Gah! Stop saying that. I'm *not* sorry you're pregnant. I don't expect everyone to stop procreating just because I can't." I sniff.

"You're right. I'm not sorry I'm pregnant, but I *am* sorry that it must be making you think of your pregnancy…of Noah."

Stupid tears burn my eyes.

She steps closer. "I know I said it a million times before, but I'm so sorry for what you went through. I'm not as far along as you were, and I'd be devastated if I lost the baby."

Stupid tears escape my eyes. I squeeze them shut, but that doesn't do anything but make more fall.

"Hey," she says gently, touching my shoulder.

I collapse against her, hugging her tight, sobbing all over her hair and shirt.

"Shhhh. I'm so sorry, Quinn, so sorry."

She holds me while I cry, for minutes, maybe hours, until the tears work themselves out. As soon as they subside, I move back, looking at the mess my snot has left behind.

"Ugh, gross. Let me get you a new shirt."

She chuckles. "Don't worry about it."

I grab some tissues and blow my nose repeatedly until I get myself under control.

"I have a proposal."

I raise my eyebrows in question.

"How about you go take a shower, because you stink, then we eat some pizza and ice cream and you have some wine?"

I lift my arm and sniff at my armpit. *Yikes*, I really do stink. "Okay."

After I'm freshly showered and Monica has changed into some of my clothes, we lounge in my living room, sitting on the floor around my coffee table, eating pizza and ice cream at the same time. Surprisingly, the combination is not bad.

Monica shovels a spoonful of ice cream into her mouth, closing her eyes in bliss as she savors the treat. "God, ice cream is so good. I could eat it for breakfast, lunch, and dinner."

"I like that plan. I think I'm going to do it." I shovel my own spoon into my mouth.

"So what happened with you and Charlie? You guys were so good together."

More stupid tears threaten to fall. "Can we not talk about this?"

"Did he not react well when you told him about the baby?"

I choke on my ice cream, some of it going down the wrong pipe. "What makes you think I told him about the baby?"

"Well, after Max and I announced the pregnancy, you and Charlie disappeared. I was worried about you so we went to look for you and we saw you. You both looked upset, so I figured he was comforting you. That's why I didn't stay and talk with you that night, because I thought Charlie was going to take care of you, but then Max said you guys broke up. What happened?"

I close my eyes, not wanting to tell Monica Charlie's business. "He doesn't know about the baby. I meant to tell him, but there was never the right time."

She raises her eyebrows and puts her spoon down, the metal clanking against the bowl. "So what was that about then?"

"It's not my place to tell you, but he was upset for his own reason."

Her eyebrows go up even higher. "You're going to leave me hanging? You know I won't tell anyone."

I sigh, wanting to tell her about it, but knowing I'll feel like shit if I do. "I can't, babe. I promised him."

"So then, what happened with you guys?"

I shrug. "It just didn't work out."

"I've been debating ways to kill him, but I need to know the reason so I can be prepared with the correct ammunition."

"I just didn't want a relationship anymore." My excuses are shit and she sees right through me.

"So that's why you haven't showered in forever and have been dodging me? Bullshit. I know he hurt you. What did he do? Did he cheat on you?"

I think of Tobias and Tallah, but Charlie was right—that didn't feel like cheating at all. "No, he didn't cheat on me."

"Good, because if he cheated I'd cut his dick off."

I chuckle at her threat. "No need to cut his dick off."

"Good, because that'd be kind of awkward. So if it wasn't cheating, what was it? Did he lie? If he lied, I could cut his tongue out."

"No. Please don't cut anything off of him."

"I'm on your side, babe. I want to help."

"Can we not talk about this?" I shove a slice of pizza in my mouth and take a huge bite.

Monica's quiet for a minute, her spoon playing with the ice cream melting in her bowl. "Do you remember when I was a stupid idiot and broke it off with Max?"

"Yes."

"Well you're the one who barged into my house and helped me pull my head out of my ass. I'm attempting to return the favor, here."

"Funny how our roles are reversed now."

"Stop deflecting. Spill the details."

I sigh dramatically, knowing she won't give up until she has the story. If the shoe were on the other foot, I wouldn't give up until I knew the truth either. "Things were going great with us. We clicked in the bedroom, but we also clicked out of the bedroom. He made me feel…normal."

"You are normal, dumbass."

"No, I mean, he made me feel like I could just be myself, and he got my quirks. Reid used to get so pissed when I worked in the studio all night when he got home from work. He thought I should arrange to paint when he was at work so that when he got home, I could spend time with him, but Charlie understood that it doesn't always work out that way. He'd just hang out in the studio with me, snapping pictures or working on websites."

"Sounds pretty…perfect. I'm failing to see what wasn't working out."

"He wants kids."

She coughs, eyes bulging out of her head. "Excuse me? Did you just say *Charlie* wants kids?"

"Yes. I know everyone thinks he's a big goof and totally irresponsible, but he isn't. He's a good man, talented and smart and…he wants kids."

"So that's why you broke up with him?" She gapes at me.

"Of course!" I shout. "I can't give him a family!" My voice breaks, more stupid tears welling up in my eyes. *How the fuck can I have any more tears?*

"But you didn't tell him about your hysterectomy?"

"No, there was never a good time, and then when I learned he wanted kids I figured, what does it matter if he knows about that? I didn't want to have to make him choose between a family or me. What kind of choice is that?"

"One that he should make for himself, don't you think?"

"He can find someone new, someone with a uterus."

"But Quinn, you took that choice away from him."

I freeze at her words. "What?"

"You took his choice away. I think he should have all the facts and make the choice himself. I think you'd be surprised at what his choice would be."

I took his choice away from him.

His words from the night he told me about Anna ring in my ears.

"What happened to my *choice? Didn't I deserve to even* know *about it?"*

I'm as bad as Anna. Well, it's not exactly the same thing, but I did take his choice away.

Oh shit. Shitty shit shit.

"And now you're getting it."

My eyes snap up to hers, heart pounding, stomach sinking. "I fucked up."

"Yes, you fucked up."

"He's going to hate me."

"You need to talk to him."

"No, I don't know how to tell him."

"Well you have to talk to him soon. He's leaving on Monday."

"What? Leaving?"

"You mean to tell me you don't know about his promotion?"

"He got the promotion? And accepted it?" *Wow.* I'm not surprised he got the job, but I am surprised he took it.

"Yes."

"Well, that's good, isn't it?"

"The promotion is good, yes, except for one small detail."

"Would you just spit it out already!"

"The job is in New York. Logan and Max are helping him pack tomorrow. He leaves Monday."

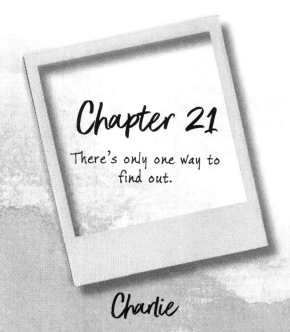

Chapter 21

There's only one way to find out.

Charlie

Boxes are stacked up everywhere in my house. HR set me up with a furnished apartment to start, so I don't need to take my furniture right away. Dom is going to help me sell this place later, so for now, I'm just packing up the essentials and leaving the rest.

"Well, the basement is done," Max reports, wiping his hands on a rag.

"Upstairs bathroom is done," Logan chimes in.

I finish taping the box in front of me and place it on top of the nearest pile.

"Then I think we're officially done. You guys up for a beer?"

"Of course."

I grab three from the fridge and we head to the back deck. The furniture has been packed away into the garage, so we sit on the steps instead.

"I still think you should stay." Max bumps my shoulder with his.

"Not this again."

"It's just not going to be the same without you here," Logan complains.

"New York City is not that far away,

just a short plane ride. Besides, I'll be back for the bachelor party and the wedding in just a couple weeks."

"You promise you're coming?"

"I promise."

"You are aware that Quinn is going to be there, too, right?"

"I am aware, but thank you for reminding me."

"Monica was with her last night, you know." He glances at me warily as if unsure how much he can say.

"Oh?" I'm not sure how much I want to know.

"She's really upset."

"That's interesting. Considering it was her choice, not sure what she has to be upset about." My voice is hard.

"Easy, easy." Max raises his hands as if to say, *I come in peace.* "I thought it might give you some consolation to know she's not happy about it, and Monica said she didn't know about the move."

"Well how would she know? I accepted the position after she broke up with me." Part of me is glad she knows—maybe it will give her a reason to realize she made a mistake. Maybe I want her to try to stop me from going. "How's Sparky doing, Logan?" My abrupt subject change tells them I don't want to talk about Quinn anymore.

"He's good. That dog will eat anything though. He's moved on from eating Tate's shoes to eating my socks."

"Your socks?" Max asks.

"My dirty socks. I was cleaning up the yard the other day and I kid you not, he shit out an entire sock."

"Gross, yet somehow impressive." Max chuckles.

"At least socks are cheaper to replace than Tate's shoes."

"That's true."

We chat some more about mundane things and I realize this is what I'm going to miss the most—my best friends. We talk and talk until we start repeating ourselves and I realize they don't want to leave either.

"I'm going to miss you guys," I tell them, smiling wide.

"I hate you for leaving," Logan says without malice.

"We're going to miss you, too. Don't be a stranger, okay? Maybe we'll have happy hour on Skype."

"Okay, you're on."

I hug each one, chest to chest, and if our eyes are a little glassy, no one comments.

Quinn

Charlie is all over my house.

He's in my bedroom.

He's in my studio.

His pictures are on my website.

I can't even pick up a paintbrush without thinking about him.

I'm in love with Charlie Nelson, and he's moving away tomorrow.

Tomorrow.

Every cell in my body screams at me to go see him, to beg him to stay, to convince him what I said before was bullshit, to tell him I can't bear the thought of not being with him.

But…

That would require me to tell him everything, and when he knows I'm just as bad as Anna, I'm not so sure he will pick me.

Look at Reid. He was my *husband*, and when life got tough after losing Noah, he didn't stick around. He fucked someone else in our bed. I shudder remembering how devastated I was when I saw him. After that, I built walls around my heart and never wanted to give anyone a chance to hurt me again.

Charlie has somehow gotten through those walls, but I still don't want to make myself 100% vulnerable to him when I'm not sure he will pick me in the end.

Reid choosing another woman devastated me, yes, but I survived and moved on.

If I give Charlie the choice to be with me without a family or move on to find a family with someone else and he doesn't choose me…I'm not sure I could survive it.

I tried to get out of attending the open house this month, but Suzanne insisted I come, excited about a new exhibit and new prospective clients.

Looking at myself in the mirror, I give myself a pep talk. *You can do this. You can rejoin society for a couple of hours and not cry. You can talk to people with a smile on your face and be pleasant.* I try a smile on for size, but it just makes me look like I'm constipated.

Whatever.

I might be sad, but I manage to get myself to Art Redefined. I plan to lay low today, just show Suzanne I'm there, smile for some new clients then feign a migraine and get back home. I'll be here for 20 minutes, tops.

I make my rounds in the front gallery, trying to remember what pieces I brought for this exhibit. When I look at the feature wall, my mouth falls open.

My art is on the feature wall.

Not only that, pictures of me surround my art.

Pictures of me in my studio, hair in a messy bun, paint splattered all over my clothes, a look of determination and fierce focus on my face. My hand holding a paintbrush as I blend a color on the canvas. My wrist wiping sweat away from my face, leaving a smear of paint behind on my forehead. Each piece has two or three pictures of me around it, and they show me creating that very piece.

He has showcased my hard work with his pictures.

And everyone is buzzing around the exhibit. Among the small crowd gathered in front, I spot my parents. I stare at them, thinking I must be hallucinating. I blink, but they're still there, staring at my work like everyone else.

"There you are!" Suzanne greets me. "What do you think? It's magnificent, isn't it?"

I nod, unable to form a coherent sentence yet. I'm completely overwhelmed.

"You're not going to believe this, but your exhibit just sold out."

My eyes widen. "Sold out? But they've only been for sale for like 20 minutes."

She beams at me. "Sold out. And guess what else."

"I'm not very good at guessing."

"Everyone who bought a piece bought the pictures of you making it."

"Really?"

"Really. They love Charlie's photographs!" she confirms with a nod. "I've been talking to your parents, too! It was so nice of Charlie to send them tickets."

Charlie sent my parents tickets?

They turn and catch me staring at them, open-mouthed. I don't try to hide my shock, as they have never come here before. They've seen me paint and draw before, of course—I've been doing it ever since I could hold a pencil—but they never supported my career choice.

Slowly, they approach, and Suzanne leaves us to talk.

"Mom, Dad, what are you doing here?"

"Well, that friend of yours, Charlie, he sent us some tickets in the mail along with a letter," my mom says.

"A letter?" *What could he have possibly said to my parents?*

"It would seem he's quite taken with you."

"What did he say?"

They glance at each other and my dad clears his throat. "He had some very strong opinions."

Strong opinions?

"At first I was quite upset at the nerve of him," my mom huffs.

"But he did make a couple of valid points."

"Oh? Are you going to share those with me?"

"That good parents show their children unconditional love, that you deserve our support even if we don't agree with your choices." She looks away when she says the words, but I see her eyes shine.

I wrap my arms around my waist and stupid tears threaten to fall, but I'm not letting them off the hook with one nice gesture.

"You haven't been very supportive."

They both sigh, as if they practiced doing it in unison. "The divorce was hard for us to accept."

"It was hard for me, too."

"I realize that," my mom says, eyeing the people walking around us, uncomfortable about talking like this in front of strangers.

"What your mom is trying to say is that we will try to do a better job showing you support."

"Actions speak louder than words."

"You're right," my dad agrees.

"Would you like to come to dinner next weekend?" My mom finally meets my gaze.

"Is Reid going to be there?"

"No, just the three of us—unless Charlie would like to come, too."

"I think the three of us would be nice."

"See you then. You did a great job here today, Quinn." My mom nods to the exhibit behind her.

"We're proud of you."

I nod, taking in those rare words. I don't reach out to hug them. I don't tell my mom my heart is breaking. I don't ask my dad for advice on how to fix my stupid mistake. We just don't have that kind of relationship.

But I'm beyond touched that Charlie told my parents off and sent them tickets to my show.

And I'm glad they made an effort. It's a good place to start.

My insides ache, telling me every cell in my body misses Charlie.

Charlie isn't Reid. I need to talk to him before he leaves. I need to tell him how I feel.

Monica's right, he deserves the right to choose.

I'm just afraid I've fucked up any chance I had with him by holding back the truth.

There's only one way to find out.

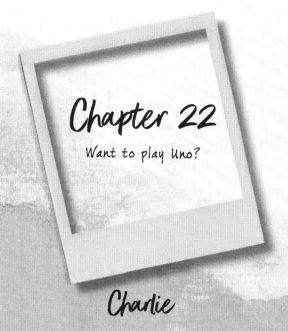

Chapter 22

Want to play Uno?

Charlie

I check the clock on the wall for the hundredth time in the last five minutes. The open house started an hour ago, and I wish I could have been there to see Quinn's reaction to the exhibit. Suzanne texted me a picture of it, and I love how everything came together. I wonder if Quinn's parents used the tickets I sent them.

I check the time again, unable to stop myself from hoping beyond hope that Quinn will come talk to me. No time has passed. I need to find something to distract myself, except everything I own is packed in boxes. I debate going for a run to work off some of this nervous energy, but I can't leave. What if she actually stops by and I'm gone?

Just when I'm about to go stark raving mad, I hear a knock at the door. For a second I think I made it up because I want it so bad, but then I hear it again.

Heart in my throat, I make it to the door in three long strides and throw open the door. My heart sinks when I see Max.

"Hey."

He must notice how I deflate when I

realize it's him. "Am I catching you at a bad time?"

I sigh. "No, come on in. What's up?"

"Oh, nothing. I just thought that today is the last time I can come over for no reason, so here I am."

A small smile tugs at my lips. "Here you are."

"What are you doing?"

"Nothing."

"Nothing?" He raises his eyebrows.

"You really want to know?"

He sits on my couch and kicks his legs up on the ottoman. "Tell me—unless it involves you jerking off, then I don't want to know."

"I was just checking the time obsessively. The open house at Art Redefined started over an hour ago." I explain the details to Max, the pictures I took, the way Suzanne made Quinn's art and my pictures a feature exhibit, the tickets I sent to her parents. "I wish I knew what was going on."

"You miss her."

I grimace. "I'm trying not to."

"You fell hard for her, didn't you?"

"You and Logan called it."

"Well, she's making a mistake, and I bet she's going to realize it."

"But is she going to realize it before tomorrow?"

He shrugs. "Maybe, but maybe not. All that matters is that she realizes it, don't you think?"

"It'd be nice if she realized it soon," I mutter.

"Want to play Uno?"

I raise my eyebrows. "Uno? Random much?"

"What? I figured everything was packed here so I brought a game." He takes out a small box of playing cards.

"I haven't played Uno since we were kids."

"Me neither. I was helping my mom clean out the basement the other day and she was about to throw these away. I had to rescue them."

We have to read the instructions on the box to refresh our memory of the rules, then Max deals and we play Uno.

Surprisingly, it helps. The time passes while we play. Since there are only two of us, the *reverse* and *skip a turn* cards don't have as much impact as they would with more players, but we still get the thrill of making the other person pick up four cards. We're so into the game I almost miss the knock on the door.

Then it happens again, louder, and I freeze.

Max smiles. "You going to get that?"

I try not to hope it's Quinn. "It's probably Logan."

"Nah, he and Tate are at his parents' house. I stopped there before I came here to see if he wanted to come."

My heart beats, a wild thrashing thing bumping against my sternum. I'm not embarrassed that Max sees me practically run to the front door.

When I pull it open, I could cry with relief. Quinn stands on my front step, so beautiful it hurts to look at her. *She came.*

"Hi," she says in a small voice.

"Hi." Is it too early to grab her and kiss her? I mean, why else is she here?

"Can I come in?"

I step out of the way and open the door in invitation.

When she hears rustling sounds inside, her face floods with horror. *She thinks I have someone over.*

"It's Max," I tell her.

Relief washes over her and Max joins us by the door.

"Thank God you're here, Quinn."

"Um," she hedges, not sure what to say.

"He's been so grumpy without you. I hope you two kiss and make up. See you later!" He waves and lets himself out.

I chuckle and we stand there, facing each other awkwardly.

"Charlie, the pictures…they were amazing."

"Did you like them?" My throat is tight, but I manage to form words.

"Yes. We sold out tonight."

"What?"

She nods, smiling. "All my pieces and all your pictures sold. Suzanne is over the moon."

I smile at her, proud of her success. "That's great. Congratulations."

"You too."

A beat passes and I'm dying to know more. *Why is she here?* "You want something to drink?"

"I'd love some water."

We move silently into my kitchen where I get two water bottles. She looks at all the boxes with wide eyes.

"Monica told me you got the position in management. I can't believe you're moving."

Please beg me to stay. I'll stay for you. "That's the plan."

"Well." She squares her shoulders and takes a deep breath for fortification. "I just needed to talk to you before you leave. I have to…tell you some things."

"Okay." I wait patiently.

"I miss you," she starts.

Thank fuck. I force myself to remain seated where I am. I need more.

"I miss you too, Red."

"But I need to tell you a story and I need you to let me get it out."

I nod slowly, curiosity running wild with what she might need to tell me. "Go on."

Quinn

Charlie looks at me with his gorgeous blue eyes and waits for me to continue. I don't know where to start, but I know I need to just get on with it. Heart hammering in my chest, I start at the beginning.

"When Reid and I were married, we wanted to have a family."

He looks surprised, but keeps quiet as promised.

"I got pregnant."

His eyes widen in shock. "You were pregnant?"

I nod, trying not to cry. "I had a complication that required surgery. My son, Noah, lived for eight hours." This time, I'm not surprised when hot tears fall down my cheeks.

He gapes at me. "I'm so sorry, Quinn. Why didn't you ever tell me?"

"When they operated on me, they couldn't stop the bleeding in my uterus. They had to do a hysterectomy."

He stares at me, not quite getting it.

"They had to remove my uterus, Charlie. I can't ever have kids again." My heart breaks all over again and I clasp my hands together to stop them from shaking.

His face is full of regret, but behind that, tenderness shines in the way he looks at me, and I try to squash the seed of hope that expression puts in my heart.

I stutter through the rest of it. Burying Noah. My subsequent depression. How I lost my art for a while. Reid's affair and then our divorce.

When I finish, silence stretches between us, ringing in my ears, and I'm desperate for his reaction, but I give him a minute to absorb everything.

"I'm so damn sorry for what you went through, Quinn, but why are you telling me this now? Why didn't you tell me this when I told you what happened with Anna?"

I shrug. "That was such an emotional night, I wanted to comfort you, not dump my sob story on you. That wasn't the right time."

"Then why didn't you tell me some other time?"

I shrug, not having a good answer. "I was waiting for the right time to tell you, but there's never a good time to tell that story, you know?"

"Why did you break up with me, Quinn?" His eyes are searching and I want to know so badly what he's thinking right now.

"I never knew you wanted kids, Charlie. If I had known, I wouldn't have let it get so far. When you hinted at wanting to have a second chance at becoming a dad, I knew I had to give you a chance to find someone else, someone you can have a family with."

"So let me get this straight: you broke up with me, not because you don't love me, but because you can't have kids?"

I shrug. "You said you want to have a family. I want you to be happy."

"And you thought I'd be better off without you? You thought *you* would decide what I want instead of being truthful and letting *me* decide?" His voice has an edge of steel and my stomach sinks with dread. I knew it. He thinks I'm no better than Anna.

"I can't give you a family, Charlie."

"And you think I want a family so bad I'd leave you because you can't have kids?"

I nod, miserable.

"I'm glad you had so much faith in me." The tenderness is gone, replaced with anger, and the small flicker of hope I had dies out.

"It wasn't about that—"

His eyes harden. "You knew how much I hated the fact that Anna took my choice away, and yet you did the same exact thing."

"I'm so sorry. I realize I didn't go about this the right way, but I needed you to know the truth. I love you, Charlie." I don't even try to wipe the tears as they fall.

"You promised me you wouldn't lie to me. You knew it was my deal breaker, just like cheating is yours."

"I didn't lie."

"You told me you didn't love me, and you withheld some pretty big facts about yourself. How am I supposed to trust you?"

The lump in my throat is about to choke me. I knew he wouldn't forgive me.

"I'm sorry. I promise to be truthful with you forever if you give me another chance."

"Give you another chance to lie to me? To decide what's best for me?" He laughs and it's an ugly sound. I know his answer before he says it out loud. "Tempting, but I'll pass." He stands up and walks toward the door, his long strides taking him away from me.

Tears blur my vision as I make my way to the door, and I'm pissed because I want to look at him one last time. Blinking rapidly, I try to clear them and stand in front of him.

His face is taut with anger, nostrils flaring with each breath. Despite his anger, he's still beautiful. My fingers itch to touch him, but I know it wouldn't be welcome. "I love you, Charlie. I hope you find someone who can make you happy, someone better than me." I turn to walk out of Charlie's life forever.

Monica thought I'd be surprised at his choice, but I knew all along that he wouldn't choose me.

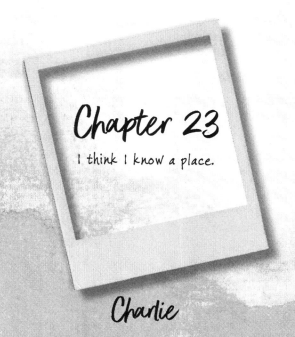

Chapter 23

I think I know a place.

Charlie

"Good morning, Mr. Nelson."

"Charlie, please. Mr. Nelson is my father." I smile stiffly at a woman whose name I can't remember. My mind swims as she takes me through her presentation and I struggle to pay attention. I catch so many errors, I can't write them down fast enough. My first impulse is to take over the project and do it myself, but that isn't my job anymore. My job is to manage my team and let them do the work. I grit my teeth as I try to give her pointers on what to improve tactfully. I was brutally honest yesterday, and that woman left my office in tears and called HR, so I'm working on toning down my kneejerk reactions.

It's hard. I want to tear up her proposal, but I don't.

I hate this job.

I hate my new apartment.

I hate New York City.

Mostly because Quinn isn't here.

But then I remember, I hate Quinn, too.

Or rather, I hate what she did. How dare she think she knew what was best for me? Especially when what she thought was best for me was for her to leave me so I could find someone else to make babies with.

As if I'm in some rush to have kids.

Okay, yes, I did have thoughts of having kids with Quinn, and when I thought she was pregnant, I liked the idea, but that was before I knew she couldn't have kids.

When I think of what she went through, having to bury her premature son, my stomach churns with sorrow. I can't even imagine burying your child and learning you can't have any more kids all at the same time.

And her fucking ex-husband cheated on her months later while she was depressed and grieving. I remember his offhanded comment about me not knowing the whole story. As if knowing everything that happened makes it okay for him to do what he did. What a fucking tool. I want to rip his dick off and pummel his face with it. How could he be so cold?

I touch my chest, trying to soothe the ache again, but it's no use. I feel hollow, grumpy, and unhappy.

My phone beeps with an incoming text.

Dom: Hey, you around

Me: I'm here, what's up?

Dom: Good news, you got an offer on your house.

Me: Is it a good one?

Dom: It's solid, but the buyers are in a rush, they want to be in by the end of the week.

Me: I'm not due back home until next weekend, I won't be able to pack up the rest of my stuff.

Dom: No worries, I can take care of it for you.

Me: You think I should close?

Dom: If you're still serious about selling, this is a great offer. The bank can fax you the documents to sign by lunch.

Me: Okay, do it.

When I get the fax, I try to remember how much Quinn hurt me.

When I fax it back to the bank, I try to ignore the knots in my stomach. I can't afford to pay rent for my new apartment plus the mortgage for my house. This is a smart decision.

"Hey man, how's New York City treating you?" The familiar sound of Max's voice makes my stomach ache with homesickness.

"Hey. It's…okay." I try to conceal how unhappy I am.

"Just okay?"

I sign. "I'm not going to lie, being a manager sucks balls."

"That bad?"

"Yeah, I think my team is the dumbest team in the company. I just want to redo all the projects myself."

"I'm sure you'll like it better as you get used to it." Max, ever the optimist.

"Maybe."

"You never told me what happened with Quinn. You're still grumpy as fuck, so I'm assuming you two didn't get back together?"

I clench my jaw. "No."

"Well that sucks. I was sure she was there to tell you she missed you."

I lean back on my couch and squeeze my eyes shut. I debate brushing him off, but my mouth has other ideas. Before I know it, I've told Max the whole damn story. I know I shouldn't have told him Quinn's story, but I trust Max not to blab about it, and I just need to get the story out.

"Wow, that's horrifying. I can't believe Quinn went through that."

"Yeah."

"And you're still pissed at her why?" he asks.

"Because she took my choice away from me! She lied to me! How can I ever trust her again?"

I hear him take a deep breath. "Look, I agree with you that she should have told you earlier. You shared a painful part of your past and she should have been open with you about hers."

"Exactly."

"But she realized she made a mistake. It seems to me like she was putting the choice back in your hands by telling you."

"How do you figure?"

"She loves you. All of her choices have been selfless. She let you go when she thought you wanted kids, and then she apologized and told you probably the most painful thing she has ever endured in hopes that you might forgive her and see past her mistake. She was giving you the chance to look past her flaws and still choose her."

"She hurt me."

"I get that. Believe me, when I thought Monica cared more about her job than me, I was gutted."

"So how did you trust her again?"

I can almost see him shrug though the phone line. "Because I couldn't breathe without her."

Holy fuck. That's exactly how I feel.

"The way I figure it, we all make mistakes, but it takes guts to admit you were wrong and lay yourself bare for someone else. She gave you the power to hurt her, too."

My heart starts to beat faster.

"Anyway, I'm sorry it didn't work out for you two. I won't make you keep talking about it. You still planning to come home next weekend?"

"I'll be there."

He goes on to tell me the agenda, but I don't hear much. Max's words keep echoing in my brain after we hang up.

"It seems to me like she was putting the choice back in your hands by telling you."

"She gave you the power to hurt her, too."

I rub my chest again. This time I don't just feel hollow, I feel sick with regret.

I think I made the wrong choice.

Quinn

I stare at the blank canvas in front of me, trying to muster up the energy to lift my paintbrush, dunk it in some color, and drag it across the white space.

I stare at it so long, my vision blurs.

I can't think of anything to paint. The colors look all wrong. My charcoal pencils are not that much more inspiring. After two hours of staring at different canvases around my studio, I give up. I take off my paint clothes and crawl into my bed, hugging the pillow Charlie used to use to my chest and burying my nose into it. His smell is gone, but it doesn't stop me from hoping I might find a trace of his woodsy, spicy scent lingering somewhere.

It's been almost two weeks since Charlie moved to New York. For some stupid reason, I still held on to a small kernel of hope that he may have just been mad at me and when he calmed down, he'd call me.

When I drove by his house in a moment of weakness and saw the sold sign in his front yard, I knew he wasn't planning on coming back.

Monica keeps telling me that I'm strong, that I've survived bad shit before and I'll survive this, but how can a heart survive so much pain? How will I face him at the wedding festivities and not fall apart? I want to tell Monica that I'm not strong enough, that I can't be her maid of honor, but that would crush my best friend and I can't do that.

Good thing I have five days to pull myself together before he's due to be in town. I close my eyes and ask the universe to grant me a good dream this time, one of Charlie looking at me with love and mischief instead of hurt and anger. For once, the universe grants me my wish.

Charlie is kissing me, his tongue sweeping into my mouth to play with mine. I know it's a dream, but I kiss him back with all I am, touching him everywhere all at once.

The sound of knocking threatens to end my dream, but I cling to him, begging him not to let me go. The knocking turns into pounding and the Charlie of my dreams fades away, slipping right through my fingers.

I wipe my face, blinking at the clock. Who would be here at 11 PM on a Monday night? Worried that it's Monica, or worse yet, Max because something happened to Monica, I race to my front door, fastening my robe on the way.

When I open the door, I'm sure I'm still dreaming, because Charlie is on my doorstep with a suitcase at his feet. He takes me in, starting at my face then traveling down my body. I'm sure I look like a hot mess, and I tighten my robe self-consciously, trying to remember the last time I brushed my hair or washed my clothes. My eyes dart all over his face, absorbing his beautiful features. Are those circles under his eyes? His expression gives me no clues about why he's here.

My heart pounds in my chest at his unexpected visit. *What is he doing here?*

"Hi," I start tentatively.

"Can I come in?"

I open the door and step aside, trying to calm the stampede of elephants in my stomach.

He parks his suitcase next to my door then turns to face me, pinning me with his gaze. "I moved to New York."

I nod. "I know."

"I hate it there," he spits out, breaths coming quicker with his irritation.

"You do?"

"I wanted to get away from you, give myself a fresh start."

I close my eyes to shield myself, but the words still land, piercing me with pain.

"It didn't work." He rubs the center of his chest. "It feels like there's something missing, some vital organ. Maybe it's one of my lungs, because I swear I can't breathe without you."

My eyes fly open, not understanding. Is he saying he misses me? Or is he here to torture me?

He walks toward me, big body invading my space. He scans my face as if trying to find something. "Do you still love me?" he whispers.

I meet his gaze, those gorgeous eyes the color of the ocean. "Yes." The elephants in my stomach are running, knocking into each other.

He closes his eyes in relief and blows out a breath. Eyes back on mine, he says, "But you thought I want to have a family so bad I'd leave you because you can't have kids?"

"Having a family is a big deal, a deal breaker for most. I didn't want you to settle for a childless relationship with me when you can easily find someone else."

His eyes flare. "I don't want anyone else!"

"You don't?" Hope starts to burn in the pit of my stomach.

"What do you want, Quinn?"

I thought that was obvious. "I want you."

He touches my face and I tremble at his proximity. "You hurt me."

I nod. "I know I did. I'm so sorry. I thought I was doing the right thing."

"You were wrong."

A tear slips out despite my best efforts. "I know."

He wipes my tears. "I want you, too."

My heart stops. "What?"

"I'm in love with you, you silly woman. I want you, too."

"But what about—"

"Kids?"

I nod. "Don't you want to have a family?"

"I want *you* to be my family. The rest we can figure out. I don't want to have a family if you're not in it."

Tears start falling faster now. "You say that now, but you don't know how you'll feel in 10 years."

He pulls me to him, surrounding me with his strong arms. "You don't know how you'll feel in 10 years either. Maybe you'll be sick of me."

"Not possible." I wrap my arms around his waist and hold on tight.

"I love you, Quinn Fitzpatrick."

"I love you, Charlie Nelson."

He steps back to look at me, his smile so wide his dimples flash at me. I laugh at the sight, touching them with my fingers.

Then he kisses me, slow and sweet at first. We breathe each other in, and I touch him everywhere, reacquainting myself with his body.

Our kisses get deeper, and all the pent-up emotion turns into fireworks. We feast on each other, he sucks my tongue into his mouth, and I bite his lower lip. He tugs my lower back toward his body, bucking his pelvis so his erection rubs my stomach. The feel of his hard dick makes me desperate to have him inside of me. I fumble with his belt buckle, unwilling to break our kiss. He helps me, unbuckling the button, unzipping his fly, and freeing his cock. We move over to the couch where I straddle him.

"Fuck, Red. I need to be inside you," he mumbles between kisses.

"I need you inside me."

His hands lift my pelvis just a fraction, pulling up my robe, and he rips my underwear off, the sound of the fabric tearing the hottest thing ever. Then I feel the blunt head of his cock against my pussy and I sigh in relief. He rubs it back and forth over my slit, coating himself in my wetness and arousing me with his piercing in the process.

"Now, Charlie."

He positions himself and I sink down. The feel of him gliding inside, stretching me so full, makes us both moan. *Fuck, he's so big.* I rock my pelvis back and forth, keeping him buried deep, loving the way he fills me.

"God, I missed you." He licks his way down my neck.

"I missed you, too," I tell him, sliding up and almost off his cock then sinking back down. *Mmmm.*

"I missed your pussy." He meets me halfway, thrusting up into me.

"I missed your cock."

He opens my robe, baring my nipples, sucking them into his mouth, pinching and pulling and biting. The sensation zings from my nipples to my clit and I angle my body toward him, giving him easier access to my tits and making my clit slide along his shaft with every thrust.

"Tell me you're mine," he demands.

"I'm yours."

He clamps his mouth on the part of my neck that meets my shoulder and sucks hard. I know he's replacing the hickey that faded away and I love it.

I feel him grow impossibly harder and he bucks into me, hands on my hips to help me ride him.

"I want to come inside of you."

God, I want that, too. The tingling starts and I know I'm close. "I want to come on your cock."

"Oh fuck, oh fuck, oh fuck," he chants, chasing his pleasure.

I shatter first, limbs trembling, vision blurring.

He wraps his arms around my waist, thrusts into me once more, and stills, groaning in pleasure as his cock pulses inside me.

Paralyzed and sated, I melt in a heap on top of him, and we catch our breath together. When I regain control of my limbs, I attempt to get off of him, but he just wraps his arms around me, keeping me where I am. He adjusts his position on the couch while I'm still straddling him, his cock still inside of me.

When I feel him start to soften I try to lift up again, but he just buries himself in deeper. I chuckle at this.

"Sorry, Red, but I'm not leaving your pussy for a while."

"Fine with me."

He smooths my hair away from my face and I lay my head in the crook of his neck.

"I love you," he whispers.

"I love you too."

"I have to tell you something."

I look up, wary, but nod for him to continue.

"I quit my job and moved out of my apartment."

I don't know why this makes me smile, but it does. "Really?"

He smiles back at me, showing me those dimples that I love so much. "You're smiling at the fact that I'm currently jobless and homeless?"

"Is there anything I could do to make you move back here?"

"You wouldn't know of a place I could stay, would you?" I feel his cock harden again and he pushes his pelvis into mine.

I groan and nod, my recently sated body perking back up. "I think I know a place."

Epilogue

One year later

Charlie

If someone had told me a couple years ago that I would end up with a beautiful, smart, talented woman, I'd have scoffed and said I wasn't looking for a relationship. If someone had told me I'd have my own photography business, I'd have laughed, thinking it was way over my head and out of my reach, but as Logan said so long ago, sometimes the best things happen when you aren't looking for them.

My love for Quinn burns brighter every day. She believes in me, and that makes me believe in myself. She's my best friend, my partner in crime, and my biggest fantasy, all rolled into one.

I moved in with Quinn the night we got back together; my house had already sold and we wanted to be together anyway. Quinn encouraged me to collaborate more with Art Redefined, and I still do, but I needed more than that. My brother Dom helped me with the legal side of things and together we formed Nelson Designs. A lot of my clients from Picture This followed me, and my customer base has only grown since then.

A wet, sticky hand slaps my face, snapping me out of my thoughts.

"Gaaaah!" Oliver complains.

"Sorry little man," I coo at the six-month-old. "I didn't mean to ignore you."

He smiles up at me with a toothless grin and a big glob of drool splats onto my wrist.

"Dude, that is so gross. I can't wait until you learn how to control the drool."

He just laughs and yanks my nose, and I'm impressed with his strength. I think his little nails just drew blood.

"Ouch!" I tell him. "Easy there, Oli, I need my nose." I blow a raspberry into his hand to distract him and bounce him on my knees the way he likes. He squeals and yells as if to say, *This is so much fun, Uncle Charlie, do it again!*

Sure enough, once I stop bouncing, his smile disappears, quickly replaced by a frown as he pats my legs, urging me to do it again.

Max plops down in the chair next to mine, smiling down at his son. "You need me to take him?"

"Heck no, Oli and I are hanging out. I'm teaching him about the birds and the bees."

Max laughs. "I think he's a bit young for that talk."

"Look over there, Oli!" I point to a blue jay as it streaks through the sky and lands on the peak of the house. "That bird is called a blue jay."

He turns his head, chubby cheeks and all, and his bright blue eyes actually follow my finger and find the bird I'm pointing at. He squeals in delight as it flies away.

Max laughs again. "The birds and the bees, huh?"

"Hey, every little boy needs to know the basics of nature. It's never too early to start with these talks, didn't you know that?"

Soon Oliver fixates on his dad and whines, reaching his chubby little arms out, telling his dad he wants him to pick him up.

I hand him over, watching my best friend hold his son. Oliver is Max's spitting image with his dark hair and blue eyes. Max stands Oliver up on his lap, holding his waist to steady him.

"Hey buddy, did you have fun with Uncle Charlie?"

Oli touches Max's nose and yells some indeterminate sound.

We both laugh at the cuteness of his little baby boy.

If you had told me a year ago that I could hold a baby and feel nothing but happiness, I wouldn't have believed it, but I can. I still have the occasional dream about my baby, but I've made peace with my past, and I'm looking forward to the future.

Quinn

Would you look at that?" I nod my head toward the back yard. Monica walks over and looks out the window where Charlie and Max are shirtless, wearing only their swim trunks, playing with Oliver.

"I think my ovaries just exploded," Monica says.

"Fuck, mine, too."

Monica shoots me a sideways glance.

"What, Dr. Spencer? I do have ovaries, you know," I joke.

We both bust up and watch our men some more. I love seeing Charlie with Oliver, the way he talks to him as if he's an adult, and Oliver loves it, too. Monica's pregnancy forced me to deal with my feelings of inadequacy. It was the best thing that could have happened, because I found a therapist and got some professional help—boxing up my feelings was not working. Therapy wasn't magic, but I've come to accept my reality, and I can see other pregnant women and babies without feelings of jealousy and anger.

Charlie and I decided to buy a home together instead of staying in my condo, and bought this house about six months ago. A definite selling point was the outdoor kitchen and pool in the back yard, making our place the summer hangout spot.

"Do you think you want to have another one?" I ask Monica.

"Not right now, but eventually. I hated being an only child."

"Well, you look fantastic, almost better than you did before you got pregnant."

"Oh stop it, my hips are so much wider," she complains.

"Your hips are not wider! But your tits are huge."

She laughs and throws a kitchen towel in my face. "What? I can't help but notice they're gigantic. I bet Max is enjoying that particular side effect of nursing."

She blushes. I love pushing her buttons. "He hasn't complained."

I laugh. "You ready to eat? Let's get the boys to fire up the grill."

We collect the food and bring it outside, setting up the table for our cookout.

Logan and Tate show up just in time to join us. Logan and Charlie still argue over whose best man speech was better, but Max and Monica refuse to weigh in on it. As I sit next to Charlie with our friends in our home, I want to pinch myself. This is bliss.

"You ready babe?" Charlie yells for me as he so often does.

"Just about," I holler back.

Tonight is date night and butterflies tickle at my insides. We are meeting up with Tobias and the thought makes me tingle in all the right places. This is only the third time we've asked Tobias to join us, and my mind races with the possibilities of what might happen tonight.

When Charlie and I got back together, he told me we could stop the threesomes if I wanted to, but I didn't want to. It's dirty and fun and exciting. Why should we stop if we both want it?

Life has taken so many choices away from us, and I like that *we* get to define our happily ever after.

Maybe my happily ever after doesn't include marriage or kids.

My happily ever after is Charlie Nelson. He never stops showing me how much he loves me, and I'll never stop showing him how much I believe in him.

It may be unconventional, but life gave me a second chance at happiness, and I'm not letting it go.

The End

Dedication (Part Two)

To all of the people who have experienced a miscarriage, unexpected hysterectomy or abortion, I'm so sorry for your loss. Losing a child is hard no matter the circumstances. It's something that stays with you forever. I hope you are able to heal and find peace. *hugs*

Acknowledgements

Thank you so much for reading Unconventional!!! I hope you liked Charlie and Quinn's story as much as I do.

Authors who self-publish are referred to as "Indie Authors" but I did not do this alone. Some fabulous, talented people helped me in the creation of this book and I'm so grateful to each and every one of them!

I have to start with my husband. He is just so supportive and amazing. Thank you for letting me chase this dream!! I love you!

Being an author is really hard, and I would have quit a thousand times if it weren't for Kim Bailey, Suzanne West and Saffron Kent. You guys are there to encourage me, lift me up when I'm down, give me advice and endless support. Thank you for critiquing my book and not letting me give up when I was SO close. I love you all so hard and I'm so amazed that I get to call you talented authors my friends.

Thank you to my beta readers. Christy Baldwin, Melissa Buyikian, Felicia Eddy, Serena McDonald, Pavlina Michou, Jackie Pinhorn & Desirae Shie. Thank you for taking the time out of your busy lives to help me. Thank you for not blowing smoke up my ass and telling me what worked and what didn't. Your input made this story into what it is now. I appreciate you!!

Serena McDonald, thank you so much for all of your help. You're so passionate about books and supporting the authors you love and I'm honored to be among them. Thank you for helping with my reader group and inspiring me to learn how to post hot GIF's.

Thank you to all the bloggers that helped to promote this book. You are rock stars!! I know there are so many amazing authors and wonderful books out there. Thank you for taking a chance on a new author and blogging about my book. To those of you that signed up for an ARC and reviewed my book, thank you so much!

Najla Qamber, thank you for being so patient with me during the cover making process. I know I drove you nuts creating this cover, changing my mind a million times, but I'm so happy with the end result. The cover and teasers are PERFECT for Charlie and Quinn's story, thank you so much for working with me!!

Caitlin with Editing by C. Marie, you smooth me out in the most wonderful ways. I'm so grateful to have an editor who doesn't change my voice, just helps me say what I want to say in a much cleaner, more grammatically correct way. Thank you for working with me.

Bex at editing.ninja, thank you so much for proofreading! I always think I caught every mistake before I send it to you, but you prove me wrong!! Thank you so much for helping to polish up my baby!!

Julia at Jersey Girl Co, thank you for formatting my book. Formatting is that final step that completes the package, giving it a polished and professional feel. You are so talented!!

I'm so grateful to everyone that helped me with this book!!

Join my reader group, Bella's Babes, to talk more about my books, get bonus content and be the first to know about my upcoming projects. Warning: we talk about dirty books, post pictures and GIF's of hot guys and I occasionally ask invasive questions. Come join the fun, I'd love to get to know you!

If you like Tumblr as much as Charlie and Quinn do, I made a page in honor of this book. **Warning:** it is highly NSFW and contains explicit, naughty, hot AF sexiness!! If you want to see some of the GIF's and pictures that make me think of Charlie and Quinn, check it out.

NSFW Tumbler: *http://bit.ly/Unconventional_Tumblr*

About the Author

Isabel Love is a hopeless romantic. She loves reading books that are sweet and dirty and everything in between. A husband, two kids, and a full-time job keep her busy by day, but by night, she can be found with her Kindle in hand, reading "just one more chapter."

To get updates on sales and new releases, sign up for her newsletter (http://eepurl.com/ctfAU1).

Stalk her on social media:

Website: http://isabelloveauthor.com/
Bookbub: http://bit.ly/IsabelLoveBookBub
Amazon: http://bit.ly/IsabelLoveAmazon
Facebook: http://bit.ly/IsabelLoveFacebook
Twitter: http://bit.ly/IsabelLoveTwitter
Instagram: http://bit.ly/IsabelLoveIG

Other Books by Isabel Love

Untouchable
Unforgivable – coming soon!
(Read on for excerpts!)

Excerpts

An Excerpt from *Unforgivable* by Isabel Love

There are two sides to every story. You heard Charlie's side in Unconventional. Read on for an excerpt of Anna's side. Unforgivable is coming next!!

Unedited and Subject to Change
Copyright © 2017 by Isabel Love

Prologue
Anna
16 years old (10 years ago)

Positive? What? This has to be a mistake.

My fingers shake as I open the next box and follow the instructions again.

Still positive.

This can't be happening. Nausea swirls in my belly and my lunch threatens to make an unwelcome reappearance.

One more time, I take out the pregnancy test, dunk it in the plastic cup I peed in and wait the required three minutes.

Positive. All three test strips have a pink plus sign displayed in the window, staring at me.

I hear my mom's voice in my head. *"You're far too young to have such a serious boyfriend, Anna. Please be careful. Getting pregnant would ruin your dreams."*

But we *were* careful. Charlie used a condom every. Single. Time. He promised he would take care of me. We have it all planned out. We're going to go to college in Columbus so that I can go to Ohio State for their pre-med program and he can go to Columbus College of Art and Design. Then, I'll continue on to medical school and he'll start building his photography portfolio. Once I'm a full-fledged obstetrician and he has a graphic design firm, we'll get married and have four kids. That's our plan.

But now that's all going to change. Because I'm pregnant.

Pregnant.

Being 16 and pregnant is not a part of our master plan.

These thoughts float around in my brain, but I can't comprehend them. I feel my stomach for any bump or difference, but it's still the same. Of course, my period is only one week late, so I can't be very far along.

But still. How will I finish my junior year of high school pregnant? How can I go to college with a baby? Med school? Residency? Fellowship? How can I do any of it with a baby to take care of?

The nausea is back, but worse than before. Saliva pools in my mouth and I know I'm about to vomit. I lift up the lid of the toilet seat just in time. My stomach clenches and I wretch over and over again. My throat is on fire and my nostrils burn. The acrid smell of vomit makes my eyes burn. Shit, I hate throwing up.

Even when my stomach is empty, I continue to heave. When they finally subside, I flush the toilet and stand on shaky legs. I brush my teeth to rid my mouth of the disgusting aftertaste and splash cold water on my face, just as my cell pings with a text message.

Charlie: Be there in 5. I got your favorite soup.

I close my eyes and try to hold back tears. How am I going to tell him? He thinks I stayed home from school today because I have the flu. And caring boyfriend that he is, he left school to bring me soup.

Without wasting another minute, I gather up the pregnancy tests and put them back in the grocery bag they came in. I stow them under the sink and rush back to my bedroom. My heart is beating a mile a minute as I get under the covers and pretend to be asleep.

Minutes later, my bedroom door creaks open.

"Anna?" Charlie whispers as his footsteps approach the bed.

I keep my breathing as slow and even as I can. I hear him slip off his shoes, pull the covers up and the mattress dips as he slides into my bed. His warm body presses up behind me and he smooths my hair back. Needing his comfort, I turn towards him and burrow my face into his chest, absorbing his warmth. He smells of woods and spice, and I breathe him in to fill up on his familiar scent.

"Hey, Sweets. You doing okay? You feel warm." He kisses my forehead tenderly.

I can't speak past the lump in my throat, so I just wrap my arms around his waist and hold on.

"You poor thing. I'm so sorry you're sick, but I'll take care of you," he tells me. This makes me want to cry even more. "What do you want first? Soup or a sponge bath?"

Despite my inner turmoil, I chuckle. Leave it to Charlie to offer a sponge bath when I'm sick.

He hears me huff and assumes that is my response. "Okay, soup it is. Good idea, this way it doesn't get cold. Soup first, then sponge bath."

When I don't move to get up, he pulls back and reaches for my chin. He tilts my face up towards him and studies me. Even though it's dark in here, I can see his blonde hair all messed up from his hands running through it, his ocean blue eyes twinkling with mischief and his perfect lips, smiling at me just enough to make those dimples pop. As he takes me in, his smile fades and concern takes over, a wrinkle forming in between his eyes as he studies me. "What's wrong, Sweets? You look sad."

I try to find the words to tell him that I'm pregnant. That I'll likely have to drop out of high school. That our dreams can't become a reality.

Instead I tell him, "I love you."

His smile is the sun, beaming down at me. His eyes shine with such love and devotion, it makes my stomach somersault.

"I love you, too. So much. I'm going to make you so happy, Anna. I was thinking about our house. What do you say we have a hot tub in the backyard?"

We do this all the time - plan what we're going to have in our house. What colors will go on the walls. Every month or two it completely changes, but we love to go back and forth telling each other what we want our home to be like.

Thoughts of our future house make the nausea return. Because who knows if we can ever make our dream house a reality? What kind of future will Charlie have when his baby mama is making minimum wage as a cashier at the grocery store?

What kind of future will this baby have with two teenage parents?

I close my eyes and swallow thickly, nodding at Charlie's suggestion of a hot tub. Tears fall down my face despite my best efforts to hold them back.

"Hey. Talk to me." He pulls back to look at my face, noticing my tears. "What's the matter, baby?"

The words get stuck in my throat and shrug.

He sees my hesitation and grows more concerned. "You know you can tell me anything, right?"

I nod, knowing I need to spit it out.

Instead I say, "I'm scared." This much is true. I'm scared out of my mind right now.

"Of what?"

"I want it all so badly. What if we can't make it happen?"

"We will do whatever it takes to make it happen. I'd climb mountains for you, Anna."

"But what if I can't climb? What if I fall?"

"Then I'll carry you." His words fill me with hope. And then dread. Because while he has the strength to carry me, my current situation will only drag him down. I'll be a ball and chain, preventing him from accomplishing his dreams. He'll give it all up for me, I know. I just don't want to be the reason he has to. I don't want him to resent me.

Whatever it takes.

I'd do anything for him, too; anything to make our dreams come true. I think I know what to do.

Sign up to be notified when *Unforgivable* is available
http://bit.ly/UnforgivableAlert

Goodreads: *http://bit.ly/UnforgivableGR*

Did you read Max and Monica's story?

"What's your name?" he asks me.

"Can we just dance?" I deflect. I'm not looking to start anything; an anonymous dance is all I want tonight. I'm never going to see this guy again, so exchanging names and getting to know each other is pointless.

He nods, not put off by my refusal to tell him my name. His blue eyes stare into mine, and I am hypnotized. His intense gaze sets my body on fire, and his lips—God, they're full. As he bites his lower lip, I get the urge to bite it, too. I watch those lips curve into a knowing, sexy grin then my gaze moves from his mouth to his eyes and I feel myself flush. Electricity sparks hot between us, and my body feels like a live wire.

His big hands splay across my back and he leans down to talk directly into my ear. "Can I kiss you?"

I nod and lean up to meet his mouth with mine. Soft—his lips are so soft. His fingers thread into my hair and he pulls me even closer. My eyes flutter shut and I'm lost, my world reduced to the feel of his lips pressing into mine, gently at first, then hungrily.

His tongue licks against my lips and I open my mouth, our tongues tangling. My fingers find their way up his neck and I allow myself to touch his face. Mmmm, his stubble *is* soft. God, everything about this guy feels good. We kiss and kiss and I feel boneless, breathless. I'm clutching at him and he's gripping me tightly. It's like his mouth is a magnet pulling me to him.

He makes me forget that we're in a crowded club. That I'm a respectable physician in charge of a department. That I don't need a man to be happy. That I usually feel as if I'm juggling a million pieces in the air every day and if I don't stay on top of everything, all the pieces will come tumbling down. I forget everything; his kiss melts it all away.

Instead, I feel...alive. Surrounded by this strong man, in his arms, practically fused to his mouth, I feel...safe. Electric and desired. Judging by the size of the erection rubbing my stomach from behind his jeans, he is as turned on as I am. We grind into each other, and his heart beats so fast I can feel it thump against my chest.

Soon enough, our bodies start to move in a way that mimics sex. His hands skim down my body, from my hips to my bare legs. His touch is hot, waking up each of the nerve endings in its path. He squeezes my thighs then starts trailing his fingers up again, feeling my bare skin. Up and up, his fingers reach the hem of my dress, and he inches it higher, exposing more skin. Both of his hands end up just under my ass, touching the elastic of my underwear.

Oh, God. I'm so wet. Just one inch farther and he'll be able to feel what he's doing to me. I feel his groan rather than hear it, the vibration in his throat a pained sound. He rests his forehead against mine and closes his eyes, hands still touching me, toying with the edges of my panties.

"Can I touch you?" he rasps into my ear.

I should push him away. I should be appalled that a total stranger wants to feel me up in the middle of a crowded dance floor. I should disentangle myself from him right now and leave.

But I don't want to.

An Excerpt from The *Unrequited* by Saffron A Kent
Copyright © 2017 by Saffron A Kent

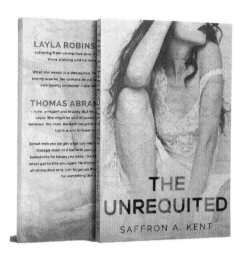

I'm hit by a storm of desire to kiss him better. It's a tornado, an avalanche in my body, and in one breathless moment, I decide to go for it. It's okay. I can take the blame for it later.

I break the rules and reach up and kiss him. A feathery peck on his plump lips, it's a kiss of solidarity, a kiss that intends to tell him I understand—but one isn't enough. It only manages to ratchet up my lust. So I give him another, this time on the corner of his mouth, and then another one on his jaw.

It's not *enough*, these small, barely-there touches. I want more, but I won't take it. I'll be good; I'll only give.

Abruptly, he fists my curls and stops me. I look at him fearfully, ready to apologize—not for the kiss, but for being the kisser. His gaze reflects passion, stark, raving need, and I shiver, despite wearing layers and sweating with his heat.

"Are you trying to kiss me, Layla?" he rasps, flexing his fingers on my makeshift ponytail.

He couldn't tell? Blush rises to the surface and I know I'm glowing like a neon sign. Swallowing, I nod. "Yes."

He inches closer to me, still not touching—as impossible as that is—but infinitely closer. "You want to kiss me, Miss Robinson, you do it right."

Oh God, does he have to call me that? Now, here? My spine arches on its own and my heavy tits graze the contours of his shuddering chest.

"H-How?" I ask innocently, belying the daring action of my body. His stern, professor-y voice is doing things to me, making me wild, uncontrolled.

For a second, he's silent, just watching. I'm afraid he'll back out from whatever this is, whatever insanity we're about to commit—but then I sense the shift in the liquor-laced air as he opens his mouth and growls, "Like this."

Goodreads: *http://bit.ly/TheUnrequitedGR*